Set Down In Malice
A Book Of Reminiscences

by

Gerald Cumberland

Set Down In Malice
A Book Of Reminiscences
by Gerald Cumberland

ISBN: 978-93-61155-11-6

Published by

DOUBLE 9 BOOKS
2/13-B, Ansari Road
Daryaganj, New Delhi – 110002
info@double9books.com
www.double9books.com
Tel. 011-40042856

ABOUT THE AUTHOR

Gerald Cumberland, a British author, journalist, poet, and composer, uses the alias Gerald Cumberland. Kenyon was a poet, essayist, and author of some police fiction. Kenyon, a trained musician, was the Daily Critic's drama and music critic for several years. In 1901, under his own name, he published a study of the work of writer and playwright Hall Caine, followed by a work for beginner musicians in 1904. His musical compositions included The Maiden and the Flower Garden (1914), a children's operetta. Julius Harrison's orchestration of his Cleopatra cantata helped the young Harrison gain fame as a composer. In 1919, under the pseudonym Gerald Cumberland, he published his "Books of Reminiscences," two major critical essays on musical life in England, as well as some police writing. His book Set Down in Malice was largely based on two extended talks with Edward Elgar (1906 and 1913), as well as a meeting with G.B. Shaw in A Terrible Walk.

CONTENTS

CHAPTER I
GEORGE BERNARD SHAW

IT was when I was a very young man indeed that I caught and succumbed to my first attack of Shaw-fever. I do not remember how I caught it; something in the Manchester air, no doubt, was responsible for my malady, for a handful of "intellectual" Manchester people had most daringly produced a complete Shaw play, and, though I had not witnessed the play, I had read it, and it was with delight that I saw *The Manchester Guardian* saying about *You Never Can Tell* just the very things I had myself already thought. I found that in my suburban circle of friends I was regarded as harbouring "advanced" ideas. Shaw, I was told, was "dangerous." This bucked me up enormously, and I thereupon wrote a long essay on Ibsen's *A Doll's House* and, desiring further to astonish and bewilder my friends, got into communication with Bernard Shaw with a view to having the essay published in pamphlet form. When it was known in Manchester suburbia that Shaw had written to me, a boy still at school, my friends could not decide whether I was cleverer than they had hitherto supposed or Mr Bernard Shaw more foolish than seemed possible.

I have never completely recovered from that first attack of Shaw-fever; like ague, it sleeps in my bones and, from time to time, makes its presence known by little convulsions that are disturbing enough while they last, but which generally die pretty quickly.

It was in the middle of 1901 that I wrote to Mr Shaw about the particular brand of socialism from which at that time I was suffering. It must have been a very raw and crude brand, and my letter to Bernard Shaw must have amused him considerably. Certainly his reply was most diverting. Here it is:

"By all means give 'every penny you can spare to those who are most in need of monetary help.' If you will be kind enough to send it to the Treasurer of the Fabian Society, 3 Clement's Inn, London, W.C., you may depend upon its being wanted and well used. If you prefer relieving needy persons, I can give you the names and addresses of several fathers of families who can be depended on to absorb all your superfluous resources, however vast they may be. By making yourself poor for their sakes you will have the satisfaction of adding one more poor family to the existing mass of poverty and contributing your utmost to the ransom which perpetuates the existing social system. You will go through life consoled by an inexhaustible sense of moral superiority to bishops and other inconsistent Christians. And you will never be at a loss for friends. Where the carcass is there will the eagles be gathered.

"A world of beggars and almsgivers—beautiful Christian ideal.

"You are not a prig—only a damned fool. A month's experience will cure you."

But though I think this letter amusing now, I am convinced I did not think so at the time I received it. I know not in what terms of pained surprise and hurt vanity I replied to it, but a few days later I received the following short note:—

"Yes: you are an ass; and nothing will help you until you get over that.

"'A has money, B is without. If A doesn't share with B he is—well, I call him a thief.' Just what an ass would do. Pray what do you call B if he accepts A's bounty?

"I strongly recommend you to become a stockbroker. You believe that doing good means giving money; and you fancy yourself in the character of Lord Bountiful with a touch of St Francis.

"Yes, a hopeless ass. No matter; embrace your destiny and become a philanthropist. It is not a bad life for people who are built that way."

That, I think, most effectively closed the correspondence, as, I have little doubt, it was intended to do.

During the next few months, having approached Messrs Greening & Co., the publishers, I was commissioned by them to write a book on Mr Hall Caine for their *Eminent Writers of To-day* series. The book being completed and published before the end of the year, I conceived the idea of writing another about Mr Bernard Shaw, and communicated with the dramatist, informing him of my intention and asking him if he would provide me with biographical details. This he consented to do, and on 19th December 1901 wrote to me from Piccard's Cottage, Guildford, saying: "If you will let me know when you are coming to London, I will make an appointment with pleasure and give you what help I can."

A few weeks later I went to Guildford, but I went there with a guilty secret hidden in my breast. The secret was this. My publishers did not care about issuing a complete book devoted to Bernard Shaw and all his works. I gathered, much to my amazement, that they did not think him of sufficient importance. The astounding idea was then suggested that half my book should be concerned with Bernard Shaw and the other half with Mr George Moore. Now, at the time of my visit to Guildford, I had not imparted this information to Mr Shaw. I did not anticipate that he would like the suggestion and I thought it wiser to disclose it to him by word of mouth rather than by letter.

I came upon Mr Shaw taking photographs in the little front garden of Piccard's Cottage. It was a winter's day and an inch of snow lay upon the ground; yet he wore no overcoat. He insisted upon taking my photograph. He took me sitting. He took me standing. And when he had grown tired of playing with his new toy, he suggested that we should go into the house.

There a hideous surprise awaited me. Lying upon the sofa of the study was an open copy of the current week's *Candid Friend*, a most brilliant and most ruthless paper edited by Mr Frank Harris.

"There is something there," said Shaw, nodding in the direction of the sofa, "that should interest you, I think."

I sat down, took up the paper and looked at the open pages. To my horror I saw a most brutal, murderously clever full-page caricature of Mr Hall Caine on one side, and on the other a long and most hostile review of my stupid little book on the famous novelist…. Shaw, tall and erect, stood looking at me a little malignantly, and, on the instant, I was on my guard.

I read the review word by word and examined the caricature very closely. The article was amazingly good, but, as I read it, I did so wish it had been written about a book by somebody else. Frank Harris himself, I think, had written the article and Frank Richardson had drawn the caricature. I looked up at Shaw and smiled.

"Awfully good, don't you think?" I said.

He nodded, and by his manner seemed to express approval of the way in which I had come through the ordeal. He showed me some photographs he had taken—not very good photographs. One, taken by his wife, I think, showed Bernard Shaw with his arm round a female scarecrow; leaning slightly forward, he was leering at it with narrowed eyes.

During lunch Shaw devoured a large number of vegetarian dishes and drank water, whilst Mrs Shaw and I ate meat and drank wine. It was, I think, the mellowing influence of a basin of raisins that loosed his tongue and set him talking without cessation. He spoke of Karl Marx and Granville Barker, of Mrs Annie Besant and Janet Achurch, of Mr Sidney Webb and the Fabian Society, of Morocco and Ancoats, of Shorthand and Wagner, of *The Manchester Guardian* and H. G. Wells … in a word, of Shakespeare and the musical glasses.

I rather gathered that he had "got over" Karl Marx years ago, and I inferred that he considered the work of this writer indispensable for young cubs to sharpen their teeth upon, but that he was by no means the last word in socialism. I think he thought that Bernard Shaw was the last word. For Granville Barker he had even then a great regard, and, speaking of him, he offered me some cider, a bottle of which Barker had drunk some days previously; as he offered the cider he said that Barker had "ridden over" — whence, I know not — on his bicycle and that the cider had made him half tipsy.... The thought of Mrs Annie Besant appeared to afford him vast amusement, but he spoke in terms of high regard of Janet Achurch.

"But she uses her voice wrongly. It is quite the finest voice on the stage and, perhaps because she knows it is so fine, she is always trying experiments with it. For a Shakespeare passage, for example, she will plan out what I may call a scheme of sound; sound that will rise and fall with the passion and decline of the words, that will intensify and grow dim as the mood waxes and wanes. But the scheme, the design — for it *is* a kind of design — is nearly always too elaborate, too involved. It is full of detail, and the detail is apt to become more prominent than the general outline. She will start off most magnificently, lose herself a little, recover herself, lose herself again, and then abruptly strike a woefully wrong note. Perhaps her ear is wrong; perhaps excitement betrays her. But, with all her faults — and even her faults are more interesting than other people's excellencies — she remains a superb actress."

Of Mr Sidney Webb I remember nothing that he said, nor have any of the loving words he spoke of the Fabian Society remained in my memory. He spoke of it a great deal, both at lunch and during our subsequent walk, but somehow or other the Fabian Society has always seemed to me a bloodless and dull sort of institution, and while he talked about it my thoughts wandered, and I mused rather sadly over the psychology of this man whose moral earnestness was so much greater than my own.

But I pricked up my ears when the word "Morocco" fell from his lips, though in the event he said very little about it. I found he had no great belief in the value of travel as a means of education, an expander of the mind. He himself had never travelled; places and countries so precisely fulfilled all your expectations that, really, what was the use of going to see them? Facts, people and ideas: nothing else aroused his curiosity.

Of shorthand he said ... well, you don't particularly want to know what he said of shorthand, do you? And in *The Perfect Wagnerite* he has said all that it is necessary for him to say about Wagner. Last of all comes H. G. Wells.

Now, I have not the remotest idea what Shaw thinks of Wells in these days, yet I would give a good deal to know. But sixteen years ago the older man had for the younger an almost reverential admiration. At the time of my visit to Shaw one of Wells' books was appearing serially in, I think, *The Fortnightly Review*. Wells was busy looking into the future, and the future that he saw seemed, in some respects, so disagreeable yet so likely that Shaw was dismayed at the prospect. "A great man, Wells," said Shaw; "do you know anything about him?"

I told him the little I knew and, as we had finished lunch, I asked Mrs Shaw's permission to light a cigarette.

Almost immediately after, we started on our walk.

Never shall I forget that terrible walk. I believed then, as I believe now, that Shaw was deliberately pitting his powers of endurance against my own—the powers of endurance of a middle-aged vegetarian against those of a young meat-eater. He walked with a long, easy stride, swinging his arms, breathing deeply through his wide nostrils. His pace, which never for a moment did he attempt to accommodate to mine, was at least five miles an hour. He forgot, or he did not choose to remember, that I had that morning travelled by the slow midnight train from Manchester, that I had crossed London, that I had reached Guildford by a weary Sunday train from Waterloo, and that I had just eaten an enormous lunch. I panted and struggled half a pace behind him. I became stupendously hot. I made unexpected and unathletic sounds, like a man who is being smothered. Blissfully unconscious of all this was Shaw.... I wonder?... No; blissfully conscious of all this was Shaw.

He talked steadily the whole time, but I was suffering from an inhibition of all my mental faculties. Yet, at the back of my mind, I kept saying to myself: "You know, you have not yet told him that he is to share your book with George Moore." And each time I told myself that, I shuddered somewhat.

It was not until we had neared Mr G. F. Watts' house that Shaw moderated his pace a little.

"That," said he, in a curiously low voice—the kind of voice one uses in churches—"that is where G. F. Watts lives."

And he pointed to some high chimneys that overtopped a belt of trees, and stopped and gazed. But I was in no mood of reverence and, though I have frequently struggled to induce a feeling of rapture when gazing upon the large canvases of Watts, I have never been able to do so. So I pulled out my handkerchief and wiped my perspiring forehead.

"Hot?" asked Shaw grimly.

"Of course I'm hot. Aren't you?"

"Warm. Just nicely warm."

Presently we came to a tall tower of terra-cotta bricks which, Shaw told me, had been erected by the villagers under the direction and at the instigation of Watts himself. We stopped in front of this and, as it was one of the "sights" of the district, I felt that I was expected to say something wise or, at all events, something complimentary about it. I could say neither.

"Which do people imagine it to be—useful or ornamental?" I asked.

"I wonder," said he.

"For it is neither," I ventured.

But his thoughts were otherwhere, for he began a long, technical exposition on the art of making bricks and tiles. His talk became art-and-crafty. I was carried back to my childhood days, my kindergarten days. I heard the name of William Morris and I sighed most profoundly.

Shaw won that walk by a neck. Having reached Piccard's Cottage, he put me in a kind of conservatory, gave me a blanket and a deck chair and told me to go to sleep. But already I *was* asleep....

When I awoke it was quite dark, and, feeling rather miserable, I groped my way back to the house. There I found Mr and Mrs Shaw in the study, she frowning at her desk, he standing on the hearthrug and looking at her most quizzically.

"Well, how much is it?" she asked. "Four times into two hundred. The cheque *must* go by to-night's post. I've done the sum three times, and on each occasion I've got a different answer."

"Is it two hundred pence or two hundred pounds?"

"Don't be absurd, George. Even you know that you can't get a furnished house like this for two hundred pence a year."

"Four times into two hundred—let me see—fifty. Yes, fifty. You can safely write down fifty pounds."

That little incident safely over, we turned to tea.

I induced Shaw to talk about his own work, and I quickly discovered that, unlike most authors, he had no feeling of bitterness that he had had to spend years in hard work before he won public recognition.

"A writer of originality must expect to have to wait. If a writer is acclaimed immediately—I mean a writer on social and artistic subjects—he may be pretty sure that he is saying things that have been said before. He may be saying them better than anybody else; nevertheless, they are the same things. My own success has been gained, and is very largely maintained, by the force of my personality and by the tradition about myself that has gradually grown up in the mind of the public. For example, if I were to write an article and give it to you to copy out and offer to editors in your own name, you being the professional author, I doubt very much if a single editor would look at it twice. A good deal, you see, *is* in a name."

It was when Mrs Shaw, having sipped her tea, had left the room, that I broached the subject of my book.

"Publishers are curious people," I remarked meditatively.

He sat silent.

"My own publishers in particular. They are now fighting shy of a book solely about you."

I paused and glanced at him. But he was gazing at me with eyes of a mild malice and he was very silent.

"Yes," I continued. "To put it bluntly, they think that a book solely about you would not be a success. So that they propose the first half of the book should be concerned with you and the second half with George Moore."

"And the title?" he asked gently.

"Why? What do you mean?"

"Well, don't you think *The Two Mad Irishmen* would go rather well?"

I floundered. If he was going to be witty or sarcastic, or anything horrid of that kind, I should be nowhere at all. To cover my confusion—and, as it chanced, to make that confusion worse—I began to talk very rapidly.

"I know their suggestion is awfully stupid, but then publishers do make stupid suggestions. That, I suppose, is why they are so successful. Of course, George Moore and yourself——"

"Oh, George has worked awfully hard," said Shaw reasonably. "I don't suppose there is a more conscientious artist living. He has dug out of himself everything there was to be got. No one could have tried more. As a worker, George is magnificent. But, really, when you suggest a book——"

"No! No! I don't suggest it for one moment," I interrupted.

"Then what are we discussing?"

"Well, in the first instance, my publishers suggested——"

"Ha! 'In the first instance!' No; it really cannot be done. If you wish to write the book nobody, of course, can stop you, but if you do you must not expect me to countenance it. I shall wash my hands of the whole business."

And, in spite of some further conversation, that remained his unshakable attitude.

An hour later he walked with me down to the station, I resolving all the way that I would persuade my publisher to accept two books. Shaw droned on about Sidney Webb and the Fabian Society.... So many people have talked to me of Sidney Webb. I wonder why. I have heard Sidney Webb speak; he knows all about figures and dates and money and wages, and so on.... But of human nature he knows nothing; he knows less than a child, for a child has at least intuition. Figures don't go very far, do they? Of course, by manipulation, you can make them go all the way....

But, as I was saying, Shaw talked about Fabianism and Webbism all the way to the station.

He was good enough to wait till the train started, and the last I saw of him as I leant through the window was a long, lean figure standing under a lamp. The figure wore no overcoat, but I noticed, even when a hundred yards separated us, a pair of thick, home-knitted woollen gloves....

P.S.—The book was never written, for my publishers could not be persuaded to take G.B.S. at his own or my estimate.

Mr George Moore, on being approached, wrote me from Dublin, saying, inconsequently enough, that he had never asked anybody to write about him nor had he ever asked anybody to refrain from doing so. On the whole, he thought it better that if A (myself) wished to write about B (Mr George Moore), it would be an excellent arrangement, provided that:

(1) A was an intimate friend of B's, or

(2) A was a complete stranger to B.

I was left, most courteously, to infer that I (A), being a complete stranger, had better remain so.

I did.

I have done.

CHAPTER II
MISCELLANEOUS

MRS ANNIE BESANT, like her Himalayan Mahatmas, is lofty, remote, and difficult of access. Only once was I admitted to The Presence. What drove me there was, first of all, curiosity, and, secondly, a feeling of great respect for her which I had retained from boyhood. I admired her courage, her independence, her friendship with and loyalty to Bradlaugh; moreover, I have always held in high regard those who, from temperamental or spiritual discord with their fellows, have kicked over the intellectual traces and run a race of their own. Annie Besant, whatever else she may be, is a woman of courage, of vast resource and of indomitable will.

But alas! my hour's interview with her did much to sap and destroy my devotion. First of all, I must say that, previous to meeting her, I had been for a short time an Associate of the Theosophical Society. I was never admitted to membership of that body because I never claimed the privilege; my associateship originated in my desire to hear Orage lecture and in my anxiety to study some curious and not unintelligent people at first hand. Nothing is at once more distressing and more repellent to me than affectation, and the affectation of most members of the Theosophical Society whom I met was really appalling. The people were also grotesque. The men had dyspepsia and bald heads, and the women wore djibbahs and a look of condescending benevolence. They read Madame Blavatsky assiduously and gabbled nonsense to each other.

Mrs Besant made an appointment for me one Saturday afternoon at the Midland Hotel, Manchester. I was shown into a private sitting-room which, upon entering, I took to be empty. But, after a few moments had passed, I observed a snake-like movement in a corner of the room, and a thin, pale lady advanced languidly towards me, holding out a lifeless hand which hung nervelessly at her wrist. I glanced at her in surprise and noticed that she wore a djibbah, a long necklace of yellow stones, a most insincere smile, and vegetarian boots.

"Mrs Besant will be with you shortly," she said, scrutinising me carefully. Having, as it appeared to me, taken a mental inventory of my clothing, she glided to the door and, smiling at me once more, disappeared. I took her to be a sort of bodyguard.

The entrance of Mrs Besant was brisk and businesslike. She had a firm handshake; she looked a capable business woman—a woman accustomed to issuing commands and having them implicitly obeyed. Of medium height, she was plump and heavily built; her pale face, surmounted by perfectly white hair, was of an intensely serious cast, and I saw no humour in her eye.

Our conversation, a little halting at first, began to flow quite easily when I mentioned her Autobiography and asked her why she had not issued a second volume.

"You see," I said, "it stops just at the most interesting period of your life. You have never stated fully how you became convinced of the truth of theosophical doctrines. I, for one, cannot understand your position."

"It isn't very necessary that you should," she observed calmly.

"Who am I, you mean, that I should presume to understand you?"

"Yes; perhaps I meant something like that. People who are intended to understand me will understand me. The rest don't matter. In any case, this is not a subject that has much interest for me."

"But, surely, if you think you have discovered the truth, you are anxious to spread it? As a matter of fact, I know, of course, that you are anxious on this point, or you would not lecture and write."

"You are quite right," she said, leaning forward a little. "I spread the truth, but, then, the truth is not for everybody. Much of it falls on stony ground."

"And it will continue to do so," I half interrupted, "until you have proved that the alleged miracles of Madame Blavatsky are really true. Was Madame Blavatsky a charlatan or was she not?—on the answer to that question all modern theosophy stands or falls."

She smiled at this attack of mine and at the violence of it.

"It *is* proved," she answered; "it is proved up to the hilt. I and thousands of others are entirely satisfied."

"And Madame Coulomb?—was she a mountebank? And were the mysteries of Adyar frauds?"

"Everyone is entitled to his own opinion about those matters. I have my own view; you, no doubt, have yours. And now," she added, a little wearily, "let us have tea and talk about the weather."

Such was the substance of our talk. I gathered the impression, right or wrong, that Mrs Besant had brought herself to a state of mind when no evidence, however strong, that was opposed to her beliefs would shake her faith for a moment. She desired most fervently to believe in the *bona fides* of Madame Blavatsky, and believe she did. The Theosophical Society does not—or it did not in those days—demand from its members the acceptance of any particular doctrine; you could accept as little or as much as you wanted and still remain one of the faithful. But Mrs Besant went the whole hog.

Bernard Shaw once told me that, meeting Mrs Besant years after the Bradlaugh days, he said to her, half jokingly:

"You surely don't believe one quarter of the rubbish you write and talk, do you?"

Her answer was to look at him coldly and turn on her heel. Which, after all, was perhaps the wisest answer she could give.

A kindly old man took me to his studio and began to talk of Dickens. He spoke of those Victorian days as though they were the greatest that have ever been. He knew Anthony Trollope and all his works and looked askance at me because *Barchester Towers* was the only Trollope book I had read.

And then he took me to an easel and showed me his latest work—a "pretty-pretty" picture of a girl in a garden; the sort of picture that, according to my mood, either excites my laughter or throws me into a fury of rage.

But Marcus Stone was very old, and his ideals, being those of yesteryear, left me untouched. The young can never understand the old and, as I listened to him talking of art and literature and life, I told myself that we to-day are centuries away from the mid-Victorian days. If he had not been so old and kindly I should have wished to say:

"Do you want to know what all you people were like fifty years ago?— well, read *Punch* for, say, the year 1870."

But though my friends tell me that I am brutal, and I know I am ill-mannered, I could not find it in my heart to speak those words.

The amiable but rather weak Mr P. W. Wilson, who used to do "Lobby" work for *The Daily News*, having declined a whisky, entered into conversation with me at the hotel at Criccieth. He told me that till that morning he had been staying with Mr Lloyd George, but that, Mr Masterman, Sir Rufus Isaacs and other people of importance having turned up, he himself had had to seek refuge in the hotel.

The occasion of the assembly of these wits was the opening of an institute at Llanystumdwy, the little village near Criccieth, where the Prime Minister spent his childhood days. Mr Lloyd George had given the institute to the inhabitants of the village and was himself to open it publicly the following day.

Mr Wilson's amiability and his self-satisfaction at enjoying the friendship of Mr Lloyd George rather put me out, and I felt a strong desire to disturb his sleek smoothness.

"I hope," said I, "that the suffragettes will not be brutally treated to-morrow, but I am very much afraid they will."

"Of course," observed P. W. W., between draws at his pipe, "if they create a disturbance here, in the very midst of Lloyd George's worshippers, they must expect a stiff time of it."

"Yes, and they will get it. The organised gang of roughs from Portmadoc who are coming here to-morrow armed with clubs will see to that. The uneducated Welsh, their passions once aroused, are little better than savages...." I hesitated a moment. Then, as impressively as I could, I added: "We must prepare ourselves for dreadful sights to-morrow. I should not be very surprised if one or two women are not torn limb from limb. And if they are, the responsibility will, in my opinion, rest mainly with Mr Lloyd George himself."

P. W. Wilson took his pipe from his mouth and looked at me with some concern.

"How do you make that out?" he asked.

"Well, hitherto he has not done very much to soothe the irritation of meetings he has addressed which have been interrupted by suffragettes. Lloyd George has not very much magnanimity. Moreover, in this particular matter, he evinces but a shallow knowledge of human nature. He would win the approval of all men of generous and chivalrous natures if— —"

I allowed my voice to die away to nothing.

Wilson, really disturbed, moved a little uneasily on his chair, rose, scratched his head, sat down again and sighed.

"I must tell him," said he. "I must warn him that, at the very beginning of his speech, he must appeal to the audience to deal gently with any interrupters.... Torn limb from limb.... You really think that?"

I felt a little sorry to have disturbed him so much, and yet I knew that I very much preferred an anxious, harassed Wilson to a Wilson who was smooth and sleek.

Next morning at breakfast he was again smooth and self-satisfied.

"I have seen him," he whispered, like a conspirator; "I have seen him. It is arranged. Everything is all right."

Later on that morning I was myself received by Mr Lloyd George in his house. I went prejudiced against him and determined at all hazards not to allow myself to be won over by that charm of manner of which I had heard so much.

But in five minutes I had succumbed. He has a wonderful gift of making you feel that he thinks you are the most interesting and most intelligent person he has ever met. What he really does think, I suppose, is that you (of course, I don't mean you; I mean myself) are an unmitigated bore, and while his eyes are smiling at you he is really saying to himself: "Why doesn't the fellow go?..." Yes, he has charm. He does not fuss and he is not over-emphatic in his manner. And he is a most deferential listener. He will even ask you your opinion about matters of which he knows ten times more than yourself, and he will do you the honour of arguing with you.

That afternoon, at the formal ceremony of "opening" the institute, my warning concerning the suffragettes was nearly prophetic. Mr Lloyd George, of course, did all in his power to quell the mob's anger, but the women were violently assaulted, their breasts beaten, their clothes ripped from their backs, their hair torn by the roots from their heads.... On the edge of the mêlée I saw P. W. Wilson standing deploring it.

It has always seemed to me an extraordinary thing that, in company with Dr Walford Davies, I should have been asked some years ago to be a guest at the annual dinner of the Church Diocesan Music Society. I am always ready for adventure, of however hazardous a nature, so I accepted the invitation even after I had been told that a speech was expected from me.

Bishop Welldon, arriving late—in fact, I believe he had dined elsewhere—plumped himself on a chair next to me, and immediately began to dominate everything and everybody within a radius of twenty yards. He is one of those distressing people who *will* be jocular. And his jocularity is rather noisy. He laughed a great deal and rubbed his hands together. And he asked me a question and then asked me another before I had had time to answer the first. And, really, he did talk so awfully loudly.... I had come across him before in trams and shops and places of that kind, and it was always the same; he invariably talked *at* you.... Even in the Manchester Cathedral, where Dr Kendrick Pyne introduced me to him, he shouted at me and never allowed me to finish a sentence.

But I perceive that I am becoming petulant, and I ought not to do so for, as a matter of fact, the dinner was a screamingly funny affair. I had prepared a fierce and warlike speech, a speech attacking the Society whose food I had just eaten and whose wine was still warm in my veins. I am, I suppose, quite the worst speaker in the world; so I had memorised my speech and, so good I thought it that I had vastly enjoyed doing so. But alas! when the minute drew near for me to deliver it, I found myself in an atmosphere of such conviviality, such kindness, such flattering attention, that I could not find it in my heart to deliver the words I had prepared and memorised. Yet an impromptu speech of a different tenor was impossible. I simply hadn't the talent to do it. My name was called and I rose to my feet.

My speech was offensive: it was meant to be. But offensive though I knew it to be, I did not know how offensive it really was. I mentioned the name of Wagner and, as I did so, I saw Dr Walford Davies shudder most violently. Though I attacked the Church for her unimaginative attitude to music, though I stamped on hymns and hymn tunes, though I slanged the microscopic brains of many organists, though I said that nearly all Cathedral music was to me anathema maranatha, nobody except Bishop Welldon appeared to care in the least, and he did not care half so much as poor, virginal Walford Davies, who, at the name of Wagner, shuddered and put his glass aside.

Davies spoke: earnestly, like St Francis; frenziedly, like Savonarola; passionately, like Venus ... no! no! no! ... passionately, like St Paul. Eschew Wagner! That's what it all came to.... "Eschew...." Hate the sin, love the sinner, but most certainly "eschew" both. His cheeks were very white, his lips pale. He trembled a little. Wagner, it appeared, was one of the devils. Ab-so-lute-ly pernicious.... Have you ever noticed how accurately you can estimate a man by his adjectives? Dr Walford Davies used "pernicious" eleven times, "poisonous" twice, "very-much-to-be-distrusted" once, "naughty" once ("this naughty man!" was the phrase), "unlicensed" thrice, and "immoral" fifteen times.... I must say, *en passant*, that I am writing from memory and that my memory for figures is atrocious; still, these adjectives, collectively represent the impression his speech left on my mind.

After dinner (well, neither after nor before dinner) one does not ardently desire a speech of that kind. It fell flat. A fat organist from Bolton (or was it Bacup?) winked me a fat wink. The man on my left—a young musical doctor from Cambridge—dug his elbow into my ribs.

And then came Bishop Welldon's speech. He was extraordinarily clever. He said some of the most cutting things imaginable. He was scathing. He hurt me. Reaching for my glass, I hastily swallowed the large brandy I had been careful to ask for beforehand. He made epigrams, epigrams adapted most skilfully from the writings of his friend, John Oliver Hobbes. And he spoke so well; he had presence; he had a manner; he, like Sir Willoughby Patterne, had a leg ... and a leg that was gaitered. Perhaps it was the gaiters that did it. One has heard a good deal lately about the Hidden Hand, but what about the influence of the Hidden Leg? The leg hidden under the table? The gaitered leg hidden under the table? Most of the diners, remembering that Bishop Welldon was indeed a bishop—though, truly, only, so to speak, an ex-bishop, and an ex-bishop only of Calcutta, and now possessing only the powers of a dean (whatever those powers may be!)—most of the diners, I say, recollecting that Bishop Welldon was indeed a bishop, looked at me with eyes of faint hostility or did not look at me at all.

I was very young, said Bishop Welldon. I was enthusiastic; I was inexperienced; I was "artistic"; I was a jumper-at-conclusions.

When he finished and, with one of his good-natured smiles, turned and looked at me, I was crumbling bread very rapidly, rolling the bread into soiled little pills, putting the little pills all in a row.

Later on in the evening Bishop Welldon, a little group of jolly people and I myself sat and smoked and drank very inferior coffee. Dr Walford Davies did not join us. He shot little pointed darts at me from his eyes, but (as, of course, you must have anticipated) when he and I parted he was most studiously polite.

And, on my way to my tram, I hummed Davies' *Hame! Hame! Hame!* to myself and pondered over the mystery that enables a man to write such a wonderful, soul-searching melody and yet possess an intellect of quality only ... well, so-so.

> Here a little child I stand,
>
> Heaving up my either hand ...

Do you know Walford Davies' setting of that Grace, the setting he made some years ago for one of the daughters of the late Canon Gorton? If you do, if, as I do, you adore its Blake-like simplicity, its Ariel freshness, you will not mind his hatred of Wagner. Only, it is rather strange, don't you think, that we outsiders who love Wagner (and I believe, don't you, that all intense lovers of Wagner must be rather outsiderish?) should be able to love Walford Davies also, though he (most unhappy!) can't or won't love us?

But it is being borne in upon me that for the last five minutes I have been writing like the adorable Eve in *The Tatler*. Let me, for her sake, begin another chapter.

CHAPTER III
FRANK HARRIS

IT must have been five or six years ago that a friend came to me with the news that Frank Harris had expressed a desire to see some of my verse. Precisely what my friend had told Harris about me, I do not know; something very exaggerated, perhaps; something complimentary, doubtless; something that piqued Harris's curiosity, it was evident. As Harris is one of the few modern writers for whom my boyish admiration has survived manhood, I felt subtly gratified that he should take even a fleeting interest in me, and I sat down at once and copied out various poems that had already appeared in *The Academy*, under Lord Alfred Douglas's editorship, and in *The English Review* in the days of Ford Madox Hueffer, and, more recently, when edited by Austin Harrison. With my verses I sent a letter, hypocritically modest as regards myself, honestly full of admiration as regards Harris. He replied from his villa in Nice, sending me a long letter in which he did me the honour to enter fully into the supposed merits and demerits of my work. Of one poem he said that it was not sufficiently sensual, and I have never been able quite to understand what he meant, for I had, with some particularity, described seven naked ladies swimming in a pool, and I had felt that my verses had obviously enough expressed my feelings.

The correspondence continued until, one day, Harris wrote to tell me he was returning to London and to invite me to visit him there. In the event, however, my first meeting with Harris was in Manchester, whither he came to lecture on Shakespeare to the local dramatic society. Jack Kahane (a great friend of mine) and I met him at the Midland Hotel upon his arrival, and from the very first moment he intoxicated me. Whilst he changed from his travelling clothes to evening dress he talked and ejaculated, beseeching us to remain with him as he had had "a rotten journey from London and felt unutterably bored." I remember very little of what he said except that, with some venom, he called Browning "a not unprosperous gentleman." He refused to eat or drink before his lecture and, presently, we went down to the large room in the hotel where he was to speak.

We found there a mixed assembly. Everybody in Manchester, it should be explained, writes plays; at least, I never yet met a man in that delectable city who does not. Moreover, they "study" them. They weigh and compare the merits of Stanley Houghton and Ibsen, Harold Brighouse and Strindberg, Allan Monkhouse and Bjornson, Arnold Bennett and Hauptmann, Laurence Housman and Brieux, and so forth. They search for "inner meanings"; the more earnest of them hunt for "messages"; the more delicate seek to perceive Fine Shades. They are veritable disciples of Miss Horniman— priggishly intellectual, self-consciously superior. And, of course, the rock of their salvation is St Bernard. Innocuous people enough, but impossible to live in the same city with.

To this assembly of earnest, pale men and spectacled women Harris was to lecture, and I looked from them to Harris and from Harris to them with joyful expectations. From the very first sentence he was fiery and provocative, throwing out daring theories, anathematising all forms of respectability, upholding with unparalleled fierceness a wonderful ideal of chivalry and nobility and condemning, *en bloc*, the whole human race, and particularly that portion of it seated before him. Ladies rustled; men stirred uneasily. Then, having delivered himself of a passage of hot eloquence, he paused. A clock ticked. He looked defiantly at us and still paused. A fat lady in the front row, palpably embarrassed by the long silence and, no doubt, feeling that she had reached one of the most dramatic moments of her existence, banged her plump hands together and ejaculated: "Bravo!" A few other ladies of both sexes joined her, but Harris was not to be placated. Thrusting out his chin, he began again. And this time he attacked the Mancunian literary idol, Professor C. H. Herford, a great scholar, but a more than suitable object for Harris's ridicule. Herford is a man who has not lived fully: a semi-invalid, asthmatic, bloodless and spectacled; a man of books and rather dusty books; in effect, a professor. He had recently reviewed Harris's book, *The Man Shakespeare*, in *The Manchester Guardian*, and had called it "a disgrace to British scholarship." Why this should have annoyed the author I cannot tell, but Harris is at times a little unreasonable. Indeed, "annoyance" but feebly describes the feeling that spent itself in scalding invective and the most terrible irony. Each sentence he spoke appeared to be the last word in bitterness; but each succeeding sentence leaped above and beyond its predecessor, until at length the speaker had lashed himself into a state of feeling to express which words were useless. He stopped magnificently, and this time the room rang with applause. It is probable that not half-a-dozen people present believed his attack on Professor Herford was justified; indeed, it is probable that not half-a-dozen were qualified to form any opinion of value on the matter. Nevertheless, they applauded him with enthusiasm, and they did so because they had been deeply stirred by eloquence that can only be described as superb and by anger that was lava hot in its sincerity. Briefly, the lecture was an overwhelming success.

I was soon to discover that Harris, like all the men of genius I have met, is vain. I do not mean that he overrates his gifts: he does not; nor that his recognition of his own genius is offensively insistent: such is very far from being the case. I mean that he is inordinately proud, innocently and childlikely proud, of things that are not of the least consequence. At supper in the French Restaurant the head waiter slipped noiselessly across to the table at which Harris, Kahane and I were sitting. (Harris is the kind of man who acts as a magnet to all head waiters—a high tribute to his dominating personality.) When our orders had been given the waiter, turning to go, said: "Very good, Mr Harris." On the instant Harris looked up. "So you know me?" he asked. "Yes, sir. I have had the pleasure of waiting on you in Monte Carlo and, if I am not mistaken, in New York as well." It is difficult to describe the naïve pleasure Harris took in this: it stamped him at once as a man of the world—he who, of all people, required, in our opinion, no such stamp.

For six hours we talked—talked long after every other visitor in the hotel had retired, and we were left alone in the Octagon Court in a pool of dim light. Harris is the only brilliant talker I have met who has not made me feel an abject idiot. To begin with, though he has a pronounced strain of violence, almost of brutality, in his nature, he is always infinitely courteous. He will listen to your (I mean my) feeble contributions to a discussion with interest which, if feigned, is so admirably feigned that you are completely deceived. And he can keep this sort of thing up indefinitely. Moreover, though his mind is agile enough, his speech is rarely quick; it is slow and deliberate, but without hesitation, without a single word of tautology.

I cannot hope, after so long a lapse of time, to reproduce, however faintly, the true quality of Harris's conversation, but I remember the substance of it most vividly. In his lecture earlier in the evening he had mentioned Jesus Christ, and the reference to our Saviour had been so original in its implication, yet so reverent in its manner, that I felt he must have much that is new to say on a subject that has aroused more discussion than any other during the last two thousand years. So I broached it tentatively. He was aroused immediately, and skilfully drew me out to discover if I had anything new to say. I had not. I merely voiced what must be an age-long regret, that only one side of Christ's nature has been presented to us in the Gospels; that the feasting, joyous Christ has been only faintly indicated; and that His tolerance towards the weaknesses of the body's passions had always been shirked by those of the priestly craft. I thought it possible that at some future crisis in the world's history Christ might come again and, on His second coming, present to the world a more complete embodiment of all the potentialities inherent in human nature.

With much of this Harris agreed, though I soon perceived that his mind had for long been intuitively building up, and giving true proportion to, those elements in Christ's nature that are only hinted at in the Gospels. He was all for a full-blooded, passionate Jesus, for a Jesus who had tested the body's powers, for a Jesus who was crucified by passion before He was crucified by Pilate. In a word, he applied to Jesus the same intuitive method that he had already applied to Shakespeare. The danger of this method, of course, is that one is tempted (and it is almost impossible not to succumb to the temptation) to project one's own personality into that of the man one is studying.

"My next book shall be about Jesus Christ," said Harris. "No man in these days has written honestly about Him."

"Shall you write as a believer?" I asked.

"Most assuredly," he replied.

Then Harris told us some stories—stories he had written, stories he had yet to write. I remember Austin Harrison once saying to me: "Frank Harris is the most astounding creature! He will tell you a story and tell it so marvellously that, when he has finished, you say to yourself: 'That is the most wonderful thing I have ever heard.' And you say to him: 'Why, in God's name, don't you write that?' Well, he does write it, and when you read it you see that, after all, it is by no means so wonderful a thing as you had thought it." But this is only half true. The story that is told is a very different thing from the story that is written: so different, indeed, that one cannot find any basis for comparison. In telling a story Harris is elliptical; a faint gesture serves for a sentence; a momentary silence is an innuendo; a lifting of the eyebrows, a look, a dropping of the voice, a slowness in his speech—all these take the place of words. He is an exquisite actor and he is at his best when he is sinister and menacing. One need scarcely say that the effect of one of Harris's stories, told in private, with only one or two listeners, is extremely powerful, for his personality, so quick to melt and suffuse his speech—colouring it and vitalising it—is strong and strange and full of tropical richness....

But the actor's gift is not rare, whereas that combination of talents that makes a great short-story writer is met with only once or twice in a generation. Harris's claims to greatness in this direction cannot justly be denied, though of late years there has been a noticeable tendency to treat his work as though it were not of first-rate importance. His choice of subject, the violence of his thought, his strict honesty of mind, his open contempt for many of his contemporaries—these have brought him enemies whose only method of retaliation is to decry work they will not understand.

But Harris could not be happy without hostility. There is something of the jaguar in his nature; he must, for his soul's peace, have his teeth in the flesh of an enemy. And, if he is not fighting an individual, he is offending society at large. Years ago, so Harris told me, when he was editing *The Fortnightly Review* with such distinction, he printed one of his own short stories in that magazine—a story that, for one reason or another, gave great offence to a large section of readers. Within twenty-four hours he had a hornet's nest about his ears, and the directors of the firm, Messrs Chapman & Hall, who published the *Fortnightly*, met in solemn conclave to discuss what should be done with so injudicious and reckless an editor. Needless to say, Harris stood by his guns, and one can imagine the splendidly arrogant way in which he would uphold his right to insert anything he chose in a magazine edited by himself. But discussion made matters only more critical, and Harris told me he would have been compelled to hand in his resignation if an unforeseen event had not occurred. That event was the entrance of George Meredith, who, at that time, was a reader for Messrs Chapman & Hall. As soon as his eyes lit on Harris he held out his hand, and walked quickly up to him, saying: "My warmest congratulations! Your story in the new number is quite the finest thing you have done—an honour to yourself and the *Fortnightly*!" That left no further room for discussion and, needless to say, Harris retained his editorship of the great magazine.

My first meeting with Harris was of the friendliest nature, and on his return to London he wrote to me thanking me for something I had written about him in *The Manchester Courier*. (I noticed with amusement that *The Manchester Guardian*, unable, no doubt, to forgive Harris for attacking Professor Herford, had absolutely ignored the Shakespeare lecture, except to announce baldly that it had been given.)

Very soon after this meeting in Manchester I went to live in London, and called on Harris in Chancery Lane. He was running a curious illustrated weekly, entitled *Hearth and Home*, and I remember sitting in a little back room in his office turning over the files of his magazine and wondering what on earth he hoped to do with such a production. It was tame; it was watery; it was feeble. I looked at him quizzically.

"What do you think of it?" he asked.

"Well, don't you see?..." I began hesitatingly; "don't you see that ... well, now, look at the *title*!"

"Title's good enough, don't you think?"

"Oh yes, good enough ... good enough for Fleetway House. Why not sell it to Northcliffe? But you've got no Aunt Maggie's column, and no Beauty Hints, and no Cupid's Corner! Oh, Harris!"

He laughed, and invited me out to lunch.

I never discovered what strange circumstances had conspired to make him the possessor of this extraordinary production. No doubt he bought it for nothing, with the intention of rapidly improving it and selling it for something substantial later on. But I believe it died soon after—perhaps urged on to its grave by some verses of mine which were printed close to an advertisement of ladies' — —.

On our way out of the office we were joined by a very beautiful lady who, it soon transpired, shared my admiration for Harris's genius. We jumped on to a bus running at full speed and alighted, a couple of minutes later, at Simpson's.

Harris should write a book on cookery. Perhaps he will. Harris should run a hotel. But he has already done so. Harris should be induced to print all the indiscreet things he says over coffee and liqueurs....

It was a close study of Simpson's menu that started the cookery discussion. The Beautiful Lady and I were told what was wrong and what was right with the menu. And then there began a discourse, profound, full of strange knowledge and recondite wisdom, a discourse that Balzac should have heard, that the de Goncourts would have envied. We listened, amazed. And a waiter, having rushed to our table in the stress of his work, stood anchored, his mouth slightly open, his whole attention riveted on the Master from whom no gastronomic secrets were hid. Truly, Harris was amazing!

After a considerable time his enthusiasm evaporated and we began to eat. And then ensued a long talk, full of indiscretions, of most enjoyable malice. Harris told us many things that, perhaps, it would have been wiser if he had kept to himself. But, in spite of his venom, his real hatred of certain individuals, he never for a moment permits himself to be blinded to the quality of a man's work.

"So-and-so is the most detestable person," he said, speaking of a well-known writer, "but he is one of the few real poets alive." Again: "X is the most generous-hearted man I have ever met; it's a pity he can't learn to write."

Mention of Richard Middleton, who had only recently died by his own hand in Brussels, troubled him, and it was clear that he had not yet recovered from the shock of this tragedy.

"He killed himself in a mood of sheer disgust—disgust at his lack of success. True, he was still young, and was becoming more widely known month by month; also, he had many friends. Nevertheless, life did not give him what he asked and, tired of asking, he ended life. I remember him coming to me just before he left England. He wanted to get away. Some mood of loathing had come to him; he was fretful, yet determined. I offered him my villa at Nice; it was empty, the caretaker would attend to his wants and he would have ample leisure for his work. He hesitated, stayed in London a day or two longer and then disappeared to Brussels.... I know the poison he used, and a score of times I have gone over in my mind the tortures he must have endured."

Harris paled; his face twitched and, involuntarily, as it seemed, his shoulders twisted themselves. Brooding, he was silent for a few minutes, and then, collecting himself with a little shudder, began to speak of other things.

A little later the Beautiful Lady departed and we were left alone.

"And now," said Harris, "tell me about yourself. What are you doing? Why have you left Manchester?—but there is no reason to ask that. Tell me this—are you making enough money for yourself?"

"Well, I've lived in London just one week," said I, "and my tastes are rather expensive. Just before I left Manchester a very experienced journalist told me I should be making a thousand pounds a year at the end of eighteen months; another, equally experienced, declared I should never make more than six pounds a week. I hope the second one won't prove correct."

He mused for a few moments.

"You ought to make a thousand pounds a year pretty easily, I should think," he said at length. "Whom do you know?"

I knew nobody, and said so. He thereupon took a piece of paper from his pocket and wrote a list of names; at the top of the list stood J. L. Garvin; at the bottom, Lord Northcliffe.

"Northcliffe's away," he said, "buying forests in Newfoundland to make paper with. However, he'll be back in a week or two, and in the meantime I'll write you a letter to give to him. And now we'll take a taxi and see people."

Harris gave up the whole of that day to me and, largely owing to him, I had within the next few days more work offered to me than I could possibly get through. From time to time, months later, good things would come my way, and nearly always I could trace them to something generous and fine that Harris had said of me.

It was chiefly because he was so generous with his time that I so rarely called upon him. Often I would curb a strong desire to see him, feeling that however embarrassing my visit might be, he would, out of a quixotic kindness, throw up his work and come with me to talk. For this reason I had not seen him for some little time, when, one morning, I received a letter from him reproaching me for my absence. "Why have you hidden yourself for so long?" he asked. "I go to the Café every night; come, you will find me there."

"The Café," of course, was the Café Royal. It so chanced that, that very afternoon, my duties took me to a symphony concert in the Queen's Hall; the concert over, I found myself passing the Café Royal on my way from the Queen's Hall to Piccadilly Circus, and turned in on the remote chance of finding Harris.

At the end of the passage, near the windows where French papers are displayed, I found a crowd of a dozen excited men, all talking and gesticulating. The rest of the Café was empty, as one would expect at that time of the day. In the middle of the small crowd was Harris, who caught my eye almost at once. He came to me, and I saw that he was rather agitated.

"Come and sit over here, Cumberland," he said. "I've just been through a beastly quarter of an hour."

It appeared that a well-known and very distinguished *littérateur* had quarrelled with him in the Café.... Blows had been exchanged....

We talked of money—an ever-absorbing topic both to Harris and to me. He told me his books had brought him practically nothing. For *The Bomb*, if I remember correctly, he received fifty pounds—certainly not more than one hundred pounds.

"If I had been compelled to live by what my books have brought me," he said, "I should have starved. Yet it is not long ago that Arnold Bennett assured me that I should be able to earn five thousand pounds a year if I gave my whole time to fiction. But Bennett is wrong. My books, ever since *Elder Conklin* was published, have been enthusiastically praised, but they have not had large sales. Most authors must find book-writing the most unremunerative work in the world. I put an enormous amount of labour into *The Bomb*, as I do into all my books, and the labour was not made any the less from the fact that much of the earliest part of the book is autobiographical. In my young manhood I worked as a labourer, deep under water, at the foundations of Brooklyn Bridge; it is all described in my book."

Though I went to the Café Royal at frequent intervals after that I very rarely saw Harris there. He had abandoned *Hearth and Home*, or it had abandoned him, and he was now throwing away his brilliant gifts on *Modern Society*. I was elected an honorary member of the Cabaret Club, run by Madame Strindberg, the widow of the great Swedish writer, and I used to look in there occasionally in the early hours of the morning, expecting to run across Harris, who, I heard, also visited that exotic, underground and rather riotous place. But I never chanced to see him, and two or three months must have passed without my hearing of him.

In March, 1914, I went to Athens for a holiday. Something brave and wonderful in that city, some ancient Bacchic madness, some fierce exaltation of soul took hold of me, and I remember sitting down one night, after a visit to fever-stricken Eleusis, to write to Harris, feeling the necessity of expressing myself to one who would understand. The reader may be amused that I should think Harris akin to ancient Greece, but if the reader is amused he does not know Harris. Only A. R. Orage is more Greek in spirit than he is. In reply Harris wrote at great length, full of the fervour of a young student. He told me that in his young manhood he had spent a year of study in that wonderful city, and urged me to visit him on my return to England.

But I was destined not to see him again. Very soon after my return to England he got into trouble with reference to something libellous that he had published in *Modern Society*. He was kept in prison, if I remember rightly, for about a month. I sought permission to visit him there, but was refused, and I was staying in Oxford when he was released.

Soon after the war broke out he wrote me the following letter from Paris:—

> 23, Avenue du Bois de Boulogne, Paris,
> *29th Aug.* '14.

My dear Cumberland,—I'm just back from the frontier.... This war of nations is going to test every man as by fire before it's over. It will be long in spite of Mr Kipps and Bernard Shaw. The Russian masses will hardly come decisively into action (they have scarcely any railways and no good roads) till next May or June, and long before then, or rather in a couple of months from now, the French will be pressed back to within twenty miles of besieged Paris, when I hope the English forces on the flank will stop the German advance. Then will begin the slow process of driving the Germans home, which will be quickened by the Russian weight behind Cossack pricks. Fancy one *man* having the power to set 400 millions of men fighting for their lives. And then they talk of man as a rational animal!!

Don't say you like what I wrote in *The Daily Sketch*; all my best things were carefully cut out and filled up with drivel, till my cheeks burned.

Your sketch of me is very kindly; the fault you find in me is not a fault. Jesus, Shakespeare, Napoleon—all the greatest men have known their own value and insisted on it—perhaps because they have all *come to their own and their own received them not*. When you have done great work you feel it is not yours, but given to you; you are only a reed shaken in the wind; you can judge it as if it had nothing to do with you. Moreover, you see that this failure to recognise greatness is the capital sin of all time, the sin against the Holy Ghost which He said could never be forgiven. Modesty is the fig-leaf of mediocrity—don't let us talk of it. Remember how Whistler scourged it.

I'm writing now on *Natural Religion*—my best thing yet: I've done more than Nietzsche: don't think I'm bragging. I am the Reconciler; though my cocked nose and keen eyes may make you think me a combatant. Twenty years hence, Cumberland, if your eyes keep their promise, you'll think differently of me. I remember as a young man getting Wagner to praise himself and saying to myself that no man was ever so conceited as the little hawk-faced fellow with the ploughshare chin. Did he not say that the step from Bach to Beethoven was not so great as that from Beethoven to Wagner! And yet for these fifteen years past I have agreed with him and find nothing conceited in the declaration. Only weak men are hurt by another man's conceit; are we not gods also to be spoken of with reverence?

> To see the world in a grain of sand
>
> And Heaven in a wild flower,
>
> To hold Infinity in your hand
>
> And Eternity in an hour.

The question for you is, have I quickened you? Encouraged you to be a brave soldier in the Liberation War of Humanity? Did virtue come out of me? or discouragement? Now at nearly sixty I am about to rebuild my life: my own people have stoned and imprisoned and exiled me. Well—the world's wide. In October I shall be in New York, ready for another round with Fate. Meanwhile, all luck to you and all good will from your friend,

Frank Harris.

Remember this word of Joubert: there is no such sure sign of mediocrity as constant moderation in praise. Ha! Ha! Ha! Yours ever,

F. H.

There is not in this letter a single word to indicate that he was not, heart and soul, in sympathy with the Allied Cause. Late in September, 1914, I was myself in Paris, having visited Amiens and the Marne. I took the earliest opportunity of calling upon Harris, but discovered that he had left his rooms a few days earlier, leaving no indication of his next resting-place. On calling upon the American Consul I discovered that my friend had already sailed for the States.

Subsequently he wrote bitterly about England in an American paper. I never had an opportunity of reading his articles, but I read various extracts from them in British newspapers, and was astounded both by the views they contained and by the manner in which those views were expressed.

Years ago Ruskin wrote Rossetti a curious letter: he said he could regard no man as friend who did not value his (Ruskin's) gifts as highly as he (Ruskin) did. Harris, no doubt, adopted the same kind of attitude towards England. England refused to accept him at his own estimate and, at length, in fierce disgust, Harris turned his back on a country which he deemed unworthy of him.

CHAPTER IV
MISCELLANEOUS

YVETTE GUILBERT!... Yvette Guilbert! I suppose that only a writer who really can write can say anything useful or dignified about this most wonderful woman.... And yet I must try. Do you remember that extraordinary breath-catching passage in *Villette* where Charlotte Brontë describes the acting of Vashti—Vashti who was Rachel—Vashti who went to London when Charlotte loved Héger?... That, I always think, was a great event. Little Currer Bell, with her most modest mind and her most proud heart, sitting, so breathlessly, on one side of the footlights, and Rachel walking from the wings, beyond the footlights, and, like an empress, speaking, thinking like an empress, and, like a veritable woman, loving and hating.... Do you remember that passage? If you do, perhaps you will think, as I do, that, after all, only women can write of women. Did not Jane Austen create Elizabeth Bennet? And who was it who wrote the *Sonnets from the Portuguese*? And even, after all, Aphra Behn ... well, *she* knew something about women, didn't she?

So that I feel only a woman can write at all convincingly of Yvette Guilbert. I must just gossip and prattle a little while.

I must have heard Yvette Guilbert a score of times. The first occasion was in the Midland Hall, Manchester, eight or ten years ago, when she sang to an audience of about two hundred frigid people who, apparently, knew as much French as I know of the language of the Serbs, and as much about Art as the pencil with which I write knows about the thoughts it records. Ernest Newman was there and, that night, wrote an article for *The Manchester Guardian* that must have more than compensated Guilbert for the smallness of the audience. For she loves praise, even the praise she gives herself, as the following letter addressed to myself will testify:

Je reçois votre aimable lettre et votre *admirable article*!! Je ne peux pas vous dire toute *la joie* que je ressens en lisant que vous comprenez *si bien* mes efforts! Je n'ai jamais *su être hypocrite* et j'ai toujours manqué de diplomatie dans la vie à cause de cela; aussi, je n'hésite pas à vous dire que je *crois* sincèrement mériter vos bonnes paroles parce que je passe *ma vie entière à me dévouer* à mon art sans jamais de vacances. Mon amour pour le travail et la Beauté et tout ce qui est *pure* en art est tout le "mateur" de mes forces intellectuelles. Merci d'avoir deviné ce que le public ne voit pas toujours. Mes mains dans les vôtres.

Yvette Guilbert.

Guilbert has no singing voice, and yet she sings. Her singing voice is small ... ever so small. Yet clear, distinct, expressive and, in the lowest register, most deep and thrilling. How little mere "voice" matters! Only consider. Here, on one hand, we have Madame Clara Butt with, I suppose, one of the most wonderful organs that this world, or any other world, has ever listened to. But would you walk five miles to hear her sing? I wouldn't. You, I hope and believe, wouldn't either. Would you walk five miles to hear Blanche Marchesi sing—Blanche Marchesi, whose voice, as mere voice, is like a hundred other voices? Of course you would. Voice matters little. It is the temperament, the intellect, behind the voice that counts. And the eternal struggle that Yvette Guilbert has had to undergo has been the struggle to make her comparatively small voice express the wonderful things of her imagination.

A gesture. A look. An inflection. Two paces on the platform. A little cry ... a little cry of dismay. A superb and beautiful signal that tells us the Mother of God is big with a Child. A tiny silence. A moment of jauntiness. Something arch and irresistible. Something tragic that makes you clench your fists....

One day Yvette Guilbert wrote to ask me to call on her. I did not go. One feels so foolish in the presence of genius. One's vanity is hurt. One is afraid of being found out.

In the early days of the war I visited Sir Victor Horsley several times at his home. I was interested in shell shock, in the influence that the horror of war has on certain types of human nature, and he was good enough to supply me with a great deal of information. Quiet and undemonstrative, he used always to stand, or move slowly up and down the room; in the long talks we had together, I do not remember his sitting down once.

I don't think I ever met a man more careful to express his exact meaning; he appeared to have a horror of exaggeration and he qualified nearly every statement he made. In discussing scientific subjects such scrupulous carefulness is, of course, not only wise but necessary, and when, later on, I wrote a newspaper article on the effect that the strain and horror of war have on the human brain, Sir Victor showed himself very anxious that, in quoting his views, I should do so in language that could not possibly be interpreted in two different senses.

He told me what my own experience in France and Salonica in 1915–1917 confirmed later on, that it is frequently the neurotic, the artistic, the excitable man who most quickly adapts himself to, and is least disturbed by, the incredible cruelties of warfare, whilst the phlegmatic type of man is more liable to be broken by those cruelties. Sir Victor Horsley suggested that this was, in some measure, due to the fact that the neurotic man has, in imagination, tasted the terror of war before he has actually experienced it; that he has, as it were, prepared his mind for the shock it is to receive. The unimaginative man cannot do this, so that when his turn comes to go to the trenches and witness stark horrors, his nervous system reacts most violently.

Sir Victor spoke a good deal to me about the evil influence of drink, and continually regretted that rum was served out to our soldiers. On this subject, of course, though I disagreed with him profoundly, I did not attempt to argue, though I pointed out that Napoleon had won many of his campaigns by almost drugging his men with spirits. To this he made no reply, though he shook his head gravely and seemed to ponder a little.

My last interview with him was in his long, bare dining-room, where, as we stood before the fire, he described to me in a low, serious voice two or three war cases of mental trouble (functional, of course, not organic), and I could see that the war was, so to speak, closing in around him and enveloping him with its violent appeals, its tragic interests.

Mrs Pankhurst I met only once, but the impression she has left on my mind is that of a most vivid personality. I saw her in many ridiculous situations that would have made almost any other person look positively foolish; but Mrs Pankhurst's sense of personal dignity is so strong, her personality is so imperious, and, above all, she possesses so much humour and good sense, that it is impossible to imagine any situation, however grotesque, that would render her ridiculous.

My interview with her was at the close of a day during which she had worked incessantly. She was tired, and her face was lined and rather dim. An hour earlier I had seen her in Oxford Street, Manchester, seated in an open, horseless carriage, a dozen enthusiastic girls pulling at the shafts, a few ribald boys following and shouting small obscenities. I admired the perfect way she carried off the trying situation. She sat perfectly calmly, as though nothing in the least unusual were happening, as though, indeed, it were her daily custom, and the daily custom of all women, to be dragged through the public streets by a band of young ladies.

We sat under a lamp at a large table. The things we discussed are now of no consequence, for the need for their discussion no longer exists. I can only give my impression of her.

She struck me as being unutterably weary, weary bodily and perhaps mentally. Her personality suggested a body and a spirit being driven by an implacable will, a will that had no mercy for herself or for others, a will that no power could break. I could not help wondering, as I looked at her, whether she had not her moments of doubt, of self-distrust. She must have had, for all men and women have. But those moments would be few and short. Though she spoke to me very quietly, without a gesture, with one rather tightly clenched hand on the table, I felt the sheer *power* of her, the power that a quenchless spirit always gives to its owner.

Fanatic? Well, yes, if to be indifferent to the opinion of other people and to be absolutely sure of yourself is to be fanatical. Certainly, she was strange and grim and relentless. And yet one could not doubt her tenderness, her deep sympathy, her devotion to humanity. Yes, a strange woman, but perhaps not so very strange. The qualities I saw in her are common qualities; the difference between her and others was simply that she possessed those qualities in an unusual degree.

Jacob Epstein, after flouting the artistic conventions for at least ten years, is being taken to the heart of the public. The impossible is happening, and it is happening because of the war. The war has forced reality upon us; it has made us love beauty rather than prettiness, truth rather than make-believe, the soul of things rather than their appearances.

Epstein, I think, could never be said to be in revolt against any of the artistic tendencies of the time. He simply did not follow those tendencies or permit them to influence him. But three or four years ago, when I first met him, he had the appearance, the manner, and even the thoughts of one who is in revolt.

I remember discussing with him some very curious and, indeed, rather alarming designs of his which were being exhibited at a little gallery whose name I have forgotten. The designs were openly and widely described as "indecent"; to me they were not indecent: they were merely meaningless. I could see no idea behind them.

"They are not designs," said Epstein, a little petulantly, I thought.

"Then what *are* they?" I asked. "What do *you* call them?"

"I am not aware that I call them anything."

"But what do they *mean*?"

He smiled curiously and (we were sitting in the Café Royal) lit a cigarette.

"Ah! That is for you to find out. Surely you don't expect an artist to explain himself?"

Of course he was perfectly right, and I was more than foolish to ask him these questions. But I flogged at it.

"Now, your busts! Especially that wonderful head of Augustus John's son!—beautiful, marvellous! But those extraordinary red drawings."

"I cannot explain them," said he, "but I would certainly like you to understand them, for it seems to me that you are not unintelligent."

He gave me a quick, sly look, and we began to talk of John. I am afraid that Epstein must have qualified his opinion of my intelligence, for he asserted, in contradiction to what I was saying, that John was on the wrong tack, and we failed to come to any agreement about this most wonderful of living painters.

Like most artists, Epstein is pronouncedly inarticulate. He is, I suppose, as much a mystery to himself as he is to others. But his work is, of course, a hundred times more interesting than himself.

I used to see him often, but we rarely did more than acknowledge each other's existence, and when I saw him the other week in khaki, sitting in the Café Royal, it was clear to me that, though he said he remembered me, he had only a vague recollection of my personality and had completely forgotten my name.

I have often thought it strange that while singers like Madame Patti and Madame Tetrazzini should conquer the world—and by the world I mean every section of the musical public, vulgar and fastidious alike—another and, to my mind, a very much finer artiste, Madame Ackté, should be regarded with delight only by those whose musical experience is wide and whose minds have been tutored by comprehensive study. Personality, after all, is almost everything in Art, and Madame Ackté has a personality that dwarfs into insignificance nearly all singers who are her equal in technical attainments and in musical subtlety.

Her great part is Salomé, in Richard Strauss's opera of that name. With the wonderful intuition of a healthy, robust mind she has divined all the perverted wickedness of that most tortured woman. Her acting is among the finest things of our day.

No one could guess, in talking to this quiet, almost demure woman, that she has in her such fires of passion, such powers of portraying devastating wickedness. She has charm, graciousness, simplicity. Like Yvette Guilbert, she has worked hard almost every day of her life. Her talk is all of music and acting. She seems most unmodern. Her ingenuous love of praise is delightful, and if you notice the little subtleties in her singing and acting that most people do not notice, she is your friend for ever.

CHAPTER V
STANLEY HOUGHTON AND
HAROLD BRIGHOUSE

BUT perhaps you have forgotten who Stanley Houghton was? Well, not so long before the Great War he was famous, both in England and America, as the author of *Hindle Wakes*, he was universally alluded to as a charming personality, and he promised to become one of the most prosperous playwrights in England. Then, while still young and not yet accustomed to his fame, he died in Italy. Thereupon some thousand newspaper-writers recorded his death and wrote about him some of the most lamentable nonsense it has ever been my misfortune to read.

Let me tell you all about it.

I was introduced to Stanley Houghton in Manchester by Jack Kahane— the latter a most brilliant and engaging personality who knew everybody: or, rather, everybody knew him.

"This," said Kahane, indicating Houghton, "is one of Miss Horniman's pets. She is doing a play of his this week at the Gaiety. Now, let me see, Stanley, what is the name of your little play?"

Houghton laughed deprecatingly.

"Oh, I saw it last night," said I, "and jolly good it was. But I've seen another play of yours besides *The Younger Generation*; it was founded on a story by Guy de Maupassant. That, also, was tremendously amusing."

He frowned, and I understood from the way that he looked over my head that I had displeased him. For a moment he was silent, then:

"I've just been reading some of your verses in *The English Review*," said he; "quite nice, quite nice."

So then I examined him closely and saw a tall, fair youth, with plenty of straw-coloured hair, a prominent, rather crooked nose, and a manner of painful self-consciousness. I believe that, from that moment, we distrusted each other most heartily. We parted a few minutes later and I think Houghton must have shared my suspicion and regret that we should often have to meet after that date. Kahane was and is (though he has been in France these three years and I in Macedonia) my most intimate friend, and had lately "taken up" Houghton, and whenever Kahane did a thing he did it pretty thoroughly. And friends of a friend are bound to tumble across each other continually.

Later in the day I protested to Kahane.

"What on earth has induced you to take up this man Houghton?" I asked.

"He amuses me," said Jack. "And, really, you know, one or two of his little things are quite promising. When he bores me I rag him. And then he loses his temper. *Il m'amuse*, and that's all I require from him."

Shortly after I was elected a member of a funny little coterie in Manchester, called the Swan Club. Kahane had founded it. There were twelve of us altogether: Kahane; Stanley Houghton; Harold Brighouse (whose play, *Hobson's Choice*, is making "big money" in London at the moment of writing); Charles Abercrombie (now a Lt.-Colonel and a C.B.); Walter Mudie, the best of good fellows; Ernest Marriott, artist; W. Price-Heywood, accountant and leader-writer; myself and a few hangers-on of the Arts. We used to meet for lunch at a shabby little restaurant in Peter Street, Manchester, opposite the Theatre Royal, and we did our utmost to induce each other to talk about ourselves.

In this little coterie Houghton was a veritable whale among the minnows. He was also a fish out of water. From the very first his success spoiled him. He would take himself ponderously. Brighouse worshipped success, so he worshipped Houghton. The rest of us, if we worshipped anything at all, worshipped genius, and as Kahane was the only one among us who had a touch of that divine quality, we rather tended to worship him. But Kahane frittered away his gifts; he made a lot of money by dint of working about an hour a day and by the sheer force of his personality. For the rest he played and played hard. He talked; he ragged; he listened to music and saw plays; he fell in love; he indulged harmless vices; and he wrote two wonderful plays, full of faults, but streaked with originality, with fire and with colour. In effect, he could beat both Houghton and Brighouse at their own game, and they knew it. But, at that time, playwriting with Kahane was only a game; with the other two it was deadly earnest.

Houghton and Brighouse were something (and, I gathered, something not very brilliant) in the city. Quite what that something was I do not know, though I remember seeking out Brighouse once in a dark warehouse smelling of damp cloth. Every afternoon Houghton and Brighouse would close their ledgers, or petty-cash books, or whatever it was they did close, and rush off home—Brighouse to catch, perhaps, his six-five p.m. train to Eccles, and Houghton to jump gymnastically (he played hockey, I believe) on to a passing tram bound for Alexandra Park. After a hurried meal, out with the MSS., the notebooks, the typescript and to work! And how hard they *did* work!

I remember Brighouse telling me some years ago that he had written more than thirty plays, but I cannot conceive that anybody but himself has read them all. Brighouse slogged, and he beat so long at the door of success that at last it opened to him. Houghton also slogged, but in a dandified way. He was clever, he was cute, and he played his cards well.

Houghton was, not without full justice, called the leader of the Manchester School of dramatists. He was hard; he was unimaginative; he was unromantic. But he was extraordinarily apt, and he had a neat and tidy brain. Close must have been that union of souls that bound his soul to the soul of Miss Horniman. Miss Horniman never (well, hardly ever) produced a romantic play, and Stanley Houghton never wrote one. He was out to "make good," and Miss Horniman helped him to go one better.

I need scarcely say that Houghton was, so far as his plays were concerned, an industrious man of business. When the real artist has finished a work, he ceases to take interest in it; but, with Houghton, when a play was completed his interest in it immediately intensified. He sent his plays everywhere: to the provinces, to London, to America, to agents. As soon as a play came back, "returned with thanks," out it went again by the next post. And he pulled strings—oh! ever so gently, but he pulled them.

Though quite a few of his plays had been produced in the north, and though he had written some clever dramatic criticism for *The Manchester Guardian*, he was unknown in London till the Stage Society produced *Hindle Wakes*. Then Fame came to him and knocked him off his feet. It is impossible to imagine a man more conscious of his success. His consciousness of it made him, on occasion, tongue-tied. In conversation he could be ready, and his repartee was frequently brilliant, but during the years I knew him his attitude always suggested that he anticipated and feared attack. I saw him once at the bar of the Gaiety Theatre, Manchester, in the midst of a group of friends. I was not of their company, but I noticed that he stood silent, erect and strained, his head a little thrown back, his face set. Then, and on many other occasions, it seemed to me that he longed to break down the feeling of awkwardness—to throw off the obsession of self-consciousness—that overcame him.

But I must confess that I rarely saw him in company in which there were not two or three who were hostile to him; therefore I saw him but seldom at his best. Not infrequently, there was a "dead set" against him, and if the banter were edged with malice (as it not infrequently was) he withered like a lily under the grip of a frost. The truth is, he was not modest and he could not feign modesty. His vanity was neither charming nor aggressive; it was cold and distant, without geniality, without humour. Genius is one of the wombs of vanity, but Houghton had no genius; there was not a trace of magic in him; he was merely extraordinarily clever, closely observant and possessed of an instinctive sense of form and of literary values.

There came a day when it entered my head to interview him for *The Manchester Courier*, a paper for which I wrote musical criticism. He accepted my proposal with alacrity, invited me to the Winter Garden of the Midland Hotel, and provided me with coffee, liqueurs and cigars.

He began by telling me that this was the first time he had been interviewed for the Press.

"An uncomfortable half-hour awaits you, then," said I, and, on the instant, he began to fidget.

I noticed that he was dressed for the occasion; he looked prosperous and literary and there hung about him just a suspicion of cosmopolitanism. Not only sartorially was he prepared; his mind was in tune to the occasion and the right pose was donned. That is to say, he was determined not to appear conceited or self-satisfied; but he did not succeed. He made light of his success in a heavy, emphatic way. He praised *Hindle Wakes* with faint damns, and suggested that this play would soon cease its successful run in London. He was careful not to evince any pleasure in his success, any natural buoyancy of spirit, any momentary delight. In a word, he was dull, tactless and insincere. There was nothing boyish or charming or graceful in his words; he had on all his heavy armour and it banged and clanged as he moved.

When the interview was over he invited me to his father's house for the evening meal. I went. I went out of curiosity. He did not amuse me, but most certainly he did interest me.

When we had finished our meal he took me to his study. Near the window was a typewriter; in the typewriter was a sheet of paper half covered with script. There were very few erasures.

"I always compose straight on to the machine," said Houghton.

"Ah yes," said I, "and so did J. M. Synge. It has always seemed to me remarkable that Synge should do that; in your own case, of course, it is not quite so remarkable."

"It is a comedy for Cyril Maude" (I think he said Cyril Maude). "He wired to me the other day to go up to London to see him. Yes; he wanted a comedy, and he wanted me to write it. That was about a fortnight ago. Well, the thing's nearly finished; in another week it will be on its way to London. Rather quick work, don't you think?"

"Quite. But all that you have told me I know already, and, really, you must know that I know. You see, Brighouse comes to the Swan Club day by day, drinks his beer—you know, the conventionally British pint he *will* have in a pewter mug— —"

"Yes; Harold is very British," interrupted Houghton.

"Isn't he? Well, as I was saying, Brighouse drinks his beer, fixes his eyes on his plate, and then spasmodically tells us all the news about you. He told us, for example, about Cyril Maude giving you a hundred (or was it a thousand?) guineas for the sight of a new comedy; he told us about *The Daily Mail* wanting articles from you at some colossal figure; he told us about the host of people who send you wires every day; he told us about— —"

Houghton stirred uneasily, but he looked intensely gratified.

"He told us about everything," I added, after a slight pause. "What you tell him he tells us. But why don't you come and tell us yourself, Houghton? We never see you at the Swan Club nowadays. It must not be said of you that you desert old friends, that success has made you careless of those you once liked."

He darted a glance at me and decided, as was indeed the case, that I was attempting to be ironical.

"The truth is," said he, "that the company I find at the Swan Club is not always very congenial. One or two new men have been lately introduced— —"

He looked away from me meaningly.

"Quite," said I, unperturbed; "oh, quite."

"And," he continued, "I am kept very busy with one thing and another. It is true that I have given up my business and now intend devoting all my energy to literary work, but just at the present moment I am kept at it from dawn to dusk."

Silence fell upon us, a rather oppressive silence, I think, for I remember hunting about in my mind for something to say. I noticed a copy of *The Playboy of the Western World* on the little table before us.

"Still reading Synge?" I asked.

"Yes; still reading Synge," he replied. Then, after a pause: "A great man, Synge."

"An interesting man, a curious man," said I, "but great? Only G. H. Mair, Willie Yeats and high school girls think Synge great, Houghton."

"Is that so?" asked he languidly.

I invited him to have a cigarette, but he refused. In truth, we were both very uncomfortable and, by the subtle understanding and inverted sympathy that hearty dislike engenders, we rose simultaneously to our feet, rather hurriedly left the room, and soon found ourselves in the hall downstairs. He opened the front door and we stood for a moment, looking around us.

Next day my interview with Houghton appeared in *The Manchester Courier*, with a portrait of the young dramatist. I do not remember a word of that article, but I am quite sure it was insincere, without distinction, and full of inanities; indeed, I would bet at least ten drachmæ that there occur in it such expressions as "inherent modesty," "charming personality," "interesting outlook on life," and so on. A journalist (must I say it?) is like a barrister: he is fee'd to say what is required to be said. At all events, the interview pleased Houghton, for he sent me a copy of *Hindle Wakes* with a jocular inscription on its title-page.

The friendship between Brighouse and Houghton increased in intensity, and when Arnold Bennett publicly referred to Brighouse in terms of no small admiration Houghton decided that his eager disciple could be received into the inner sanctum of his coldly fraternal breast. And Brighouse, grateful to Bennett, loudly proclaimed that *Milestones* was "the greatest play since Congreve."

"But why Congreve, Brighouse?" I asked. "Surely you mean H. J. Byron?"

But no! He said he meant Congreve.

"I do not," I said, considerably perturbed, "I do not like to think, Brighouse, that you have stained your virgin mind with Congreve."

"I've looked at him," said he icily. "He wrote comedies. *Milestones* is a comedy."

Now, I was used to Brighouse for, from the age of eleven to thirteen I had been at the same school with him, and I remembered how enormously sensitive and how self-contained and how stubborn he was. I also remembered that Rabelaisianism, or Congrevism, or, indeed, any ism that denoted the real philosophic vulgarity of the human mind, or any jolly indecent wit, was repellent to him.

"There are, I suppose, expurgated editions of Congreve, Brighouse. I imagine you as a collector of expurgated editions."

But he buried his nose in his pint of beer and refused further converse.

Now, such are the influences that one man may have upon another, it came about that the more successful Houghton became, the harder worked Brighouse. Said Brighouse to himself, I imagine: "If Stanley can do all this, why not I?" So he worked desperately, sloggingly, overwhelmingly. Yet, in spite of all his hard work, he kept a most watchful and jealous eye on his contemporaries, and I remember meeting him at one of Miss Horniman's orgies at the Gaiety Theatre when a new play of Galsworthy's was given. It was a beautiful play (Galsworthy has not written many beautiful plays), but I regret to say I do not remember its name. At the end of the first act Brighouse was disgustingly "superior," and at the end of the second he was contemptuous. So I sought a quarrel with him. There are, I think, few emotions so devastating, and so difficult to control, as the anger that surges upon one when one hears a beautiful work of art, noble, subtle and full of humanity, treated with contempt by a man whose vanity has blinded the eyes of his soul. But I do not remember making any attempt to control my anger at Brighouse; rather did I nurse and nourish it, and, when the proper time came, I poured it upon him with generosity. Harold—or "Brig," as we used to call him—is too much a man of the world not to know how to deal with an excitable man in a temper, and I remember coming away from our quarrel feeling rather foolish and having a disturbing admiration for Brighouse's dignity. After this little episode, we were always very polite to each other, and, later on, when we met in London, our meeting was not without some cordiality.

Since these days Brighouse has scored a big success with *Hobson's Choice*. He will score other successes. He will die reputed and rich. He will live, some day, in a West End flat and have a cottage in the country from which he will issue at regular intervals and take long walks in muddy lanes. I believe he will sedulously cultivate the friendship of those who may be of service to him, and he will drink his pint of beer every day of his life. He will be praised twice a year by Sir William Robertson Nicoll. Yes, he will be praised twice a year by Sir William Robertson Nicoll. And when Sir William dies, Mr St John Adcock will take up the cry. And, when the war is over, our successful young dramatist will go to America, where the money comes from.... I should like to see Harold in America.

There came a day when a new one-act play by Houghton was given at the Manchester Gaiety—a play I subsequently saw at a London music hall, its fit home; but I remember neither the play's title nor its plot. I recollect, however, that three or four men and women met in the corridor of a London hotel and talked or suggested risky things. Rather stupid, I thought it, and it certainly never occurred to me that it was immoral or nasty; it was merely a dramatic experiment that did not quite come off. But the dramatic critic of *The Manchester Guardian*—either Mr A. N. Monkhouse or Mr C. E. Montague (I think the former)—"went for" it tooth and nail on the score of its alleged immorality. The criticism was scathing: it made a wound and then poured acid into the wound. Houghton must have felt the criticism sorely, but when I met him next day he pluckily treated it as a matter of no consequence whatever.

"A reasonable man cannot expect always to be understood," said he, "and I suppose *The Manchester Guardian,* which has always been very good to me in the past, has a right to scold me if it thinks fit."

"A *scolding*, Houghton? Why, you were thrashed."

"Well, I s'pose I was. But I can stand it."

Vain men are invariably supersensitive, and for that reason I think Houghton felt every word and act of hostility; but he never showed weakness under opposition, and he could hit back when he thought it worth while.

I once witnessed a physical assault upon him after a rather rowdy dinner, when we all took to ragging each other. There was no excuse for the assault, except what excuse may be found in bitter feeling and enmity, but Houghton received the blow without a word, and we who witnessed it neither expostulated with his assailant nor expressed sympathy with his victim. Houghton paled and his large eyes gleamed, and I have no doubt that on a subsequent occasion he settled the matter with the man who was responsible for his humiliation.

Only a very few men really understood Houghton, and those were men who, like Walter Mudie, had known him intimately in boyhood. Mudie swore by him and would hear no word against him. But there was something forbidding in Houghton's nature—a barricade of reserve that he himself had not wilfully erected, but which had been placed there by Nature. It was impossible for people who met him casually a few times to form a high opinion either of his intellect or of his personality. I remember Captain James E. Agate, a most original and brilliant colleague of Houghton's on *The Manchester Guardian*, once saying to a group of people: "Don't you make any mistake about Houghton. He's not such a fool as he appears." But it is a very incomplete man who requires such a double-edged defence as that.

Though the contrary has often been stated, Houghton did not, I believe, take much interest in anybody's work except his own. He patronised a young bank clerk, Charles Forrest, who had written a promising little play that was subsequently, by Houghton's recommendation, I believe, given in Manchester and Liverpool; but when he came in contact with work that was, in many respects, superior to his own, he was airily superior and supercilious. He once asked to see a blank-verse play of my own that was given at the Manchester Gaiety, but as I was aware that he knew as much of blank verse as I do of conic sections—which is nothing at all—I refrained from passing on my MS. to him. In other men's work he looked for faults; in his own he found perfection.

I need scarcely say that when I went to London I did not seek out Houghton, who had settled down in the Metropolis some months before me. But we met in the Strand, he wearing a fur-lined overcoat and looking a trifle like H. B. Irving, and I carrying a load of review books under my arm. We looked at each other; we hesitated; we stopped. Stanley was a trifle languid and, after a few inconsequent remarks, he began telling me the history of his fur overcoat. He had, he said, bought it for five pounds or seven pounds, or some such ridiculously low price, and he had bought it second-hand.

And (Fate wills these things) whenever I hear the name Stanley Houghton I think of that rather tall, rather aristocratic, figure in the Strand wearing its second-hand fur-lined overcoat and talking, with embarrassment, about nothing in particular, standing first on one foot and then on the other.

It is, of course, impossible to predict with certainty what further successes Houghton would have achieved had he lived, but there can be little doubt that his sharp and lively talents would have produced plays even more noticeable than *Hindle Wakes*. A little more experience of life would probably have shown him the futility and the destructive effects of his intellectual snobbery. He was raw and crude, and success did not mellow or enlarge him.

CHAPTER VI
SOME WRITERS

OF all the famous writers I have met, I have found Arnold Bennett the most surprising. I do not know what kind of man I expected to see when it was arranged that I should meet him, but I certainly had not anticipated beholding the curiously, wrongly dressed figure that, one spring afternoon some few years ago, walked up the steps leading from the floor of Queen's Hall to the foyer of the gallery. I was there by appointment. I was a friend of a friend of his—Havergal Brian, a young fire-eating genius from the Potteries, and Brian had planned this curious meeting. It was during the interval of an afternoon concert of a Richard Strauss Festival, and Ackté was singing.

Bennett was rather short, thin, hollow-eyed, prominent-toothed. He wore a white waistcoat and a billycock hat very much awry, and he had a manner of complete self-assurance. I cannot say that I was unimpressed. We were introduced, and he looked at me drowsily, indifferently, insultingly indifferently. He did not speak and I, nervous, and a little bewildered by the colour of his socks, which I at that moment noticed for the first time, blundered into some futility.

"I don't see why," said Bennett, in response.

I didn't either, so far as that went. Desperately uncomfortable, I looked round for Brian, and saw him standing fifteen yards or so away, grinning malignantly.

So I plunged into a new topic—with even more disastrous results.

"I notice," said I, "that you continue writing for *The New Age* in spite of their violent attacks on you."

"Yes," he answered laconically, and he looked dizzily over my left shoulder.

Then and there I decided that I would not speak again until he had spoken. I had not sought the interview any more than he had. Presently:

"I have been working very hard lately," I heard. I turned quickly to him; he had spoken into space. I showed a polite interest and he thawed a little. He told me something of the number of words and hours he wrote a day, of the work he had planned for the next two years, of the regularity of his methods, of his disbelief in the value of "inspiration." I seemed to have heard it all before about Anthony Trollope. He was not exactly loquacious, but he communicated a great deal in spite of a rather unpleasant impediment in his speech....

Soon our interview was over, for we heard the orchestra tuning up, and we left each other with just a word of farewell and without a sigh of regret.

His conversational powers never, I believe, reach the point of eloquence. I remember G. H. Mair giving me an amusing description of a breakfast he gave to Arnold Bennett and Stanley Houghton in his lodgings in Manchester. Bennett and Houghton had not previously met, and the latter was young and inexperienced enough to nurse the expectation that the personality of the famous writer would be as impressive as his work, and impressive in the same way. It is true that very extraordinary circumstances would be necessary to make breakfast in Manchester free from dullness, but Houghton no doubt thought that his meeting with Bennett *was* an extraordinary circumstance. In the event, however, he was disillusioned.

They went in to breakfast, and Bennett sat moody and silent, crumbling a piece of bread. It chanced that on being admitted to the house Bennett had caught sight of a cabman carrying a particularly large trunk downstairs, and he began to question Mair closely about the incident, Mair explaining that a fellow-lodger was removing that morning and taking all his luggage with him.

"Yes, yes," said Bennett, a little impatiently, "but why should he have such a large trunk? It was enormous. I don't think I have ever seen so large a trunk before. It was at least twice the usual size."

He took a mouthful of bacon and spent a minute in mastication. Having swallowed:

"Absurdly large," he said challengingly. "I can't think why anyone should wish to own it. Besides, it's not right to ask any man to carry such an enormous weight. That's how strangulated hernia is caused. Yes, strangulated hernia."

The topic did not prove fruitful, and I can imagine Houghton cudgelling his brains to discover what strangulated hernia really was, and Mair saying something witty about it. But with his second cup of coffee and his marmalade and toast Bennett once more talked of the cabman, the impossible trunk, and the cabman's hypothetical hernia.

"Of course," he remarked meditatively, "the man must have *some* reason for owning such an incredibly large trunk, but I confess I can't guess the reason. And, in any case, it is bound to be a selfish one. Now, strangulated hernia— —"

And that was all that issued during a whole hour from one of the cleverest brains in England.

That Arnold Bennett is almost painfully conscious of his own cleverness there is no manner of doubt. He is stupendously aware of the figure he cuts in contemporary literature. He is for ever standing outside himself and enjoying the spectacle of his own greatness, and he whispers ten times a day: "Oh, what a great boy am I!" I was once shown a series of privately printed booklets written by Bennett—booklets that he sent to his intimates at Christmas time. They consisted of extracts from his diary—a diary that, one feels, would never have been written if the de Goncourts had not lived. One self-conscious extract lingers in the mind; the spirit of it, though not the words (and perhaps not the facts) is embodied in the following:—"It is 3 a.m. I have been working fourteen hours at a stretch. In these fourteen hours I have written ten thousand words. My book is finished—finished in excitement, in exaltation. Surely not even Balzac went one better than this!"

A great writer: no doubt, a very great writer: but you might gaze at him across a railway carriage for hours at a time and never suspect it.

But if Arnold Bennett is the least picturesque and literary of figures, G. K. Chesterton is the most picturesque and literary. His mere bulk is impressive. On one occasion I saw him emerge from Shoe Lane, hurry into the middle of Fleet Street, and abruptly come to a standstill in the centre of the traffic. He stood there for some time, wrapped in thought, while buses, taxis and lorries eddied about him in a whirlpool and while drivers exercised to the full their gentle art of expostulation. Having come to the end of his meditations he held up his hand, turned round, cleared a passage through the horses and vehicles and returned up Shoe Lane. It was just as though he had deliberately chosen the middle of Fleet Street as the most fruitful place for thought. Nobody else in London could have done it with his air of absolute unconsciousness, of absent-mindedness. And not even the most stalwart policeman, vested with full authority, could have dammed up London's stream of traffic more effectively.

The more one sees of Chesterton the more difficult it is to discover when he is asleep and when he is awake. He may be talking to you most vivaciously one moment, and the next he will have disappeared: his body will be there, of course, but his mind, his soul, the living spirit within him, will have sunk out of sight.

One Friday afternoon I went to *The Daily Herald* office to call on a friend. As I entered the building a taxi stopped at the door and I found G. K. C. by my side.

"I have half-an-hour for my article," said he, rather breathlessly. "Wait here till I come back."

The first sentence was addressed to himself, the second to the taxi-driver, but as we were by now in the office the driver heard nothing. Chesterton called for a back file of *The Daily Herald*, sat down, lit a cigar and began to read some of his old articles. I watched him. Presently, he smiled. Then he laughed. Then he leaned back in his chair and roared. "Good—oh, damned good!" exclaimed he. He turned to another article and frowned a little, but a third pleased him better. After a while he pushed the papers from him and sat a while in thought. "And as in uffish thought he" sat, he wrote his article, rapidly, calmly, drowsily. Save that his hand moved, he might have been asleep. Nothing disturbed him—neither the noise of the office nor the faint throb of his taxi-cab rapidly ticking off twopences in the street below.... He finished his article and rolled dreamily away.

His brother Cecil has the same gift of detachment. He can write anywhere and under any conditions. I have seen him order a mixed grill at the Gambrinus in Regent Street, begin an article before his food was served, and continue writing for an hour while the dishes were placed before him and allowed to go stone cold. Like most men in Fleet Street who do a tremendous amount of work, he has always plenty of time for play, and I do not remember ever to have come across him when he was not ready and willing to spend a half-hour in chat in one of the thousand and one little caravanserai that lurk so handily in the Strand and Fleet Street.

Of poets of the younger generation I have met only three—Lascelles Abercrombie, Harold Monro, and John Masefield. Abercrombie I remember as a lean, spectacled man, who used to come to Manchester occasionally to hear music and, I think, to converse intellectually with Miss Horniman. Of music he had a sane and temperate appreciation, but was too prone to condemn modern work, of which, by the way, he knew nothing and which by temperament he was incapable of understanding. He struck me as cold and daring—cold, daring and a little calculating. He appeared unexpectedly one day at my house, stayed for lunch, talked all afternoon, and went away in the evening, leaving me a little bewildered by the things he had refrained from saying. Really, we had nothing in common. My personality could not touch his genius at any point, and the things he wished to discuss—the technicalities of his craft, philosophy, æsthetics and so on—have no interest for me. If I had not studied his work and admired it whole-heartedly, I should have come to the conclusion that he had written poetry through sheer cleverness and brightness of brain. No man was less of a poet in appearance and conversation. He professed at all times a huge liking for beer, but I never saw him drink more than a modest pint, and his pose of "muscular poet" (a school founded and fed by Hilaire Belloc) deceived few.

Harold Monro I used to see occasionally in the Café Royal, and I met him a few times at the Crab Tree Club. I remember going with him, early one morning in June, 1914, after sitting up all night, to the Turkish baths in Jermyn Street. We swam a little in a tank and were then conducted to a cubicle, where I wished to talk, but Monro was heavy with sleep and soon began to breathe stertorously. A few days later he received me rather heavily at his office at The Poetry Bookshop, read some of my verses, and told me quite frankly that he did not consider me much of a poet. A sound, solid man, Monro, and he has written at least one poem—*Trees*—as delicate and as beautiful as anything done in our time.

But neither Monro nor Abercrombie, greatly gifted and earnest in their work though they be, fulfils one's conception of a poetic personality. There is no mystery about them, no glamour; they do not arouse wonder or surprise. John Masefield, on the other hand, has an invincible picturesqueness—a picturesqueness that stamps him at once as different from his fellows. He is tall, straight and blue-eyed, with a complexion as clear as a child's. His eyes are amazingly shy, almost furtive. His manner is shy, almost furtive. He speaks to you as though he suspected you of hostility, as though you had the power to injure him and were on the point of using that power. You feel his sensitiveness and you admire the dignity that is at once its outcome and its protection.

There are many legends about Masefield; he is the kind of figure that gives rise to legends. And, as he is curiously reticent about his early life, some of the most extravagant of these legends have persisted and have, for many people, become true. But the bare facts of his life are interesting enough. As a young man he grew sick of life, of the kind of life he was living, and went to sea as a sailor before the mast. He had neither money nor friends; or, if he had, he relinquished both. The necessity to earn a living drove him into many adventures, and I am told that for a time he was pot-boy in a New York drink-den. Here his work must have been utterly distasteful, but the observing eye and the impressionable brain of the poet were at work the whole time, and one can see clearly in some of Masefield's long narrative poems many evidences of those bitter New York days. How Masefield came to London and settled in Bloomsbury, becoming the friend of J. M. Synge, I do not know. For six months he was in Manchester, editing the column entitled Miscellany in *The Manchester Guardian*, and writing occasional theatrical notices. I have been told by several of his colleagues on that paper that Masefield's reserve was invulnerable; he quickly secured the respect of his fellow-workers, but not one of them became intimate with him. He lived in dingy lodgings, he worked hard and, at the end of six months, withdrew to London on the plea that he found it impossible to do literary work at night.

But if the circumstances of Masefield's life are little known, his spiritual history is more than indicated in his work. Here one sees a stricken soul; a nature wounded and a little poisoned; a nervous system agitated and apprehensive. His mind is cast in a tragic mould and his soul takes delight in the contemplation of physical violence. His personality, as I have said, is furtive. He shrinks. His intimate friends may have heard him laugh. I have not.

It must be nearly six years since I visited him at his house in Well Walk, Hampstead. It was a miserably cold afternoon in February, and though it was not yet twilight the blinds of the drawing-room were drawn and the lights already lit. Masefield's conversation was intolerably cautious, intolerably shy. In a rather academic way he deplored the lack of literary critics in England; the art of criticism was dead; the essay was moribund. He expanded this theme perfunctorily, walking up and down the room slowly and never looking me in the eyes once. It was only when, at length, he had sat down—not opposite me, but with the side of his face towards me—that, very occasionally, his eyes would seek mine with a rapid dart and turn away instantly, and at such moments it seemed as though he almost winced. Such shrinking, such excessive timidity, whilst arousing my curiosity, also made me feel no little discomfort, and I was glad when a spirit kettle was brought in, with cups and saucers, and Masefield began to make tea.

This making of tea, a most solemn business, reminded me of *Cranford*. The poet walked to a corner of the room, took therefrom a long narrow box divided into a number of compartments and proceeded, most delicately, to measure out and mix two or three different kinds of tea. The teapot was next heated, the blended tea thrown in, and boiling water immediately poured on it. And then the tea was timed, Masefield holding his watch in his hand and pouring out the fluid into the cups at the psychological second.... He ought, I think, to have taken a little silver key from his waistcoat pocket and locked up the tea-box. He ought to have taken his knitting from a work-box. He ought to have asked me if I had yet spoken to the new curate. But he did none of these things....

Though for an hour he continued talking, he said nothing—at least, he said nothing I have remembered. The extraordinary thing about him was that, in spite of his timidity, his seeming apprehensiveness, he left on my mind a deep impression of adventure—not of a man who sought physical, but spiritual, risks. I think he is a poet who cannot refrain from exacerbating his own soul, who must at all costs place his mind in danger and escape only at the last moment. I believe he is intensely morbid, delighting to brood over dark things, seeing no humour in life, but full of a baffled chivalry, a nobility thwarted at every turn.

A man of a very different type is Jerome K. Jerome, whom I met at the National Liberal Club and elsewhere in the early days of the war. Like all humorists, he is an inveterate sentimentalist; his belief in human nature is as wide-eyed and innocent as that of a child. He is an untidy, prosperous, middle-aged man—very kindly, but a little intolerant. His mental attitude is that of a man sitting a little apart from life, alternately amused and saddened by the things he sees. In the drawing-room of his flat at Chelsea he seemed a little out of place; he did not harmonise with his surroundings. But in the Club he was easy, natural, at home. More than twenty years ago I heard him lecture in Manchester; the Jerome of to-day is the Jerome of those far-off years, a little mellower perhaps, a little quieter, a little more sentimental, but essentially the same in appearance, in manner and in his attitude towards life.

I have met other humorists, but of a type very different from that represented by Jerome. Sir Owen Seaman I met at a little dinner given by the Critics' Circle at Gatti's to a colleague of ours who was on the point of leaving for the Front, and who, alas! is now no more. Sir Owen was made both by nature and training for a squarson—that useful but fast-dying gentleman who combines the duties and responsibilities of squire and parson. His personality, rather beefy and John Bullish, confirms one's expectations. He made an excellent chairman at this particular dinner.

His very brilliant assistant, A. A. Milne, I once interviewed for a now defunct Labour paper. I was invited to the office of *Punch*, and met a tall, slim, yellow-haired and blue-eyed youth, who was so inordinately shy that, after half-an-hour's perfunctory conversation, I discovered that I had not sufficient material for a paragraph, whereas I had orders to make a column article of the interview. I knew instinctively that Milne must find, as I do, a good deal in W. S. Gilbert's writings that is in deplorable taste, and I did my utmost to induce him to say something very rude about Sullivan's collaborator. But he would not "bite." He nodded and smiled at, and appeared to agree with, all the savage things I said of Gilbert, but he would say very little—and certainly not enough for my purpose—on his own account. I tried other subjects, but without success; finally, I got up in despair, thanked him for the time he had given me and prepared to depart.

"But," said Milne, eyeing me, a little distrustfully, "I must see a copy of your article before it is printed."

"Why, certainly," said I, and that evening posted it to him, expecting to see it back with perhaps one or two minor alterations.

But when my poor article arrived back (really, I thought it an excellent piece of work) I could scarcely recognise it, so heavily was it scored out, so numerous were the alterations. And Milne's accompanying letter was scathing. I remember one or two sentences. "I cannot tell you how thankful I am," he wrote, "that I insisted on seeing your article before it was printed. It does not represent my views in the least; your talent for misrepresentation is remarkably resourceful."

When the article was finally passed for publication at least seventy-five per cent. of it was from Milne's pen. He wrote one or two other stabbing sentences to me, from which it appeared that, however numerous his virtues may be, he is unable to suffer fools gladly.

CHAPTER VII
SIR EDWARD ELGAR

THE weaknesses that seem to be inseparable from genius—and, most particularly, from artistic genius—are precisely those one would not expect to discover associated with greatness of mind. It would appear that few men are so great as their work, or, if they are, their greatness is spasmodic and evanescent. Works of genius, it is sometimes stated, are created in moods of exaltation, when the spirit is in turmoil, when the mind is lit and the nerves are tense. In some cases it may be so. It was so, I believe, in the case of Wagner, who had long spells, measured by years, of unproductiveness, when his creative powers lay fallow; and it was so in the case of Hugo Wolf, Beethoven, Shelley, Poe, Berlioz and many other men whose names spring to the mind. But it certainly was not so with Balzac and Dickens, any more than it is to-day with Arnold Bennett.

There is in Sir Edward Elgar's work a strange contradiction: great depth of understanding combined with a curious fastidiousness of style that is almost finicking. Many aspects of life appeal to his sympathies and to his imagination, but an innate and exaggerated delicacy, an almost feminine shrinking, is noticeable in even his strongest and most outspoken work.... It is this delicacy, this shrinking, that to the casual acquaintance is at once his most conspicuous and most teasing characteristic.

My first meeting with Elgar was ten years ago, when, being commissioned to interview him for a monthly musical magazine, I called on him at the Midland Hotel, Manchester, where he was staying for a night. On my way to his room I met him in the corridor, where he carefully explained that he had made it a strict rule never to be interviewed for the Press and that under no circumstances could that rule be broken. His firm words were spoken with hesitation, and it was quite obvious to me that he was feeling more than a trifle nervous. I have little doubt that this nervousness was due to the fact that in an hour's time he was to conduct a concert at the Free Trade Hall. However, he was kind enough to loiter for some minutes and talk, but he took care, when I left him, to remind me that nothing of what he had said to me must appear in print.

I, of course, obeyed him, but, in place of an interview, I wrote an impressionistic sketch of the man as I had seen him during my few minutes' conversation at the Midland Hotel. Of this impressionistic sketch I remember nothing except that, in describing his general bearing and manner, I used the word "aristocratic." At this word Elgar rose like a fat trout eager to swallow a floating fly. It confirmed his own hopes. And I who had perceived this quality so speedily, so unerringly, and who had proclaimed it to the world, was worthy of reward. Yes; he would consent to be interviewed. The ban should be lifted; for once the rule should be broken. A letter came inviting me to Plas Gwyn, Hereford—a letter written by his wife and full of charming compliments about my article.

So to Hereford I went and talked music and chemistry. It was Christmas week, and within ten minutes of my arrival Lady Elgar was giving me hot dishes, wine and her views on the political situation. The country was in the throes of a General Election, and while I ate and drank I heard how the Empire was, as Dr Kendrick Pyne used to say, "rushing headlong to the bow-wows." Lady Elgar did not seem to wish to know to what particular party (if any) I belonged, but I quickly discovered that to confess myself a Radical would be to arouse feelings of hostility in her bosom. Radicals were the Unspeakable People. There was not one, I gathered, in Hereford. They appeared to infest Lancashire, and some had been heard of in Wales. Also, there were people called Nonconformists. Many persons were Radicals, many Nonconformists; but some were both. The Radicals had won several seats. What was the country coming to? Where was the country going?

Where, indeed? I did not allow Lady Elgar's rather violent political prejudices to interfere with my appetite, and she appeared to be perfectly satisfied with an occasional sudden lift of my eyebrows, and such ejaculations as: "Oh, quite! Quite!" "Most assuredly!" and "Incredible!" If she thought about me at all—and I am persuaded she did not—she must have believed me also to be a Tory. After all, had not I called her husband "aristocratic," and is that the sort of word used by a Radical save in contempt?

After lunch Elgar took me a quick walk along the river-bank. For the first half-hour I found him rather reserved and non-committal, and I soon recognised that if I were to succeed in obtaining his views on any matter of interest I must rigidly abstain from direct questions. But when he did commit himself to any opinion, he did so in the manner of one who is sure of his own ground and cannot consider, even temporarily, any change in the attitude he has already assumed.

I found his views on musical critics amusing, but before proceeding to set them down I must make some reference to his relations with Ernest

Newman. Newman, it is generally agreed, is unquestionably the most brilliant, the fairest-minded and the most courageous writer on music in England. His power is very great, and he has done more to educate public opinion on musical matters in England than any other man. For some little period previous to the time of which I am writing he and Elgar had been close friends, and their friendship was all the stronger because it rested on the attraction of opposites. Elgar was an ardent Catholic, a Conservative; Newman was an uncompromising free-thinker and a Radical. Elgar was a pet of society, a man careful and even snobbish in his choice of his friends, whilst Newman cared nothing for society and would be friendly with any man who interested or amused him.

Up to the time Elgar composed *The Apostles* he had no more whole-hearted admirer than Newman, but this work was to sever their friendship and, for a time, to bring bitterness where before there had been esteem and even affection. Newman was invited by a New York paper—I think *The Musical Courier*—to write at considerable length on *The Apostles*. As his opinion of this work was, on the whole, unfavourable, he may possibly have hesitated to consider an invitation the acceptance of which would lead to his giving pain to a friend. But probably Newman thought, as most inflexibly honest men would think, that, on a matter of public concern, silence would be cowardly. In the event, he wrote his article and sent it to America, also forwarding a copy to Elgar himself, telling him that, though it went against his feelings of friendship to condemn the work, he thought it a matter of duty to speak what was in his mind. That letter and that article severed their friendship, and the severance lasted for some considerable time.

My visit to Elgar took place during his estrangement from Newman, and when I mentioned the subject of musical criticism to him it was, I imagine, with the hope that the name of the famous critic would crop up. It did.

"The worst of musical criticism in this country," said Elgar, "is that there is so much of it and so little that is serviceable. Most of those who are skilled musicians either have not the gift of criticism or they cannot express their ideas in writing, and most of those who can write are deplorably deficient in their knowledge of music. For myself I never read criticism of my own work; it simply does not interest me. When I have composed or published a work, my interest in it wanes and dies; it belongs to the public. What the professional critics think of it does not concern me in the least."

Though I knew that Elgar had on previous occasions given expression to similar views, his statement amazed me. So I pressed him a little.

"But suppose," I urged, "a new work of yours were so universally condemned by the critics that performances of it ceased to take place. Would you not then read their criticisms in order to discover if there was not some truth in their statements?"

"It is possible, but I do not think I should. But your supposition is an inconceivable one: there is never universal agreement among musical critics. I think you will notice that many of them are, from the æsthetic point of view, absolutely devoid of principle; I mean, they are victims of their own temperaments. They, as the schoolgirl says, 'know what they like.' The music they condemn is either the music that does not appeal to their particular kind of nervous system or it is the music they do not understand. They have no standard, no norm, no historical sense, no——"

He stammered a little and waved a vague arm in the air.

"There are exceptions, of course," I ventured. "Newman, for example."

"No; Ernest Newman is not altogether an exception. He is an unbeliever, and therefore cannot understand religious music—music that is at once reverential, mystical and devout."

"'Devout'?" whispered I to myself. Aloud I said:

"A man's reason, I think, may reject a religion, though his emotional nature may be susceptible to its slightest appeal. Besides, Newman has a most profound admiration for your *The Dream of Gerontius*."

Elgar was silent for a few minutes. Then, with an air of detachment and with great inconsequence, he said:

"Baughan, of *The Daily News*, cannot hum a melody correctly in tune. He looks at music from the point of view of a man of letters. So does Newman, fine musician though he is. Newman advocates programme music. Now, I do not say that programme music should not be written, for I have composed programme music myself. But I do maintain that it is a lower form of art than absolute music. Newman, I believe, refuses to acknowledge that either kind is necessarily higher or lower than the other. He has, as I have said, the literary man's point of view about music. So have many musical critics."

"And so," I interpolated, "if one has to accept what you say as correct, have many composers, and composers also who are not specifically literary. And, after what you have said, I find that strange. Take the case of Richard Strauss, all of whose later symphonic poems have a programme, a literary basis. Do you, for that reason, declare that Strauss regards music from the literary man's point of view—Strauss who, of all living musicians, is the greatest?"

He paused for a few moments, and it seemed to me that our pace quickened as we left the bank of the river and made for a pathway across a meadow. But he would not take up the argument; stammering a little, he said:

"Richard Strauss is a very great man—a fine fellow."

But as that was not the point under discussion, I felt that either his mind was wandering or that he could think of no reply to my objection.

A little later, on our way home, we discussed the younger generation of composers, and I found him very appreciative of the work done by his juniors. He particularly mentioned Havergal Brian, a composer who has more than justified what Elgar prophesied of him, though perhaps not in the manner Elgar anticipated.

Apropos of something or other, Elgar said, I think quite needlessly and a little vainly:

"You must not, as many people appear to do, imagine that I am a musician and nothing else. I am many things; I find time for many things. Do not picture me always bending over manuscript paper and writing down notes; months pass at frequent intervals when I write nothing at all. At present I am making a study of chemistry."

I think I was expected to look surprised, or to give vent to an exclamation of surprise, but I did neither, for I also had made a study of chemistry, and it seemed to me the kind of work that any man of inquiring mind might take up. I did not for one moment imagine that I was living in the first half of the nineteenth century when practically all British musicians were musicians and nothing else and not always even musicians.

When we had returned to the house we sat before a large fire and, under the soothing influence of warmth and semi-darkness, stopped all argument. In the evening Lady Elgar accompanied me to the station, and all the way from Hereford to Manchester I turned over in my mind the strange problem that was presented to me by the fact that, though I was a passionate, almost fanatical lover of Elgar's music, the creator of that music attracted me not at all. I saw in his mind a daintiness that was irritating, a refinement that was distressingly self-conscious.

Some years later Sir Edward Elgar moved to London, and when I saw him in his new home he tried to prove to me that living in London was cheaper than living in the country.

His attitude towards me on this occasion was peculiarly strange. I represented a Labour paper, but Elgar did not know that I was at the same time writing leading articles for a London Conservative daily. He treated me with the most careful kindness, a kindness so careful, indeed, that it might be called patronising. It soon became quite clear to me that he imagined I myself came from the labouring classes, but I cannot boast that honour, and as he, the aristocrat, was in contact with me, the plebeian, it was his manifest duty and his undoubted pleasure to help me along the upward path. I was advised to read Shakespeare.

"Shakespeare," said he, "frees the mind. You, as a journalist, will find him useful in so far as a close study of his works will purify your style and enlarge your vocabulary."

"Which of the plays would you advise me to read?" asked I, with simulated innocence and playing up to him with eyes and voice.

The astounding man considered a minute and then mentioned half-a-dozen plays, the titles of which I carefully wrote down in my pocket-book.

"And Ruskin," he added as an afterthought. "Oh, yes, and Cardinal Newman. Newman's style is perhaps the purest style of any man who wrote in the nineteenth century."

"I do not think so," said I, thoroughly roused and forgetting to play my part. "The *Apologia* is slipshod. My own style, faulty though it may be, is more correct, more lucid, even more distinguished than Cardinal Newman's."

He turned away, either angry or amused.

"It is true," said I, with warmth. "Anyone who has tried for years, as I have done, to master the art of writing, and who examines the *Apologia* carefully will perceive at once that it is shamefully badly written. For two generations it has been the fashion to praise Newman's style, but those who have done so have never read him in a critical spirit. I would infinitely prefer to have written a racy book like—well, like *Moll Flanders*, where the English is beautifully clean and strong, than the sloppy *Apologia*."

"*Moll Flanders*," he said questioningly; "*Moll Flanders*? I do not know the book."

"It is all about a whore," said I brutally, "written by one Defoe."

And that, of course, put an end to our conversation. I rose to leave.

The impression left on my mind by my two visits to Elgar is definite enough, but I am willing to believe that it does not represent the man as he truly is. He is abnormally sensitive, abnormally observant, abnormally intuitive. Like almost all men, he is open to flattery, but the flattery must be applied by means of hints, praise half veiled, innuendo. If you gush he will freeze; if you praise directly, he will wince. His mind is essentially narrow, for he shrinks from the phenomena in life that hurt him and he will not force himself to understand alien things. His intellect is continually rejecting the very matters that, in order to gain largeness, tolerance and a full view of life, it should understand and accept. Yet, within its narrow confines, his brain functions most rapidly and with a clear light.

I have been told by members of the various orchestras he has conducted that when interpreting a work like *The Dream of Gerontius* his face is wet with tears.

He has a proper sense of his own dignity, and it is doubtful if he exaggerates the importance of his own powers. Many years ago, as I have related, I employed the word "aristocrat" in describing him, and to-day I feel that that word must stand. He has all the strength of the aristocrat and many of the aristocrat's weaknesses.

CHAPTER VIII
INTELLECTUAL FREAKS

IN the most tragic and most trying moments of life it is well to turn aside from one's sorrows and refresh one's mind and strengthen one's soul by gazing upon the follies of others. Those others gaze on ours.

In my spiritual adventures I have met many amazingly freakish people. Ten years ago the Theosophical Society overflowed with them. They were cultured without being educated, credulous but without faith, bookish but without learning, argumentative but without logic. The women, serene and grave, swam about in drawing-rooms, or they would stand in long, attitudinising ecstasies, their skimpy necks emerging from strange gowns, their bodies as shoulderless as hock bottles. The men paddled about in the same rooms, but I found them less amusing than the women.

"You were a horse in your last incarnation," said a fuzzy-haired giantess to me one evening, two minutes after we had been introduced.

"Oh, how disappointing!" I exclaimed. "I had always imagined myself an owl. I often dream I was an owl. I fly about, you know, or sit on branches with my eyes shut."

"No; a horse!" shouted the giantess, with much asperity. "I'm not arguing with you. I'm merely telling you. And I don't think you were a very nice horse either."

"No? Did I bite people?"

"Yes; you bit and kicked. And you did other disagreeable things besides. Now, I was a swan."

I evinced a polite but not enthusiastic interest.

"You would make an imposing swan," I observed.

"Yes. I used to glide about on ponds, like this."

She proceeded to "glide" round and round the corner of the room in which we were sitting. She arched her neck, raised her ponderous legs laboriously and moved about like a pantechnicon. Her face assumed a disagreeable expression and I thought of a rather good line in one of my own poems:

And swans sulked largely on the yellow mere.

"And how much of your previous incarnation do you remember?" I asked, when she had finished sulking largely in the yellow drawing-room.

"Oh, quite a lot. It comes back to me in flashes. I was very lonely—oh, *so* lonely."

She gave me a quick look, and I began to talk of William J. Locke, who, a few days previously, had published a new book. Resenting my change of subject, she left me and, a few minutes later, as I was eating a watercress sandwich, I heard her saying to a yellow-haired male:

"You were a horse in your last incarnation."

I met this lady on other occasions, and always she was occupied in telling men that they had been horses and she a swan—an oh-so-lonely swan.

"Why," said I to my hostess one day, "don't Madame X.'s friends look after her? See—she is arching her neck over there in the corner, and I am perfectly certain she has told the man with her that he has been, is, or is going to be a horse."

For a moment my hostess looked concerned.

"Look after her? What do you mean?"

"Well, she is obviously insane."

"On the contrary, she is the most subtle exponent we have of Madame Blavatsky's *Secret Doctrine*. Eccentric, perhaps, but as lucid a brain as Mr G. R. S. Mead's or as Colonel Olcott's. You should get her to describe your aura. She is excellent, too, in Plato. She doesn't understand a word of Greek, but she gets at his meaning intuitively. There is something cosmic about her. *You* know what I mean."

"Oh, quite, quite." (But what *did* she mean?)

"Cosmic consciousness is a most enthralling subject," continued my hostess, digging the hockey-stick she always carried with her well into the hearthrug. "Walt Whitman had it, you know."

"Badly?" I inquired.

She appeared puzzled.

"I don't quite know what you mean by 'badly.' He could identify himself with anything—the wind, a stone, a jelly-fish, an arm-chair, a ... a ... oh, everything! They were he and he was they. He *thought* cosmically. Fourth dimension, you know. Edward Carpenter and all that."

I rather admired this way she had of talking—a little like the Duke in G. K. Chesterton's *Magic.*

"Oh, do go on!" I urged her.

"What I always say is," she continued, "why stop at a fourth dimension? Someone has written a book on the fourth dimension, and some day perhaps I shall write one on the fifth."

"A book? A real book? Do you mean to say you could write a book? How clever! How romantic!"

"Well, I have thought about it. One is influenced. One has influences. The consciousness of the ultimate truth of things, the truth that suffuses all things, the cosmic nature of—well, the cosmos. Do you see? Tennyson's *In Memoriam.*"

"Yes; Tennyson's *In Memoriam* does help, doesn't it?"

"Did I say Tennyson's *In Memoriam*? I really meant Shelley's *Revolt of Islam*. The fourth dimension is played out. It's done with. It was true so far as it went, but how far did it go?"

"Only a very little way," I answered.

"Yes, but Nietzsche goes much farther. Have you read Nietzsche? No? I haven't, either. But I have heard Orage talk about him. Nietzsche says we can all do what we want. We must dare things. We must be blond beasts. Mary Wollstonecraft and her set, you know. Godwin and those people."

She waved her hockey-stick recklessly in the air and marched inconsequently away. Nearly all the Theosophists I met were like that— inconsequent, bent on writing books they never did write, talkers of divine flapdoodle, inanely clever, cleverly inane. Dear freaks I used to meet in days gone by!—where are you now?—where are you now?

A freak who ultimately lost all reason and was confined in a private asylum used to sit at the same desk that I did when, many years ago, I was a shipping clerk in Manchester. This man, whose name was not, but should have been, Bundle, had considerable private means, but some obscure need of his nature drove him to discipline himself by working eight hours a day for three pounds a week. The three pounds was nothing to him, but the eight hours a day meant everything. He was a conscientious worker, but I think I have already indicated that his intelligence was not robust. He had no delusion; he merely possessed a misdirected sense of duty.

One day he left us, and a few months later I met him in Market Street. He looked prosperous, smart and intensely happy.

"Are you busy?" he asked. "No? Well, come with me."

He slipped his arm in mine, led me into Mosley Street, and stopped in front of the large, dismal office of the Calico Printers' Association.

"That," said he, "is mine. Now, come into Albert Square."

When we had arrived there he pointed to the Town Hall.

"That also is mine. The Lord Mayor gave it to me with a golden key. Here is the golden key."

Producing an ordinary latchkey from his pocket, he carefully held it in the palm of his hand for my inspection.

"It is," he announced, "studded with diamonds. But you can't see the diamonds. Crafty Lord Mayor! You don't catch him napping. He's hidden them deep in the gold...."

I enjoyed this poor fellow's company more than I did that of a very old woman to whom I was introduced in a pauper asylum. She was sitting on a low stool and, pointing at her head with her skinny forefinger, "It's pot! It's pot!" she said.

But even she provided me with more exhilaration than do the tens (or perhaps hundreds) of thousands of real freaks who, I imagine, inhabit every part of the globe. I allude to the vast throng of people who arise at eight or thereabouts, go to the City every morning, work all day and return home at dusk; who perform this routine every day, and every day of every year; who do it all their lives; who do it without resentment, without anger, without even a momentary impulse to break away from their surroundings. Such people amaze and stagger one. To them life is not an adventure; indeed, I don't know what they consider it. They marry and, in their tepid, uxorious way, love. But love to them is not a mystery, or an adventure, and its consummation is not a sacrament. They do not travel; they do not want to travel. They do not even hate anybody.

All these people are freaks of the wildest description; yet they imagine themselves to be the backbone of the Empire. Perhaps they are. Perhaps every nation requires a torpid mass of people to act as a steadying influence.

In the suburbs of Manchester these people abound. I know a man still in his twenties who keeps hens for what he calls "a hobby." Among his hens he finds all the excitement his soul needs. The sheds in which they live form the boundaries of his imagination. I should esteem this man if he kicked against his destiny; but he loved it, until the Army conscripted him. God save the world from those who keep hens!

I know a man who has been to Douglas eighteen times in succession for his fortnight's holiday in the summer. Douglas is his heaven; Manchester and Douglas are his universe. No place so beautiful as Douglas; no place so familiar; no place so satisfying. After all, Douglas is always Douglas. Moreover, Douglas is always miraculously "there." God save the world from men who go to Douglas eighteen times!

I know a man who hates his wife and still lives with her. He is respectable, soulless, saving, a punctual and regular churchgoer, a hard bargain-driver. He walks with his eyes on the ground. He has always lived in the same suburb. He will always live in the same suburb. God save the world from men who always live in the same suburb!

I know a man ...

But this is getting very monotonous. Besides, why should I particularise any more freaks when all of them, perhaps, are as familiar to you as they are to me?

Then there is the literary freak; not the *poseur*, not the man who wishes to be thought "cultured" and intellectual, but the scholarly man who, during an industrious life, has amassed a vast amount of literary knowledge, but whose appreciation of literature is lukewarm and without zest. Very, very rarely is the great writer a scholar. Dr Johnson was a scholar, but, divine and adorable creature though he was, he was not a great writer. None of the great Victorians had true scholarship, and very few even of the Elizabethans. And to-day? Well, one may consider Thomas Hardy, Joseph Conrad, H. G. Wells, Bernard Shaw, Arnold Bennett and G. K. Chesterton as great writers; if you do not concede me all these names, you must either deny that we have any great writers at all (which is absurd) or produce me the names of six who are greater than those I have named (and the latter you cannot do). Have any of these anything approaching scholarship?

And yet in our universities are scores of men who are regarded as possessing greater literary gifts than those who actually produce literature. These learned, owlish creatures pose pontifically. Whenever a new book comes out they read an old one! The present generation, they say, is without genius. But they have always said it. They said it when Dickens, Thackeray and Charlotte Brontë were writing. I have no doubt they said it in Shakespeare's time. The present generation teems with genius, but our "scholarly" mandarins know it not. How barren is that knowledge which lies heavy in a man's mind and does not fertilise there. When one considers the matter, how essentially dull and stupid and brainless is the man devoid of ideas!

One of these bald-pated freaks is well known to me. He moves heavily about in a quadrangle. He delivers lectures. He has written books. He passes judgment. He annotates. He writes an occasional review. Funny little freak! Great little freak, who knows so much and understands so little.... When England wakes (and I do not believe that even yet, after nearly four years of war, England is really awake) such men will pass through life unregarded and neglected; they will sit at home in a back room, and their relatives and friends will love and pity them, as one loves and pities a poor fellow whose temperament has made him a wastrel, or as one pities a man who has to be nursed.

People of the Play: *A handful of literary freaks.*

Scene: *A drawing-room in Tooting, or Acton, or Highgate, or Ealing, or any funny old place where the middle classes live.*

Time: 8 p.m. *on (generally) Thursday.*

Mrs Arnold. Now that Miss Vera Potting, M.A., has finished reading her most interesting paper on Mr John Masefield, the subject is open for discussion. Perhaps you, Mr Mather-Johnstone, will give us a few thoughts—yes, a few thoughts. (*She smiles wanly and gazes round the room.*) A *most* interesting paper *I* call it.

Rev. Mather-Johnstone, M.A. Miss Potting's most interesting paper is—well, most interesting. I must confess I have read nothing of—er—Mr Masefield's. I prefer the older poets—Cowper, Bowles' Sonnets, and the beautifully named Felicia Hemans. Fe-lic-i-a! To what sweet thoughts does not that name give rise! But it has been a revelation to me to learn that a popular poet (and Miss Potting has assured us that Mr Masefield *is* popular) should so freely indulge in language that, to say the least, is violent, and I am glad to say that such language is not to be found in the improving stanzas of Eliza Cook.

Mr S. Wanley. I have read some verses of Mr Masefield's in a very— well—advanced paper called, if my memory does not deceive me, *The English Review.* I did not like those verses. I did not approve of them. They were bathed in an atmosphere of discontent—modern discontent. Now, what have people to be discontented about? Nothing; nothing at all, if they live rightly. (*He stops, having nothing further to say. For the same reason, he proceeds.*) Nevertheless, I thank Miss Potting, M.A., very much for her most interesting paper. There is one question I should like to ask her: is this Mr Masefield read by the right people?

Miss Vera Potting, M.A. Oh no! Oh dear, no! Most certainly not! Still, it is incontestable that he *is* read.

Mr S. Wanley. Thank you so much. I felt that he could not be read by the right people.

Miss Graceley (*rather nervously*). I feel that I can say I know my Lord Lytton, my Edna Lyall, my Charlotte M. Yonge and my Tennyson. I have always remained content with them, and after what Miss Vera Potting, M.A., has said about Mr Masefield in her most interesting paper, I shall *remain* content with them.

Mr S. Wanley. Hear, hear. I always seem to agree with you, Miss Graceley.

Mrs Arnold (*archly*). What is the saying?—great minds always jump alike?

Rev. Mather-Johnstone (*sotto voce*). *Jump?*

Mr Porteous (*with most distinguished amiability*). I really think that this most interesting paper that Miss Vera Potting, M.A., has read to us should be published. It is so—well, so improving, so elevating, so— —

Miss Vera Potting, M.A. (*who has already fruitlessly sent the essay to every magazine in the country*). Oh, Mr Porteous! How can you? Really, I couldn't think of such a thing.

Rev. Mather-Johnstone, M.A. (*who, being not altogether free from jealousy, thinks this is really going a bit too far*). But perhaps we do not all quite approve of women writers—I mean ladies who write for the wide, rough public.

Mrs Arnold. True! True!... But then, what about Felicia Hemans?

Rev. Mather-Johnstone, M.A. Mrs Hemans was Mrs Hemans. Miss Vera Potting, M.A., is, and I hope will always remain, Miss Vera Potting, M.A.

Mr Porteous. Oh, don't say that! What I mean is— —

(*This sort of thing goes on for an hour when, very secretly and as though she were on some nefarious errand*, Mrs Arnold *disappears from the room. She presently reappears with a maid, who carries a tray of coffee and sandwiches. The dreadful Mr Masefield is then forgotten.*]

You think the above sketch is exaggerated? Ah! well, perhaps you have never lived in Highgate, or in the suburbs of Manchester, Birmingham, Sheffield or Leeds. I could set down some appalling conversations that I have heard in suburban "literary" circles. There is a place called Eccles, where, one evening— —

In London Bohemia there are many freakish people, but, for the most part, they are altogether charming and refreshing. Quite a number of them have what I am told is, in the Police Courts, termed "no visible means of subsistence," but they appear to "carry on" with imperturbable good humour and borrow money cheerfully and as frequently as their circle of acquaintances (which is usually very large) will permit.

Frequenters of the Café Royal in pre-war days will recognise the following types:—

Picture to yourself a Polish Jew, young, yellow-skinned, black-haired; he has luminous eyes, sensuous lips and damp hands, and he dresses well, but in an extravagant style. He is a megalomaniac, and he has all the megalomaniac's consuming anxiety to discover precisely in what way other people react to his personality. One night my bitterest enemy brought him to the table at which I was sitting, introduced us to each other, and walked away.

"I am told you are a journalist," my new acquaintance began. "I myself write poems. I have a theory about poetry, and my theory is this: All poetry should be subjective."

"Why?"

"Never mind why. I am telling you about my theory. All poetry should be subjective; as a matter of fact, all the best poetry is. To myself I am the most interesting phenomenon in the world. To yourself, you are. Is it not so?"

"Yes; you have guessed right first time."

"Well, I have in this dispatch case eight hundred and seventy-three poems about myself, telling the world almost all there is to know about the most interesting phenomenon it contains."

He took from his case a great pile of MS. and turned the leaves over in his hands.

"Here," said he, "is a blank-verse poem entitled *How I felt at* 8.45 a.m. *on June* 8, 1909, *having partaken of Breakfast.* Would you like to read it?"

I assured him I should, though I fully expected it would contain unmistakable signs of mental disturbance. But it did not. It was quite respectably written verse, much better than at least half of Wordsworth's; it was logical, it had ideas, it showed some introspective power, and it revealed a mind above the ordinary.

I told him all this.

"Then you don't think I'm a genius? Some people do."

"You see, I'm not a very good judge of men—particularly men of genius. You may be a genius; on the other hand, you may not."

"But what exactly do you think of me?"

"I have already told you."

"Yes, but not with sufficient particularity. Now, put away from you all feeling of nervousness and try to imagine that I have just left you and that a friend of yours has come in and taken my place. You are alone together. You would, of course, immediately tell him that you had met me. You would say: 'He is a very strange man, eccentric....' and so on. You would describe my appearance, my personality, my verses. You, being a writer, would analyse me to shreds. Now, that is what I want you to do now. I want you to say all the bad things with the good. And I shall listen, greedily."

"But, really!" I protested. "Really, I can't do what you ask."

Disappointed and vexed, he sat biting his underlip.

"All right," he said at length, "we'll strike a bargain. After you have analysed me I, in return, will analyse you."

"You have quite the most unhealthy mind with which I have ever come in contact."

"You really believe that?" he asked, delighted. "Do go on."

"Oh, but I'm sorry I began. This kind of thing is dangerous."

"Yes, I know. But I like danger—mental danger especially."

"But drink would be better for you. Even drugs. You are asking me to help to throw you off your mental balance."

"I know. I know. But you won't refuse?"

"To show you that I will I am leaving you now in this café. I am going. Good-night."

But he met me many times after that, and always pursued me with ardour. In the end he gained his desire and, having done so, had no further use for me.

I call him The Man Who Collects Opinions of Himself. He is still in London. And he is not yet insane.

Then there was the lady—since, alas! dead—who used always to appear in public in a kind of purple shroud, her face and fingers chalked. She rather stupidly called herself Cheerio Death, and was one of the jolliest girls I have ever met. She longed and ached for notoriety and for new sensations: she feasted on them and they nourished and fattened her. Only very brave or reckless men dared be seen with her in public, for, though her behaviour was scrupulously correct, her appearance created either veiled ridicule or consternation wherever she went. Yet she never lacked companions.

"Hullo, Gerald!" she used to say to me; "sit down near me. You are so nice and chubby. I like to have you near me. How am I looking?"

"More beautiful than ever."

"Oh, you *are* sweet. Isn't he sweet, Frank?" she would say to one of her companions. "Order him some champagne. I'm thirsty."

And, really, Cheerio Death was very beautiful in a ghastly and terrible way. By degrees, all the reputable restaurants were closed to her, and in the late autumn of 1913 she disappeared, to die of consumption in Soho. Poor girl! Perhaps in Paris, where they love the *outré* and the shocking, she would have secured the full, hectic success that in London was denied her.

Are freaks always conscious of their freakishness? I do not think they are. Not even the man who wilfully cultivates his oddities until they have become swollen excrescences hanging bulbous-like on his personality is aware how vastly different, how unreasonably different he is from his fellows. He is more than reconciled to himself; he loves himself; he is what other people would be if only they could. Vanity continually lulls and soothes and rots him. The nature that craves to be noticed will go to almost any lengths to secure that notice.

It has always appeared curious to me that the ambition to become famous should very generally be regarded as a worthy passion in a man of genius. It is but natural that a man of genius should desire his work to reach as many people as possible, but whether or not he should be known as the author of that work seems to me a matter of no importance whatever. But to the man himself it is all-important. He has an instinctive feeling that if, in the public eye, he is separated from his work, savour will go from what he has created. He and his work must be closely identified.

This desire to be widely known, to be talked about everywhere, is in the man of genius accepted as natural, but it is this very desire that, in many cases, makes a freak of the ordinary man. Obscurity to him is death.

CHAPTER IX
FLEET STREET

I DON'T know why, but for many years there has been (and I am told there still is) a kind of silent conspiracy to keep out of Fleet Street as many aspirants to journalism as possible. They are discouraged by extravagant stories of the fierce competition that reigns there, by tragic yarns of men of great gifts who walk about The Street in rags. I myself was discouraged in this way and I found myself, on the verge of middle age, still hesitating in Manchester. It is true, I did not enter journalism until I was in my thirties, and I did not know the ropes. I did not know London either. Also, I was married and had children to educate and could not afford to take risks and make of life the grand adventure I have, in my heart, always known it to be.

So I hung on in Manchester, writing musical criticism for *The Manchester Courier* and contributing occasional articles and verses to *The Academy*, *The Contemporary Review*, *The Cornhill*, *The English Review*, *The Musical Times*, and many other magazines, and there is scarcely a London daily of repute for which at one time or another I did not write. But still I could find no opening in Fleet Street. The truth is, there is no regular means of finding openings in Fleet Street. If an editor is in want of a dramatic critic, a musical critic, a leader writer, or a descriptive reporter, he never advertises for one. He always knows someone who knows somebody else who is just the man for the job.

So one day I said to myself: "I will go to London at all costs. I will take a room in Bloomsbury and risk it." By a happy accident I received, a few days later, a note from Rutland Boughton, the well-known composer, telling me that he was relinquishing his post as musical critic of *The Daily Citizen*, that ill-fated paper so courageously edited by Frank Dilnot. Boughton suggested I should apply for the vacancy. I did apply. I wrote to Dilnot and received no answer. I chafed a fortnight and then telegraphed, prepaying a reply. "No vacancy at present" was the message I received. So I took the next train to London and bearded Dilnot in his den. "Yes, I'll take you," he said, "if you'll come for two pounds a week. But, if you're the real stuff, you'll receive much more." As I knew that I was, indeed, the real stuff, "I'll come," said I. "When can I start?"

I went back to Manchester and saw W. A. Ackland, the managing editor of *The Manchester Courier* and the kindest of men, expecting to receive from him a cold douche. But no! To my amazement, he encouraged me most heartily, and kept me on his staff, bidding me write a weekly article for him from London. This I did till the outbreak of the war, writing a lot of material also for his London letter.

During my first year in London I made six hundred and forty pounds. And I spent it. I spent it in eager examination of, and participation in, the many activities that the life of a great metropolis affords. Very soon—within six months—I found myself in the happy position of being able to refuse work that was offered me, for I did not wish to work all my waking hours. I wanted to play. I did play. I made many friendships. I talked a great deal, played the piano two or three hours a day, caroused, ragged in Chelsea, and lived every hour of my life.

It may be thought that six hundred and forty pounds per annum is no great sum. Nor is it. But does a doctor, a barrister, a solicitor, or any other professional man earn so much, without capital or influence, during his first year in London? Or in his second? Or third? Money-making in Fleet Street up to about seven hundred and fifty pounds a year is the easiest thing in the world for a man who has any talent at all for writing, especially if that talent be combined with versatility. The journalist is rarely intellectual; as a rule, he is merely ready and glib. I am ready and glib myself.

So I am not among those who feel inclined to discourage him who hankers after Fleet Street. No matter if you live in the waste regions of Sutherland, if you have proved yourself by inducing a number of editors of repute to take your stuff, go in and win! Really, it is very easy.

The men of Fleet Street are the best fellows in the world. Roughly, they may be divided into two classes: those who "go steady," with their eye always on the main chance, with every faculty strained to enable them to "get on" in the world; and those happy-go-lucky people who make money easily and spend it recklessly, so excited by life that they cannot pause to contemplate life, so happy in their labour and in their play that they cannot conceive a day may come when work will be irksome and playing a half-forgotten dream. There are, of course, other divisions into which journalists may be separated. There is, for example, the devoted band of brilliant young men who work for Orage in *The New Age*—a paper that cannot, I am sure, pay high rates. (What those rates are I do not know, for I could never induce Orage to print a single thing I wrote for him.) Then there are the hangers-on of journalism: people who review books in the time spared from their labours as university professors, struggling barristers, parish priests and so on. Many of these people, led by vanity or some other concealed motive, offer to work without payment.

The men who "go steady" are the editors, the leader-writers, the news editors, the literary editors, etc. For the most part they are men who have to keep late hours and clear heads, for important news may reach the office at midnight and instant decisions regarding the policy that the paper has to assume in regard to that news have to be made. A great political speech may be made in Edinburgh; a startling murder trial may close in Liverpool; a famous man may die in Paris; a strike may break out in the Potteries: in short, anything may happen. What attitude is the paper going to take up? What precise shade of opinion is going to be expressed about that political speech? What is to be said about the degree of justice that the workers in the Potteries can claim for their action? These matters have to be decided instantly, for they have to be written about instantly, and perhaps you who read the leading article next morning rarely stop to consider the conditions— the incredibly difficult conditions—under which it has been written. For this kind of work real, genuine ability is required: a very wide and accurate knowledge of affairs, rapidity of thought, a fluent and eloquent pen and a mind so sensitive that it can, without effort, reflect to a nicety the precise policy of the paper upon whose work it is engaged.

There is a story, and I think the story is true, of a new and inexperienced reporter who was given a trial on the staff of a very famous "halfpenny" paper. He was not a success, for he bungled everything that was given him to do, and he had not an idea in his head concerning the invention and manufacture of stunts. So he was tried as a book-reviewer, and again failed miserably. They made a sub-editor of him, and once more he was slow and inaccurate. Said the news editor to the editor-in-chief: "I'm afraid I shall have to get rid of Jones; he's tried almost everything and failed." "Oh! has he?" returned the editor-in-chief. "Well, put him on to writing leaders."

But even the halfpenny Press has, in recent years, come to regard its leader columns as one of the most important parts of its papers. Of this kind of work I have had little experience. A position as writer of "leaderettes" was offered me on *The Globe*, but I was not a success, for I was at the same time writing a great deal of stuff for *The Daily Citizen*, and, as both papers were equally violent in antagonistic political and social fields, I soon found myself writing solidly and regularly against my own convictions. It is true that a journalist, like a barrister, is generally but a hireling paid to express certain views, but there are few men so intellectually backboneless and ethically flabby that they can, day after day, say both yes and no to the various problems that face them.

I suppose there are few professions in which one learns more about the seamy side of human nature than one does in journalism. The one appalling vice of eminent men is vanity. Musicians, actors, authors, politicians—even judges and preachers—appear to be so constituted that they cannot live and be happy without publicity. From what source, do you think, originate those chatty little paragraphs concerning famous men and women that you find in every evening newspaper and in many weeklies? They originate from the fountain-head. If the novelist does not himself send the paragraph to the paper, his publisher does; if the actor has not written that "snappy" par., he has given his manager the material for it. At one time I wrote a weekly column of theatrical gossip for a well-known daily, and I can, without exaggeration, say that most of our famous actors and actresses did my work for me. I used scissors and paste, corrected their grammatical errors (and mistakes in spelling!), coloured the whole with my personality—and there the column was ready for the printer! Sometimes I would receive letters from notorious mimes expostulating with me because I had not mentioned their names for a month or two. Others wrote and thanked me for praising them. One lady whom I have never seen, either on the stage or off, sent me a silver pencil-case, with a letter containing the material for a very personal sketch. I put the pencil in my pocket and the sketch in the newspaper. Quite recently I was shown an article signed by a famous lady, containing a bogus account of how she had received a strange proposal of marriage. The article had been invented and written by an acquaintance of mine, but the signature was the lady's.

But more egregious than the vanity of actors is the vanity of fashionable preachers. To them notoriety is the very breath of their nostrils. They have no "agents," so they are compelled to advertise themselves without camouflage. And they do it shamelessly. I will not mention names, but at least half the fashionable preachers in London, no matter what their denomination, are guilty of constant and most resourceful self-advertisement. A little, a very little, jesuitical reasoning is sufficient to satisfy their consciences that this is done, not out of vanity, but from a desire to bring a still larger congregation to the fount of wisdom itself.... They are the fount of wisdom.

On only two occasions have I approached an author with a request for an interview and been refused. But I have taken care never to approach such men as Thomas Hardy, John Galsworthy and a few others who regard their profession with too much respect to lend themselves to a practice which, at its best, is undignified, and which, at its worst, is a method of mean self-glorification.

Of "ghosting" I have done a little and seen much. I know well a very prosperous musical composer of talent who has paid me to write many articles that he has signed with his own name. You call me an accomplice? But then it was nothing to me what he did with my articles when I had written them. Believe me, the practice is very common. The man who signs the articles furnishes the ideas: the ghost merely expresses them.

The same musical composer was commissioned a few years ago to write an orchestral work for an important musical festival. We will call him Birket. Either Birket was too busy to write the work or he felt he had not the ability to do it; whatever the reason, he went to a friend of mine—a man of far superior gifts to his more famous colleague—and offered him a certain sum to do the work for him. My friend—Foster will do for his name—consented, and the work was duly performed at the festival, conducted by Birket, and I attended in my capacity as musical critic.

How eminent men who are not writers do itch to see themselves in print! It is not enough that their speeches are reported, their paintings and musical compositions criticised, their sentences recorded by every daily newspaper, their acting, singing and what not lauded to the skies: they must themselves write: or, if they cannot write, it must appear to the public that they have written. Why? Just vanity. That word "vanity" will explain nine-tenths of the seemingly inexplicable things in the conduct of most of our public men. A man accepts a knighthood because, as a rule, he is vain; he refuses it for the same reason; he advertises that he has refused it because he is vain; and, because he is vain, he refuses to advertise that he has refused it.

A great deal has been written about the romance of Fleet Street. But romance is in a man's mind and heart, and it is true that many romantically minded men go to Fleet Street. Fleet Street gives us a sense of importance, a sense of too much importance. We like to feel that we are powerful, but only a mere handful of men in The Street have power that is worth while. What we of the rank and file write is soon forgotten, for newspaper readers are, for the most part, people who devour print greedily, neither masticating nor assimilating the things they devour. Newspapers confuse the mind and bring it to a state of drugged apathy. Did you ever meet a really voracious reader of newspapers who possessed the gift of sifting and weighing evidence, or one who had an accurate memory, or one who could think clearly and logically, or one who was not bewildered and befogged by mere words?

But even if we men in Fleet Street have no real power, we have what is much the same thing: we have the illusion of power. We come into close contact with people much more important than ourselves, and some of these people fawn on us, for we are the necessary intermediaries between themselves and the public.

But romance? Why is Fleet Street romantic? Well, as I have already said, it is because so many journalists themselves are romantic.... But I wonder if that really *is* the reason, and as I wonder I begin to think that though it is true one meets adventurous, talented and original people by the score in newspaper offices, yet, after all, it is not they who make journalism seem full of savour, of rich delight, of unexpectedness and excitement, of high romance. No; it is writing itself that is romantic: mere words and the colour and music of words; the smell of printers' ink; the wet feel of a paper fresh from the press; the sounds of telephone bells and of machinery; the joy of expressing oneself; the lovely, great joy of signing one's name to an article and knowing that in twenty-four hours it will have been read or glanced at by perhaps half-a-million people.... But it seems to me as I write that I am utterly failing to communicate to you who read the romantic nature of journalism. To you it is, perhaps, merely a slipshod profession, a profession in which there is something sordid and vulgar and as unromantic as Monday morning. To me a man who writes with distinction is the most interesting creature in the world: I cannot know too much about him; I can never tire of his talk. Actors bore me. So do politicians, lawyers, men of science, those who are professionally religious, doctors, musicians. But writers and financiers—especially Jewish financiers—are to me full of subtlety; their souls are elusive, and their minds are cunning past all reckoning. It is frequently said that the art of writing is possessed by most people. The art of writing correctly may be, but the "correct" writer is frequently not a writer at all, for he cannot compel people to read him. A writer without readers is not a writer; he is simply a man who murmurs to himself very laboriously. But the writer who can claim thousands of readers—I mean even such writers as Mr Charles Garvice and the lady who invented *The Rosary*—are in essentials more highly endowed with the true writer's gifts than many mandarins who live cloistered in Oxford and Cambridge. And I say this in spite of the fact that I have never been able to read more than ten consecutive pages of any book of Mr Garvice's that I have picked up, and that *The Rosary* seems to me a story of such amazing flapdoodleism that——

Arnold Bennett says somewhere that living in the theatrical world is like living a story out of *The Arabian Nights*. To me Fleet Street is more amazing than the bazaars of Cairo, more mysterious than the hermaphroditic Sphinx. And perhaps one of the most amazing things about Fleet Street is the easy way in which many men earn money.

Some years ago I was on the staff of a paper where I had for a colleague a dark blue-eyed young man who was our crime specialist. He had just come from the provinces, and had not even a rudimentary notion of how to write. He knew he couldn't write; he boasted of it. And he cared nothing for newspapers or books or anything even remotely connected with literature. But he had an amazing talent for sniffing out crime. I remember a great jewel robbery which he got wind of half-a-day before anyone else, and, in a way known only to himself, he obtained full particulars of the affair, writing a half-column "story" before any other paper in the kingdom even knew there was a story to write. He entertained me vastly, and I used to go with him sometimes at night when he called at Scotland Yard for news. Scotland Yard never gives away news unless it is in its own interest to do so. But I am very much inclined to believe that it was somewhere in Scotland Yard that he obtained his most valuable information. We would walk down wide corridors there together, sit ten minutes in a waiting-room, interview an official who invariably said: "Nothing doing to-night," and come away. But that was quite enough for my friend. "I must go to Poplar straight away," he would say, as we came away; or perhaps: "I can just catch the last train to Guildford"; or "There is nothing at all in the rumour of that murder in Battersea." I used to look at him in amazement and exclaim: "But how do you *know*?" "Ah!" he would reply; "they say that walls have ears. But much more frequently they have tongues."

This man was paid three pounds a week by our editor. Three times out of four he was ahead of every other paper in his news, and I was not in the least surprised when one day, after he had been in London only two months, he came to me and said: "Next week I am leaving you. I am going to *The Morning Trumpet*; they're giving me five hundred pounds a year." Five months later he was getting a thousand pounds a year from a paper that never hesitates to pay handsomely for "stunts."

I caught fire from my friend's enthusiasm, and late one night, just when I had finished a long notice of a new play, I overheard the night editor regretting to one of the sub-editors that news of a particularly horrible murder in Stepney had just reached the office when all the reporters were out on duty. "Let me go!" I urged. "But you are in evening dress," he objected. "Never mind; send me off." And ten minutes later I was being rushed in a taxi-cab at full speed to Stepney. I found the scene of the murder—a mean little house in a mean little street. Outside the house was a crowd of eager loafers, a score of reporters, and as many policemen, who, refusing to be bribed, kept us all in the street without news. However, such was my enthusiasm that I alone of all the reporters got into the house and into the cellar where the wretched woman had been butchered to death three hours earlier. I drew a hasty plan of the underground floor, interviewed a sister of the murdered woman, obtained full particulars, and then jumped into the taxi-cab to return to the office. Within an hour of leaving my desk I was back again, and in another twenty minutes I had ready as vivid and thrilling a "story" as ever I hope to write. Knowing that the paper was on the point of going to press, I did not, as I ought to have done, hand my copy to one of the sub-editors, but took it straight to the machines. Whilst I was waiting for a proof, I was summoned to my editor's room. He was frowning, and he looked very much perturbed.

"By the merest chance, Cumberland," he said, sternly, "I have been the means of saving the paper from heavy penalties for contempt of court." He paused and bit his lip. "I suppose you think your murder story a most brilliant piece of work."

"Well, I certainly was under that impression, sir," I began, "but it would seem — —"

"*Seem!*" he thundered. "You've got the facts, it's true, but then all my reporters have to get the facts. The gross blunder you've made is, first of all, in saying that the suspected man has spent practically all his life in prison— contempt of court of the vilest description. Secondly, you've said— —" He enumerated no fewer than five blunders I had made. "But, worst of all," he concluded, "you took it upon yourself to give your copy direct to the printers after midnight, thus breaking the strictest rule of this office."

It was true. In my exciting enthusiasm I had forgotten this Persian rule.

"Fortunately, I came in just in time to stop your stuff. You'd better, I think, confine yourself exclusively to your dramatic criticism."

Nevertheless, he offered me, two days later, ten pounds a week to give up my dramatic criticism and general articles (for which I was at that time getting only five pounds) and devote myself to reporting—an offer which I refused, as the work would have exhausted all my time.

It was at about this time that the idea occurred to me that a certain monthly magazine for which I had been writing regularly might, if asked, pay me at a higher rate than that which, till then, they had been giving me. So I dressed myself very carefully (clothes *do* help, don't they?) and drove up to the office in a smart hansom.

"I have called about my articles," I began, rather brusquely, to the editor, a scholarly man who knew far more about Elizabethan literature than he did about human nature. "I have found just lately that I am so busy that I have resolved to give up some of my work. Your magazine is one of those with which I am anxious to retain my connection, partly because my relationship with you has always been so pleasant."

And I stopped. It is not everyone who knows the right place at which to stop in conversations of this kind. "My relationship with you has always been so pleasant" was, most indubitably, the right place.

He tried to force me into further talk by remaining silent himself. A clock ticked: a clock always does tick on these occasions. He coughed. I looked steadily towards the window. For a full minute there must have been silence: to me it seemed an hour; to him I have no doubt it seemed eternity.

"I think, Mr Cumberland, we shall be able to come to a satisfactory arrangement," he said, when eternity had passed. "What do you say to such-and-such an amount?"

And he staggered me by mentioning a sum exactly treble the amount I had been receiving for the last two years.

As I walked into the Strand, I felt a mean and disagreeable bargain-driver, but after I had lunched at Simpson's, I said to myself: "What a fool you were not to go to see him twelve months ago!"

But though many people equally as obscure as myself earn a thousand pounds a year by their pens, you must not imagine that all the men who are famous writers do likewise. By no means always does it happen that a man combines literary genius and the power of earning money, and there are many men rightly honoured in our own day whose earnings do not involve them in the payment of income tax. The faculty of making money, no matter whether it is made out of the sale of pills or poems, tripe or tragedies, is innate. No man by taking thought can add a thousand pounds a year to his income, for money is not made by thought but by intuition.

I know a man in Chelsea who earns fifteen hundred pounds a year by writing what, in my schoolboy days, we called (and perhaps they are still called) "bloods." He knocks off a cool five thousand words a day every day for three weeks, and then takes a week's holiday—boys' "bloods," servant-girls' novelettes, children's fairy tales and newspaper serials. He is a cheerful, energetic man, whose hobbies are bull-dogs and Shakespeare, and he has five different pen-names. For the matter of that, I use three different pseudonyms, my reason for doing this being that the editor of *The Spectator*, say, might not accept my work if he knew I was writing at the same time for *The English Review* (I have written for both publications), and I am doubtful if *The Morning Post* would have printed a single word of mine if the editor had been aware that I was having a thousand words a day printed in *The Daily Citizen*. Some editors like what they call "versatility of thought," others (I think rightly) distrust it.

But I can very well believe that this gossip about money appears to you very sordid. Well, so it is. My final paragraph shall not be permitted to mention, or even hint at, hard cash.

Once again I return to my statement that Fleet Street is romantic because many of the people in it are romantic. But what is a romantic person? Alas! I cannot define one. Perhaps a romantic person is he whose soul is mysterious and elusive and whose mind is perturbed and exalted by a poetic vision of life. He must care little for the things that Mr Samuel Smiles and the "get on or get out" school value so much.... No. That will not do at all, for a great many men and women who have cared a great deal for money and worldly power were romantic. Nero, for example, and Cleopatra, and Shakespeare, and Queen Elizabeth, and Lord Verulam— —

But though a romantic man may be difficult to define, he is very easy to recognise. Ivan Heald was incorrigibly romantic. But perhaps the most romantically minded man I met in Fleet Street was the journalist who went with me to Athens in the very early spring of 1914. He had no right in Fleet Street, for he was essentially a man who preferred to do things rather than write about them. But half the men in London journalism have drifted there not so much because they have a natural aptitude for the work but because they are born adventurers, and the great adventure of Fleet Street is bound to cross the path of most roving men one day or another.

Years ago there lived in London a man who wrote books and magazine stories under the name of Julian Croskey. He had been in the Civil Service in Shanghai, had helped to finance and organise a rebellion, and had been turned out of China, whence he came to England to write. In 1901 I began a correspondence with Croskey, who, in the meantime, had gone to Canada and was living alone on a river island. Though we corresponded for years, we never met, and after a time his letters began to show signs of megalomania. But there was such genius in his letters, such brooding energy, such hate of life, and, at times, such an uncanny suggestion of terrific power, that I treasured every word he wrote to me, and, when his letters ceased, something vital and something almost necessary to me passed out of my life. I do not like to believe that he ceased writing to me because I no longer interested him. I hope he still lives. I hope he will read this book. Some day his letters must be published, for they constitute a problem in psychology at once fascinating, mysterious and demonic. And this man whom I never met remains to me the most romantic of all men I have met in the spirit.

CHAPTER X
HALL CAINE

MY acquaintance with Hall Caine began in a semi-professional way. Whilst still a schoolboy, I was commissioned by *Tit-Bits* to write a three-column interview with him. I wrote to the novelist for an interview. Perhaps the rawness of my letter aroused the suspicion that I was too young to write adequately about him even in a paper of the standing of *Tit-Bits*; at all events he refused the interview, but very kindly said that, if I was contemplating a visit to the Isle of Man, he would be pleased if I would call on and lunch with him as an unprofessional visitor. At that time, being young and ardent, I was a young and ardent admirer of his, and I believe I told him so in my letter that requested the interview.

If I went to him as an admirer I came away from that first visit to Greeba Castle a worshipper. In those days he was (but he still is!) an astounding personality. He came into the room quietly and, having shaken hands and sat down by my side, said: "An exquisite day for your walk from St John's." So impressively was this spoken, and there was such a fire in his eyes as he said it, such a weight of meaning in his manner, that I felt as though something secret and wonderful had been revealed to me. I wanted to say: "How true!" What I did say was: "Yes; isn't it?" He asked me a few questions about myself and then spoke about general matters. He probably said quite trivial, kindly things, but at the time they were uttered, and for a little while afterwards, they seemed rich and full of wisdom.

After lunch he showed me the MSS. of some of his books. I remember the MS. of *The Bondman*. It was written in a small, curiously artistic handwriting on half sheets of notepaper, which had been pasted on to much larger sheets handsomely bound. I handled the book as reverently as the young ladies of early days caressed the pages of the great Martin Tupper. There were many "blots" in the MS.—many alterations, excisions and additions, and it was clear, even from a cursory examination, that Mr Hall Caine was a hard and conscientious worker. Upon this and other books he left me to browse for an hour whilst he went to receive other callers—all of them strangers to him—who were just arriving.

Some of those visitors, as I discovered later, were a rather extraordinary crew: men and women from Lancashire and Yorkshire: I mean *absolutely* from Lancashire and Yorkshire: men and women who had made a little money and who had unbounded respect for people who had made a little more: men and women who were sound and good, but not quite educated and who were either like fish out of water, gasping and floundering spasmodically, or positively frightfully at their ease. I recollect a tall and handsome lady who prodded everything with a green parasol, and two men who, not too furtively, made elaborate efforts to estimate the amount of the author's income.

We had tea on a terrace in the grounds and in the evening I was driven back to St John's, all the other callers returning to Douglas.

The impression left by Mr Hall Caine's personality on my mind by that and many subsequent visits was overwhelming. He was vivid, alive, and full of smouldering fires; short and vehement; his eyes were large and bright; his voice beautiful and capable of a thousand inflections—an actor's voice; his temperament also an actor's; his point of view an actor's. But he never did act; invariably he was tragically (and, I must add, sometimes pathetically) sincere. He had humour, but he could not laugh at himself. His dress was eccentric; he wore a flapping hat, breeches and a jacket made of thick, everlasting, hand-made cloth. A big tie bulged and billowed somewhere about his neck. He told me on one occasion that chars-à-bancs full of trippers from Douglas continually passed along the Douglas-Peel road and that when the trippers caught a sight of him they would sometimes hail him with cries of derision and shouts of laughter.

"At those moments," he said, "I am always most dignified. I raise my hat to them and bow and their laughter immediately ceases."

That I could well believe, for there is something commanding in his personality, something well calculated to quell insolence.

A desultory correspondence and a few casual visits followed during the next three or four years, and when I was in my very early twenties I persuaded Messrs Greening & Company to invite me to write a book on Hall Caine for a popular series (*English Writers of To-day*, it was called) they were at that time issuing. Mr Caine, upon being approached by me, put no hindrance in my way, but, on the contrary, consented to give me some assistance in the way of providing me with information and a few letters received by him from eminent men. I spent several week-ends at Greeba Castle and found in Mrs Caine, always charming and ideally gifted with tact, a delightful hostess. My book was quickly written. It was a feeble, bombastic and ridiculous performance. A friend of mine (I thought he was an enemy) called it "a prolonged diarrhœa of the emotions." In this book Hall Caine took a very kindly interest, and he provided me with autograph letters written by Ruskin, Blackmore, T. E. Brown and Gladstone to insert in my book. But I was, of course, the sole author of the work, and Mr Caine had nothing to do with it save to put me right on matters of fact and to tone down some of my exuberant and sentimental praise. The silly volume, because of its subject, attracted a good deal of attention, both in this country and in America, though it was not published in the States. *The Philadelphia Daily Eagle*, for example, on the day the book was published, printed a eulogistic cablegram review of it from London. But, for the most part, my monograph was mercilessly slated. Hall Caine, in addition, was abused for consenting to be the subject of it, and I was abused for having chosen him for my subject. One paper headed its review "Raising Caine."

The truth is, at this time (1901) Mr Hall Caine, though extraordinarily popular with the public, was not much liked by a certain section of the Press. His success was envied by some, perhaps; his recognition of his own worth was fiercely and almost universally resented; and his almost unconscious habit of advertising himself—though he did not indulge this habit more than most popular novelists—could not be tolerated. Mr Caine used frequently to deplore his only too palpable unpopularity with the Press, and once or twice he asked me to explain it. His own theory was that he had a few powerful enemies who took advantage of every occasion to disseminate lies about him, but who these enemies were he never stated. As a matter of fact, he occasionally said injudicious things to reporters which, in cold print, appeared not only self-satisfied but vainglorious. A long and very well written article by Mr Robert H. Sherard, in (I believe) *The Daily Telegraph* caused him a good deal of anxiety.

Not often does one find a man of Hall Caine's very special gifts endowed with the abilities of a financier. He is as quick and as clever at driving a bargain as a Lancashire or Yorkshire mill-owner. There have always been and, I suppose, always will be a large percentage of writers who are constitutionally incapable of looking after their own affairs; they can produce, but they cannot sell. Mr Hall Caine does not belong to these. He, more than any man, contributed to the breakdown of the three-volume novel system. It was he who helped to formulate the Canadian Copyright Laws. With the assistance of Major Pond (who in these days remembers the great Major Pond?) he made tens of thousands of dollars by lecturing to the Americans.

He had the acumen and the courage to issue one of his longest novels in two volumes at two shillings net each. He was the first eminent novelist to make a practice of publishing his works in the middle of the August holidays—the supposed "dead" season in the publishing world. He has bought farms in the Isle of Man and made them pay. He has had commercial interests in seaside boarding-houses and has shown a bold but wise enterprise in many of his investments. In other words he has, to his honour, continually exhibited abilities that not one artist in a hundred possesses.

I have rarely seen Hall Caine in a light-hearted mood, but I have been with him in more than one hour of black depression.

Vividly do I remember spending a few days at Greeba Castle shortly after the time when the publication of a story of his, that was running serially in a ladies' paper, was suddenly and dramatically stopped by the editor of that paper on the score of its alleged immorality. The story was about to be produced in book form and, of course, the editor's action had provided a fine advertisement; this fact, however, did not appear to console the novelist in the least. The most sensitive of men, he was crushed by this very public charge of writing immoral literature.

For myself, when he told me all the circumstances, I merely laughed. He glanced at me sideways.

"You are amused?" he asked. "I wonder why."

"Because you are allowing yourself to be made miserable by a most trivial event."

"You call it trivial that the whole world should think me a man of immoral mind?"

"The whole world? Why, the world doesn't trouble itself about the matter in the least. Only one man accuses you of immoral writings; that man is the editor of the paper. What on earth does his opinion matter to you?"

"But his opinion will be widely read and will be widely believed."

"Will be believed, you should have added, by people who allow another man to form their opinions for them. What do *they* matter?"

He sighed.

"But they *do* matter," said he, rather forlornly. "I hate to think of people out there"—he waved a vague arm in the direction of the kitchen garden—"thinking evil thoughts and saying evil things of me."

"'They say. What do they say? Let them say,'" I quoted.

We paced up and down the terrace, his eyes fixed on the ground. At length:

"I wonder what you would think of the chapter in question," he said musingly. "You have read the story as far as it has been printed. Well, I will give you the final chapters to read."

We went to his room and he handed me a few pages of printed copy. I read them.

"Well?" inquired he, when I had finished.

"It is passionate, it is sexual," said I, "but to call it immoral is to call black white."

"You really believe that?" he asked, a little anxiously.

"I do. I assure you I do."

But the black cloud of self-distrust and misery would not be dissipated, and that night, after dinner, we sat over a slow fire, though it was early in August, and talked long and rather sadly of Rossetti, of T. E. Brown and of things that had been said by Peel fishermen.

Another occasion, when I was with the novelist on a day of some anxiety, is equally clear in my memory. I may say at this point that Hall Caine was invariably in a condition of some mental strain a few days before and after the publication of one of his stories. He was a little apprehensive of the reviewers, and he was always afraid lest the public should not remain faithful to him. In this connection I remember him saying to me once: "I can imagine no fate more tragic than for a novelist at middle age, when he believes his powers to be at their highest, to lose his hold upon his public."

He would, I think, deny that he cares what the reviewers may say; nevertheless, my experience of him tells me that he does care. In his early life as a novelist he was, perhaps, overpraised; certainly he but very rarely felt the lash of the critic's whip. So that when the critics began to condemn the work of the man they had once praised, he was not disciplined to bear their condemnation philosophically. Every taunt wounded him, every thrust went home, every sneer was a stab.

But on the occasion about which I am now writing he was not depressed so much in anticipation of what the reviewers might say as on account of the competition of another novel which had been issued a few days previous to the date fixed for the publication of a new book of his own. That novel was Lucas Malet's *The History of Sir Richard Calmady*, published, if my memory does not betray me, by Messrs Methuen.

The first question he asked me one morning before breakfast was:

"Have you read *Sir Richard Calmady*?"

"Yes," I answered.

"Well?" exclaimed he, a little impatiently, "well, what do you think of it?"

"An amazingly clever performance, but very horrible."

"Yes, isn't it?" he cried eagerly. "Horrible! Ghastly! And yet, they tell me, people are reading it."

"Partly for that reason, no doubt."

"But the public, the people, the great reading public—surely they will not respond to the appeal of a book of that nature?"

"The public, you must remember, has many hearts; it may well give one to Sir Richard Calmady."

"But *my* public?"

"Yes; even your public."

He brooded a little.

"I am told that Lucas Malet's publishers believe in the book," he said, after a longish pause, "and are prepared to spend a small fortune in pushing it. And that, of course, means that it will interfere with, and perhaps seriously injure, the sales of my own story. But it seems to me that the public—the *real* public—will never read a novel that has for its chief attraction a man with no legs."

I suggested that he should postpone the publication of his book until the rage for *Sir Richard Calmady* had died down. But no! This would not suit him. He must catch the real holiday season at its full tide. August was the best month in the year, and the first week the best week in the month, and the fifth day the best day of the week.

Hall Caine always shows great perspicacity in selecting the date of publication for his books; he will never allow it to synchronise with any other big event. Moreover, his book must be born to an expectant world; it must be well advertised beforehand. Unlike other writers, he does not work hard at a book, finish it and then hand it over to a publisher to deal with more or less as he thinks fit. In a sense, he is his own publisher, and as a rule he interests himself in the sale of a new work of his own, in its distribution, its printing and binding, etc., as much as the actual publisher himself.

It used to be a popular belief—but Arnold Bennett has done much to kill it—that an author laughs and cries with the creatures of his imagination, that he lives and dreams with them, and that when his book is finished, and the time comes for him to part from them, he does so with pain that is little short of anguish. So far as most authors are concerned, this is exactly opposite to the real facts. Before an author is half-way through his novel he is heartily sick of his characters; his beautiful heroine is an unmitigated nuisance and his hero an incredible bore. He is only too thankful to reach the end of the last chapter and leave his puppets for ever.

But this is not so with Hall Caine. His novels, as you know, do not err on the side of brevity, and though it is possible you may tire of his heroine, you may be absolutely certain that her creator never does. To this novelist the creatures of his imagination are, in one sense, more real than the material beings around him. He is wholly dominated by his imagination. His brain is peopled by creatures of his own fancy. His emotions are engaged on behalf of people who do not exist. His consciousness is confined to the little world he has created for himself and he is saturated with and submerged by fancies that his imagination has bred.

I shall never forget coming across him early one morning in the little shaded footway that winds among trees in the castle grounds to the main drive. His eyes were dim, and he had not perfect control of his voice.

"I have been finishing my book," he said, referring to *The Eternal City*, "and I wept as I wrote."

I have been with him on several occasions when he has been finishing his books, and I have always found him in alternating moods of exhaustion and emotional excitement. Whatever else may be charged against him, it cannot with truth be said that he does not put his whole soul into his work.

As a man he is the most loyal of friends and the most loyal of enemies. He can hate bitterly. I have heard him eloquent in his hate. I have heard him hate W. T. Stead and Frank Harris, and nothing could have exceeded his bitterness. But he does not nurse his hatred, and he is a man quick to forgive.

I cannot close this chapter without a word concerning his generosity. By "generosity" I do not mean only that he is free with money, but that he will give his time, the work of his brain, his advice and even himself for any good cause and for any man in need. To struggling authors he is the very soul of generosity. He struggled himself. Born on a coal barge in Runcorn, largely self-educated, having experienced the anxiety of straitened means and hope deferred, he has known intimately the hardships of life, and will do all in his power to shield others from them. On several occasions I have met people—mostly young men—who have come to him for help and advice in beginning a literary career. He is never extravagant in his praise of their work, but if he finds merit in it he is always warmly encouraging. Years before I met him face to face, when I was a boy of fourteen, I sent him a long poem I had written in the Spenserian stanza, and the first letters I received from him were careful and most helpful criticisms of this juvenile literary effort. I had written to him as an entire stranger and without any introduction whatever. In my youth and egotism I had taken his replies as a matter of course; it was only later that I recognised the most kindly spirit that prompted a busy and often harassed man to give his time and energy to a boy whose work can have had very little to recommend it.

CHAPTER XI
MORE WRITERS

I WONDER how many readers turn nowadays to the poetical works of Thomas Edward Brown, the Manx poet. Not a great number, I think. Indeed, I doubt if he ever had a large audience, though he had the power of exciting almost unlimited enthusiasm in the breasts of those whom he did attract. He was praised whole-heartedly by George Eliot, George Meredith, W. E. Henley and other famous writers, and the publication of his Letters a year or two after his death made a great stir.

In my boyhood's days I was one of Brown's most devoted disciples. He had a charming trick of infusing scholarship with the real "stuff" of humanity, that appealed to me irresistibly, and I liked the honest sensuality of his *Roman Women* and the pathos of such poems as *Aber Stations* and *Epistola ad Dakyns*. Perhaps I could not read his poems now, for, truth to tell, they "gush" almost indecently. However, he remains the most distinguished literary figure that the little Isle of Man has produced, and two or three of his lyrics will persist far into the future.

I met him at Greeba Castle, Mr Hall Caine's Manx residence, when I was still a schoolboy. It was just a few months before Brown's death, and a rather sad incident marked his visit to Hall Caine.

We were at lunch when he arrived: a rather solemn lunch: a lunch at which the guests were ill assorted. A ponderous scholar from Scotland insisted upon discussing the authorship of Homer—a subject about which our host evidently knew little and cared less. In the middle of a rather painful silence, Brown was ushered into the dining-room; he was carrying a little book of Laurence Binyon's that had just been published. His burly figure, his genial face, his ready tongue soon lifted us out of the atmosphere of black boredom that had settled upon us. In five minutes he had disposed of the Scottish scholar, had drunk a whisky and soda, and had combated Hall Caine's opinion that Binyon "had entirely missed the point" in one of the poems he (Binyon) had written.

All afternoon we talked. Brown had come all the way from Ramsey (some twenty-four miles, four of which had to be walked) to spend a few hours with his friend, and, as he was a man greedy of enjoyment, not a single moment was wasted. It soon appeared that Brown was a great admirer of Hall Caine's—it should be mentioned that Mr Caine had not then written *The Prodigal Son* or *The Eternal City*—and the novelist basked in the tactful praise that was bestowed upon him.

As we were talking, a servant came with the news that eleven Americans had arrived and had been shown into the library. Hall Caine left the room to give them tea. An hour later, he came back, exhausted but not displeased.

"One of the penalties of fame," he said, with a sigh.

"But you are not the only one who suffers from your own fame," observed Brown. "I am constantly besieged by American journalists, who come to me for private information about yourself. A very persistent lady from New York came only the other day and wished to know if you were educated."

Hall Caine laughed.

"What did you say?" he asked.

"Well, I asked her what she meant by 'education,' and she replied: 'Is he at all like Matthew Arnold?'"

Towards evening, Brown departed.

Next morning, a note arrived from him, evidently written immediately on his return home the previous evening. The note expressed the writer's regret that he had been unable to visit Greeba Castle that day; he had fully intended coming, but had been prevented at the last moment. This letter disturbed Hall Caine enormously.

"His mind is going," he said; "I have noticed several other signs of vanishing memory, if not of something worse, during the last few months."

There was, indeed, I have always thought, a streak of morbid eccentricity in Brown's intellectual make-up. A careful reader of his letters will notice many moods of fierce exaltation engendered by wholly inadequate and inexplicable causes. His sudden death was perhaps a blessing in disguise.

There are in London two or three men, not known to the general public, whose influence on modern thought is most profound and most disturbing. Of these men A. R. Orage, the editor of *The New Age*, is quite the most distinguished. What circulation his paper enjoys, I do not know; it cannot be large; probably it is not more than two or three thousand; perhaps it is not even so much as that. But the men and women who read it are men and women who count—people who welcome daring and original thought, who hold important positions in the civic, social, political and artistic worlds, and who eagerly disseminate the seeds of thought they pick up from the study of *The New Age*. Tens of thousands of people have been influenced by this paper who have never even heard its name. It does not educate the masses directly: it reaches them through the medium of its few but exceedingly able readers.

The New Age is professedly a Socialist organ, but the promulgation of socialistic doctrines is only a part of its policy and work. Its literary, artistic and musical criticism is the sanest, the bravest and the most brilliant that can be read in England. It reverences neither power nor reputation; it is subtle and unsparing; and, if it is sometimes cruel, it is cruel with a purpose. All sleek money-makers in Art have reason to fear Orage, for his rapier wit may at any moment glance and slide between their ribs and release the hot air that is at once the inspiration and the material of all their works.

Orage has more than a touch of genius. It was Baudelaire (wasn't it?) who said that genius was the power to look upon the world with the eyes of a child. Well, Orage has the all-seeing, non-rejecting eyes of a child. He has also the eternal spirit of youth. One cannot imagine him growing old. Perhaps his most interesting characteristic is his power of attracting and holding friends; he is the most hero-worshipped of men. Having once given his friendship, however, he exacts the utmost loyalty; treachery is the one sin that can never be forgiven.

I knew Orage years ago, when he was still in Leeds teaching the young idea how to shoot. He was then a prominent member of the Theosophical Society and lectured a good deal—and rather dangerously, I think—on Nietzsche. His gospel, always preached with his tongue in his cheek, that every man and woman should do precisely what he or she desires, acted like heady wine on the gasping and enthusiastic young ladies who used to sit in rows worshipping him. They wanted to do all kinds of terrible things, and as Orage, backed by "that great German," Nietzsche, had sanctioned their most secret desires, they were resolved to begin at once their career of licence. They used to "stay behind" when the lectures were over, and question Orage with their lips and invite him with their eyes, and it used to be most amusing and a little pathetic to listen to the gay and half-veiled insults with which Orage at once thwarted and bewildered his silly devotees.

He had in those days a wonderful gift of talking a most divine nonsense—a spurious wisdom that ran closely along the border-line of rank absurdity. The "cosmic consciousness" of Walt Whitman was a great theme of his, and Orage, in his subtle, devilishly clever way, would lead his listeners on to the very threshold of occult knowledge—and leave them there, wide-eyed and wonder-struck.

I have never known an editor more jealous of the reputation of his paper than Orage is of *The New Age*. No consideration of friendship would induce him to print a dull article, however sound, and when one of his contributors becomes sententious, or slack, or banal—out he goes, neck and crop. Among the contributors to *The New Age* I remember writers as different in mental calibre as John Davidson and Edward Carpenter, Frank Harris and Cecil Chesterton, Arnold Bennett and Janet Achurch. These and scores of equally distinguished people have written for Orage. Why? For money? Well, scarcely; *The New Age's* rates of pay must be very modest. For what, then? They have written because in *The New Age* they can tell the unadulterated truth and because they are proud to see their work in that paper.

To many people Norman Angell is a rather sinister figure, and the people who attack him most violently to-day are precisely those who praised him most when he wrote his first book. He has been overpraised and spoilt. His intellectual attainments are not greatly above the average, and his thinking is not always honest. In the early days of the war it used to be amusing to see him working among his spectacled and yellow-skinned assistants; he was small but magisterial, and he was always tucking sheets of foolscap into long envelopes and looking very important as he did so. I really believe that in those days of August, 1914, he had a vague idea that he and his helpers could stop the war at any moment they chose. Certainly, he was very cross with the war. Europe was behaving in her old, mad way without having previously consulted him.

"But it will soon be over," he assured me. "You see——"

He stopped and waved his hand vaguely in the direction of a typewriter, smothered in documents.

"Quite," said I uncomprehendingly. "You mean——?"

"Yes; that's it. Exhaustion. It can't go on for ever. It must stop some time."

A smile that came from nowhere straggled into his face. I felt vaguely discomfited.

"You see, we are hard at it," he said, and, as he spoke, be indicated a pale, ill-shaven youth who was wandering aimlessly about the office, his hands full of papers.

A queer little chap, Angell. Very much in earnest, of course, very sure of himself, very pushing, very "idealistic."

St John Ervine is a writer who already counts for much but who, a few years hence, will count for a good deal more. He is by way of being a protégé of Bernard Shaw, and earnest young Fabians have already learned to reverence him.

We worked together on *The Daily Citizen*, he being dramatic critic. He was not enormously popular with the rest of the staff, for he was very "highbrow"; his face was smooth, sleek and superior, and he had a habit of being friendly with a man one day and scarcely recognising him the next. My own relations with him were of the most disagreeable. A play of his was given at the Court Theatre, and I was sent to criticise it. I did criticise it: the play was ugly, clever and sordid.

"But," protested Ervine, pale with vexation, the next time he met me, "but you have entirely misunderstood my play. You can't have stayed till the end."

"It was very painful for me, Ervine," said I, "but I really did stick it out to the finish. Why do you young fellows write so depressingly? You look happy enough, Ervine— —"

"The close of my play is the part that matters. Bernard Shaw said so...."

We parted: he, with a look of successful hauteur; I, broken and crushed.

A week or so later I met him at one of Herbert Hughes's jolly Sunday evenings in Chelsea.

"You know Gerald Cumberland, of course," said someone who was introducing him to people.

He drew himself up with great dignity and stared at me through his pince-nez.

"I think," said he, "yes, I believe we *have* met before somewhere. Where was it, Mr ... er ... Cumberland?"

Shortly after, he left *The Daily Citizen*, and I was given the position which he had occupied with so much conscious distinction. I somehow think that when the war is over and we meet, he will not know me. Ervine is very much like that.

Fifteen years is a long time in the literary world, and Charles Marriott's *The Column*, which threw everybody into fever-heat somewhere about 1902, is, I suppose, forgotten. It was a "first" novel. Uncritical Ouida loved it;

W. E. Henley unbent and wrote a Meredithian letter to its author; W. L. Courtney seized some of his short stories for *The Fortnightly Review*; and I suppose (though I really don't know this) *The Spectator* wrote five lines of disapproval. It was a brilliant book; fresh, original, provocative. It promised a lot: it promised too much; the author has since written many distinguished books, but none of them is as good as *The Column* said they would be.

Marriott was living at Lamorna, a tiny cove in Cornwall, when I first knew him. He was tall, lantern-jawed and spectacled. He was interested in everything, but it appeared to me even then that he was a little inhuman. He lacked vulgarity; rude things repelled him enormously, unnaturally; he had no literary delight—or else his delight was too literary: I don't know—in coarseness. Fastidious to the finger-tips, he would rather go without dinner than split an infinitive. Since those days Marriott has gone on refining himself until there is very little Marriott left. Even the longest and the thickest pencil may be sharpened too frequently.

Many years after I met him at an exhibition of pictures in Bond Street. He was then almost old, tired, preoccupied. He is quite the last man to be a journalist; his art criticism is wonderfully fine, but a life standing on the polished floors of galleries between Bond Street and Leicester Square is soul-corroding and heart-breaking. Marriott's mind no longer darts and leaps. It moves gently, very gently.

Max Beerbohm is not so witty in conversation as one might expect. On the spur of the moment he has little verbal readiness; his mind is purely literary. He bears no resemblance to his late brother, Sir Herbert Beerbohm Tree, one of the cleverest conversationalists I have ever met.

A short, mild and debonair figure received me one May afternoon in a house which, if not in Cavendish Square, was somewhere in its neighbourhood. In my later schoolboy days Max was very much cultivated by those of the younger generation who liked to think themselves enormously in the swim. We used to "collect" Max Beerbohm's—not his caricatures, for they were far and away beyond our means; but his articles. I remember a rather startling article of his in *The Yellow Book* which I had bound in lizard-skin, and a friend of mine had all Max's *Saturday Review* articles beautifully typewritten on thick yellow paper and bound in scarlet cardboard. Max was precious, Max was deliciously impertinent, Max was too frightfully clever for words.

When I called upon him four or five years ago I had, I need scarcely say, long outgrown my early infatuation, for he had begun to "date," and was safely in his niche among the men of the nineties. But half-an-hour's talk with him revived some of the old fascination. He had "atmosphere"; his personality created an environment; he brought a flavour of far-off days. We talked quite pleasantly of his art, but he said nothing that has stuck in my memory, and my questions seemed to amuse rather than interest him. His small dapper figure gave one the impression of a schoolboy who had grown a little tired, who had prematurely developed his talents, and who had just fallen short of winning a big prize.

He led the way to the front door, shook me by the hand, looked at me meditatively for a moment, smiled faintly, and ... vanished.

Of Israel Zangwill I can give only an impression. I see him now as I saw him one hot afternoon at his rooms in the Temple. A dark man, a spare man, a man very much in earnest and anxious to be just. He was perspiring slightly, I remember, and he bent forward a little so as to hear and understand every word I said. I had a request to make: a favour to ask. He listened patiently, gave me a cup of tea, and stirred his own. For a little he ruminated. Then he turned to me and lifted his eyebrows—lifted his eyebrows rather high. I repeated my request, giving further details. I was a little confused. He studied my confusion, not cruelly, but in the way that a trained observer studies everything that comes under his notice. Then: "Ye-es," he said; "I see. I see." And then there was a minute's silence.

"I will do what you want," he remarked, at length. "I will do it willingly—most willingly."

And he did. Our little business entailed some subsequent correspondence, and some work on Zangwill's part. The work was done promptly; his letters answered mine by return of post. He gained nothing by his work, whereas the paper I represented gained a great deal.

Alphonse Courlander was one of the many young and promising writers whom the war has killed. He was one of the most hard-working journalists in Fleet Street, and if he was not precisely brilliant, he had unusual gifts and used them to good purpose. I could never read his novels, but I understand they met with a certain success, and people whose opinion I respect have spoken highly of them.

He represented *The Daily Express* in Paris at the time the war broke out. He was the most conscientious of men, and he grappled with the extra work that grew up with the war with a fierce and fanatical energy. He overworked himself, and the horror of the war appears to have got on his nerves. He disappeared from Paris and was found wandering alone in London, neurasthenic, beaten, purposeless. A week or two later he died.

Courlander was a good example of a not unusual type of man one frequently meets in Fleet Street—a type that, in the end, is bound to meet either failure or tragedy. He was too highly strung for the rigours of the game: too sensitive; too ambitious for his weak frame. The type either takes to drink or wears itself out long before middle age. Courlander was an abstemious man; perhaps if he had "let himself go" occasionally, he would have stood the strain of his work better. When I saw him, he was always busy, always up to date, always writing or going to write a novel in his spare time. He had very little inventive faculty and used to worry over his plots and worry his friends over them. "Plots! ... as if plots matter if you have anything to say!" I used to urge. And then he would look at me, mystified.

"But, Cumberland, what can you know about it? You have never written a novel."

"Oh, but I have," I would reply, "but no one will publish them."

"Ah! that's the reason."

And he really believed that that *was* the reason.

Ivan Heald was a colleague of Courlander—a colleague any man in Fleet Street would have been glad to possess. Heald was original, and he created a record in so far as he was the first and, so far as I know, the only man to be employed by a British daily paper to write a "funny story" each day. He made a wide reputation, a reputation that, no doubt, pleased him, but he had no real ambition. People who "got on" rather amused him—that is to say, if their success was won at the expense of experience of life. I never met a man more full of zest for life, a man more eager for experience, a man who retained his youth so successfully. He was vivid, careless, tolerant and, in spite of every appearance to the contrary, essentially serious-minded. It was the simple pleasures of life that attracted him.

He had no scholarship, but his mind was well ordered, and his appreciation of natural and artistic beauty was of the keenest.

I remember that when we were holidaying together at Oxford he would become almost angry with me because I could not immediately perceive the beauty of certain lines—the outlines of trees, the curve of a table-napkin, the pattern made by the ropes of a tent, and so on.

"You should get Eddie or Norman Morrow to go a walk with you," he said. "*They* would make you see things."

He loved folk-songs, Irish peasants, the plays of Synge, the Russian Ballet, the Thames, the homely comfort of a country inn. His feeling for family life was strong, and Friday evenings at the Healds', where one met his mother and sisters, as clever if not so vivid as he himself, were one of the great recurring pleasures of many men's lives.

He was wounded in Gallipoli, nursed back to health, transferred to the R.F.C., and died (in all probability, for the exact manner of his death is not certainly known) in the air. A death he would have desired. But Ivan Heald should not have died, and sometimes I am tempted to think that he still lives, that something in him still lives—something that was rich and strange and beautiful. The other day I came across one of the little notes he used to scribble to me. It is written from Ireland, and because it is so like him I give it here:

Dear Gerald,—If only I had the nice stiff paper and the delicate pen nib, I would try to write a letter to you like the ones you send me. There came a thrill yesterday. As I sat in my little parlour toying with my last month's *Ulster Guardian*, there leapt out of the page your poem, *Fashioned of Dreams You Are* [reprinted from a magazine]. It was as though the sea between us had suddenly shrunk to a couple of glasses of whisky. I shall never pass a Poet's Corner again without looking for you. There are poets here, too. An old-age pensioner describing a wonderful fish he had seen told me that it was "a gay and antic fish, fresh and smart and soople." I shall leave for home to-morrow evening and see you on Sunday night, and if there is one bottle of red wine left in the world, you and I will surely drag it out of the dust. How the bottles must wonder under their cobwebs at this strange turn of fate—that the Master Butler may either transform them into sparkling phrases and beautiful thoughts through rare fellows like us, or send them to dreary death in the paunch of fools like — —

Ivan.

Dixon Scott used to throw me into little ecstasies by his reviews in *The Manchester Guardian*, and I often used to wonder if I should meet him. Our paths crossed for a brief minute not long before we left England—he to meet his death in France, and I to sit and wait in Serbia. It was at the end of one of my evenings in the Café Royal, where one used to sip absinthe, smoke a cigar, and listen to Orage. It was "Time, gentlemen, please": 12-30 a.m.: in Army parlance, 0030 hours. We were all very merry as we crowded into Regent Street, and I heard a voice behind me say: "Dixon Scott."

I turned round immediately.

"Are you Dixon Scott?" I asked a man—a man who looked as unlike my preconceived picture of him as possible.

"Yes, and someone has just told me you are Gerald Cumberland."

"How awfully jolly," said I, "for now I have the opportunity of telling you how much I admire your wonderful genius."

"Tophole!" said he. "I love praise, don't you?"

"Ra-*ther*!" said I.

And then I fought for a taxi and saw Scott no more.

Barry Pain, like the gentleman who used to be known as Adrian Ross, leads a double intellectual life. He earns his bread by writing humorous literature; he is the king of modern jesters; but secretly (and perhaps in shame) he studies philosophy and metaphysics and is known to have written a big two-volume work dealing with the furtive processes of the human mind. He is a scholar, but Fate has made of him a manufacturer of jokes. While his tougher intellectual faculties are wrestling with the basic problems of the universe—the whence, whither and why of things—his observing eye is noting the little discrepancies of life, the jolly frailties of human nature, the absurdities of our everyday existence.

He revealed little of his capacity for humour when he entertained me to whisky and soda at his club. I found a big, bearded and rather fleshy man rolling about in a very easy chair. I had been sent to interview him by one of those very pushing newspapers that, in the Silly Season especially, run absurd "stories." I have not the slightest recollection of the particular story that took me to Barry Pain, but I am perfectly certain that it was preposterous, and I am perfectly certain that my news editor—he was Stanley Bishop, of blessed memory—expected me to bring back to the office several gems of humour tempted from the brain and stolen from the lips of the famous writer. But Pain was coy. Perhaps he does not believe in giving away jokes for which coin of the realm is usually paid.

I presented my "story" to him and tried to make him talk about it, but he looked glum and stared stonily into the empty fire-grate.

"Really," he began, at length, "I can't think of anything to say. Can you? If you can think of something very clever, put it in your article and say I said it. Yes, do say I said it. But, of course, it must be very clever."

And he lapsed into a long, depressed silence. I was very glad when a friend of his popped his head into the room and shouted: "What about that game of bridge?" I rose hastily and escaped.

It would be difficult to find a more picturesque figure than R. B. Cunninghame Graham. I always picture him sitting on a bare-backed Mexican steed, his shirt open at the throat, a long whip in one hand, a lasso in the other, his eyes, like Blake's tiger, burning bright, his boots fantastically spurred, his hat flapping in the wind, and his steed galloping *ventre à terre*. In South and Central America, no doubt, he does run wild, but in London of late years he has always been most respectable. And yet even West End respectability cannot kill his picturesqueness. He has a shining mind, and everything he says is youthful and spirited.

Most of his literary enthusiasms are for the younger—the youngest— generation, but as his mind is essentially uncritical and impulsive, his judgments are not very trustworthy. I remember his praising unreservedly a young alleged poet who in recent years has made himself known by his scholarship and impudence, and, as far as I could gather, it was chiefly his impudence that had attracted Cunninghame Graham.

CHAPTER XII
MUSICAL CRITICS

NOT until quite recently has musical criticism been taken seriously either by the London or provincial Press. In the old days of the sixties, when Wagner came to London (I am writing many miles away from books, but surely it was in the sixties that Wagner visited us?), there was not a single open-minded musical critic on the British Press. J. W. Davison, the very powerful *Times* critic, was not only a fool, but, what is much more dangerous, he was a learned fool. He treated Wagner shamefully, and he did more than his share to bring our country into musical disrepute among the cultured men of other nations. Joseph Bennett, of *The Daily Telegraph*, was a fluent writer who contrived to say less in a full column than a man like Ernest Newman or R. A. Streatfeild or Samuel Langford can say in a couple of lines. He footled gaily for many years, wielded enormous power, and did nothing whatever to advance the cause of music in England.

As a commercial asset, Joseph Bennett must have been invaluable to the proprietors of *The Daily Telegraph*. For, like Davison, he had great influence. People read him. Even in my own time, when an important new work was produced, we used to question each other: "What does Old Joe say?" And, most unfortunately, it mattered a great deal what Old Joe did say, though anyone who knew much about music was very well aware that nine times out of ten Bennett would be wrong. If he damned a work—well, that work *was* damned. No musical critic to-day wields such power as his, though there are at least a score of writers on music who have ten times his gifts. His present successor, for example, Mr Robin Legge, is incomparably a finer musician, a much more open-minded man, and a student of infinitely more culture, than Bennett. Yet his influence, I imagine, is not so great as that of his predecessor. One cannot say that Bennett stooped to his public, for Bennett could not stoop; if he *had* stooped, he would have disappeared altogether. No: he *was* the public: the people: the common people. He had the point of view of the man in the back street.

But to-day things are changed. The musical critic is no longer primarily a raconteur, a gossiper, a chatterer. As a rule, he is a man of culture, of experience, of solid musical attainments. He earns little—anything from one hundred and fifty pounds to five hundred pounds a year, though, no doubt, in very rare instances, he may be paid more than the latter figure. Musical criticism, therefore, is not a profession that seduces the ambitious man, for the ambitious man of materialistic views may more easily earn three times what the Press has to offer him by selling imitation jewellery or doing anything else that money-making people do. When E. A. Baughan, now dramatic critic of *The Daily News*, was editing *The Musical Standard* more than twenty years ago, he wrote me a very earnest letter beseeching me not to become a musical critic on account of the payment being so meagre. "If you have a desk, stick to it; if you are a commercial traveller, remain a commercial traveller" was his advice in essence. But I would rather be a musical critic on one hundred and fifty pounds a year than a stockbroker earning fifteen hundred pounds. I love money, but I love music and journalism more, and the three years I spent in Manchester with an income of three hundred pounds were full of happiness, brimful of great days when I felt my mind growing and my spirit taking unto itself wings.

E. A. Baughan is not, I think, a musician in the true sense of the word, nor does he claim to be, but I imagine that, being musical and having the itch for writing, he took the first journalistic work that offered itself. That work was the editing of *The Musical Standard*. Subsequently he went to *The Morning Leader* as musical critic, and then to *The Daily News* as dramatic critic. He is sane, level-headed, honest, but not conspicuously brilliant. His musical work, judged by a high standard, was poor. He had not sufficient knowledge to guide him to a right judgment when faced by a new problem. Hugo Wolf was such a problem, and if ever Baughan reads now what he wrote about Hugo Wolf some fifteen years ago, he must, I imagine, tingle with shame to the tips of his toes.

As a dramatic critic he has secured an honourable and enviable position. I used to meet him very frequently at first nights, and always thought him a trifle *blasé* and almost wholly devoid of imagination, subtlety and true artistic feeling. He has not the artist's attitude towards life, and he would probably bring an action for slander against you if you said he had.

I was never introduced to C. L. Graves, the musical critic of *The Spectator* and the well-known humorous writer, but on one occasion I sat next to him at a very important concert, and in conversation found him an extremely courteous but rather baffled man. His knowledge of music is that of the cultured amateur. His mind but grudgingly admits "advanced" work, and I, as a modern, regret that an intellect so charming, so gracious, so able, should be even occasionally occupied in passing judgment on work that has its being entirely outside his mental horizon. But I doubt very much if *The Spectator* has any influence on the musical life of London, though I imagine that Dr Brewer, Mr T. H. Noble, Sir Hubert Parry, Sir Charles V. Stanford and Sir Alexander Mackenzie read Mr Graves with regularity and approval.

But the man whom all of us who write about music honour most of all is Ernest Newman, of *The Birmingham Daily Post*. Here we have a first-rate intellect functioning with absolute sureness and with almost fierce rapidity. As a scholar, no man is better equipped; as a writer, he ranks with the highest; for fearlessness and inflexible intellectual honesty, he has no equal. His books on Wagner and Hugo Wolf and the volume entitled *Musical Studies* are head and shoulders above any volumes of musical criticism ever published in our language. But though his knowledge of music is encyclopædic, music is but one of many subjects upon which he is an authority. Under another name he has published a volume on philosophy which, on its appearance, created something like a sensation; unfortunately, this book ceased to be procurable within a few weeks of its publication. Poetry, French and German literature, sociology and psychology are but a few of the subjects upon which he is as well qualified to write as he is on music.

Why does he hide himself in Birmingham? Well, if you are a musical critic in London, it is impossible to do any solid work. All day and almost every day you are at concerts and operas, and you are sadly in danger of becoming a mere reporter. Newman's post in Birmingham leaves him some leisure in which to write more important work.

I never think of Newman without wondering if ever he will be given the chance to achieve the work that is nearest his heart. That work is a full and complete history of music. For this task he is intellectually well equipped, but the labour in which it would involve him calls for years of leisure. Time and again he has planned work—notably, a book on Montaigne—which, for lack of leisure, he has been compelled to abandon. He was made for finer things than newspaper work, and though he has made an indelible impression on musical thought in this and other countries, his life will be largely wasted if the latter half of it has to be spent in writing daily criticism and occasional articles.

Newman's psychology is peculiarly complex. Though there is a vein of cruelty in him, he is yet sensitive to the suffering of other people. I was with him on one occasion when Bantock told him that a certain enemy of his (Newman's) had just died. The effect of this news on Newman was to me most unexpected. He started a little. "Good God!" he said; "poor, poor devil." And for the rest of the evening he sat gloomy and silent. The thought of death is intolerable to him. His repulsion from it is as much physical as nervous. Though, on occasion, a stern and relentless critic, he reacts morbidly to criticism of himself. He is highly strung, imaginative, rationalistic; he believes little and trusts not at all, loves intensely and hates bitterly. Vain he is, also, and he clings almost despairingly to what remains of his youth.

It is some few years since I saw Newman in close intimacy, but when he was on the staff of *The Manchester Guardian* and, later on, when he removed to Birmingham, I was at his house very frequently, and a very small circle of friends used to pass long evenings in delicious fooling. In those days Newman could throw off twenty-five years of his age and become a high-spirited and impish boy. I remember one night when, a *macabre* mood or, rather, a mood of extravagantly high spirits having descended upon us, one of our company, a lady, simulated sudden illness and death. We dressed her in a shroud, placed pennies on her eyes and candles at her head and feet. But in the middle of this foolery, Newman disappeared, and when it was all over and he had returned, he was in a sombre mood. It was not because we had trifled with a terrible fact in life that he was disturbed and distrait, but because we had unwittingly cut into his shrinking mind and hurt it by reminding him of something he would fain forget. Insanity repelled him in the same violent manner, and all who knew him intimately when he was writing his book on Hugo Wolf will remember that Wolf's warped and poisoned psychology obsessed and dominated him.

But often Newman would spend an evening in playing modern songs to us—Bantock's *Ferishtah's Fancies*, Wolf's *Mörike Lieder*, and so on. I can see him now as, his clever, rather saturnine face abundantly alive, he described Richard Strauss's *Ein Heldenleben*, telling us how the music of the harps stained the texture of the music in a magical way, like one flinging wine on some secretly coloured fabric. Those evenings are to me among the most valued of my life. I remember how my wife and I used to walk home under a long avenue of trees very late in the spring nights, the gummy smell of buds in our nostrils, Newman's voice still in our ears, and our minds fermenting deliciously with a kind of happiness we had not experienced before.

Those days are gone for ever: days of a recovered youth; evenings that were romantic just because they were evenings; nights when, in silence, one dreamed long and long, the body sunk deep in unconsciousness, the soul ranging and mounting and, in the morning, returning to its home subtly changed and infinitely refreshed.... Newman opened for me a world which, but for him, I do not think I ever should have beheld; nor, indeed, should I ever have been aware of that world's existence.

I have written of Samuel Langford elsewhere in this book, and I have little to add here. He succeeded Newman on *The Manchester Guardian*, and I recall the curiosity with which many of us read his first articles, fearing that anything he might write must of necessity fall so far below Newman's high standard as to be unreadable. We were soon reassured. Langford and Newman have little in common, and there is no basis upon which one can compare them. And, at first, Langford had to feel his way, to master his *métier*, to acquire some of his literary technique....

Our respective newspaper offices were situated near each other, and on our way from the Free Trade Hall he used often to persuade me to drink with him before we began our work. "We shall do each other good," he would say. And his short, ungainly figure, with its thick neck carrying a nobly-shaped head, would make its way to the bar where, placing a pile of music on the counter, he would turn to me and talk, both of us forgetting to order our drinks, and neither of us caring for the lateness of the hour.... Next morning, he would frequently come round to my house immediately after breakfast, look in at the window of my study, and wave a newspaper in the air. I was always deep in work, for at that time I reviewed eight or ten books every week, but I remember no occasion on which I did not welcome him most gladly. And sometimes I would spend an afternoon in his great garden, worshipping flowers, and watch him as, with fumbling hands, he turned the face of a blossom to the sky and looked at it with I know not what thoughts. I know nothing of horticulture, but Langford knows everything, and often he would talk, more to himself than to me, about the deep mysteries of his science. And, saying farewell at the little gate, he would sometimes crush into my arms a large sheaf of coloured leaves and flowers, wave an awkward hand, and shamble back to his low-built, picturesque house set deep in blooms. Though twenty years my senior, neither he nor I felt the long spell of years lying between us. And sometimes I am tempted to go back to Manchester to renew a friendship for the loss of which all the great happiness that London has brought me has, it seems at times, been but inadequate compensation.

During my three years as musical critic on *The Manchester Courier* I had some curious experiences, and to me the most curious of them all was the persistent manner in which attempts were made by people in Berlin to enlist my sympathies on behalf of an extremely able musician, Oskar Fried. It almost seemed to me that a secret society existed in Germany for the sole purpose of getting Oskar Fried a job in England. Letters written in English came to me from total strangers, informing me at great length and with stupid tautology that Fried was the one hope of musical Young Germany. He had Ideals; he was a Leader; he had the Prophetic Vision; he was the man who was going to promote and lead a new Romantic Movement. "Very good," said I to myself, "but what on earth has all this to do with me?"

I was not long in finding out. A young Englishman resident in Berlin, and obviously deeply saturated with the German spirit, wrote to me to say that, in his opinion, Fried was the only man in Europe to fill the post that Dr Richter had vacated as conductor of the Hallé Concerts Society in Manchester. The letter arrived at a time when various musicians were being, as it were, "tried" as conductors of the Hallé Concerts, and my unknown correspondent was anxious that Fried should be invited to conduct one or two concerts. To this letter I sent a polite but non-committal reply. I knew Oskar Fried's name just as I knew the names of a dozen pushing German conductors; but I knew no more. My persistent correspondent, to whom I will give the name of Purvis, wrote again, sending me a typewritten copy of a book he had written on his friend. It was a highfalutin document of idolatry. Fried was his idol, and Purvis gushed and gushed and gushed again. But the whole thing was done with truly Germanic thoroughness. I felt that I was being "got at," and though I resented it, I was greatly amused. I led him on. I was anxious to see this gushing disciple, this seeming advertising agent, this, as it appeared to me, wholly Germanised Englishman. So I replied to him a second time, and one evening he called upon me. He was a boy of twenty-one with a beard, a manner that was intended to be ingratiating but was intolerably insolent, and a self-assurance truly Napoleonic. He tickled me hugely and, as I have more than a grain of malice in me, I opened out to him, flattered him heavily, and talked music with him. But, though he loved the flattery, he was level-headed enough to stick to his point—that I should do all in my power to secure for Oskar Fried the Hallé conductorship. And he ended the interview with the astonishing announcement that Fried had already been engaged by the Hallé Concerts Society to conduct two of their concerts.

By what devious and subterranean ways this was achieved, I do not know, but I have no doubt that scores of influential Germans in Manchester were approached in a similar way to what I was.

Oskar Fried, with his idolatrous lackey, came uninvited to my house. They arrived at ten and left at six. I found Fried a very remarkable man— magnetic, of forceful personality, but with the manners and point of view of a gutter-snipe. He asked me point-blank what I could do for him.

"In what way?" I asked him, through Purvis, our interpreter.

"It is obvious in what way," returned Purvis, without passing on the question to Fried.

"Well," said I, "I have already written about Fried in the papers. And, really, I have no influence. I am not very popular with the Hallé Concerts Society people, and if I were to begin to recommend Fried.... But, in any case, I have not yet heard your friend conduct. It is impossible for me to recommend a man of whose talents I know nothing save by hearsay. You see that, don't you?"

"I'm afraid I don't," said Purvis. "You are a musical critic in Manchester, whilst I am a musical critic in Berlin, and I tell you that Fried is the man you want here. Surely that is enough? You must take it from me. *I* say it."

I smiled and, glancing at Fried, watched his thin, eager face, with its peering eyes which looked inquiringly first at Purvis and then at me.

Purvis came next day and the day after that, and I began to wonder in precisely what relation he stood to Fried. When together, they seemed to be just business friends, and it occurred to me that the long typewritten *Life of Fried* that Purvis had written was merely a gigantic piece of bluff. Finally, I decided to cut both men adrift altogether, and the next time Purvis called I was out.

When I heard Fried conduct, I at once recognised his great powers: he had undoubted genius. But he was never invited to become the permanent conductor of the Hallé Concerts Society. Perchance his table manners were adversely reported upon by Dr Brodsky, or Mr Gustave Behrens, or the discreet and reserved Mr Forsyth.

CHAPTER XIII
MANCHESTER PEOPLE

IF there is one thing more than another that the ordinary person cannot endure, it is to hear a man from Manchester praising his own city. Somebody from Leeds may tell him how beautiful a town Leeds is, and he will not turn a hair; he will listen unruffled to a Liverpudlian discoursing on the peculiar glories of the great city on the Mersey; but if the man from Manchester wishes to be tolerated, he must never let fall a word in praise of the place that witnessed his astounding birth. Why this is so, I cannot explain. I merely record the fact.

So, for the moment, I will not praise Manchester. I will go even farther than that. I will agree with you that it rains there every day, that it is the ugliest city in Britain, that it is cocksure and conceited, that its politics are damnable, that its free trade principles are loathsome, and that its public men are aitchless and gross. I will, I say, agree to all this. You may say anything disagreeable you like about Manchester, and I shall not care. Nevertheless, if I could not live in London, Manchester is the city to which I would go. I have stayed in Athens, and Athens is a marvellous city; I know my Paris, and Paris is not without fascination; I have been to Cairo, and the bazaars of Cairo seemed to me so wonderful that I held my breath as I passed through them; I know Antwerp and some of the half-dead cities of Belgium, and in Bruges I have felt as decadent as any nasty Belgian poet. But these places are not Manchester. They are not so glorious as Manchester, not so vital, not so romantic, not so adventurous.... But already I have broken my word: I have begun to praise Manchester in my second paragraph. Let me begin a third.

It might be thought that the centre of Manchester's intellectual life is the University, but this is not so. Nor is it the Cathedral, nor the big technical schools, nor yet the Gaiety Theatre. These things count, but none of them precisely radiates intellectual energy. You do not (unless you wish to be disappointed) go to the Bishop for ideas, or to the man of business for culture, nor to Miss Horniman for a wide and generous view of life. For these things, and for many other things besides, you go to *The Manchester Guardian*. In *The Daily Mail Year Book*, against the entry *Manchester Guardian*, you will find these words: "The best newspaper in the world." Now, you would imagine that if *The Daily Mail* really believed that, *The Daily Mail* would strain every nerve to be as like *The Manchester Guardian* as possible. But Lord Northcliffe knows better than that. He knows, we all know, that the best newspaper in the world is not going to be the best seller in the world. The word "best," when applied to a newspaper, does not signify a newspaper that shrieks louder than any other newspaper, that has the greatest number of "stunts," that lays reputations low in the dust, that holds Cabinet Ministers in the hollow of its hand. It signifies, among other things, a paper whose editor will not sacrifice a single ideal in order to increase his circulation, who has the power of infusing his staff with his own enthusiasms, and who regards the arts as a necessary part of a decent human existence.

The Daily Mail once upon a time compelled the whole of the British Isles to start growing sweet-peas. That is one kind of power. That is the kind of power that *The Manchester Guardian* does *not* possess.

Yet, I ask you, is there a more irritating newspaper in the whole of Christendom than *The Manchester Guardian*? How many times have we not all thrown it down in disgust and vowed never to read it again, only to buy it faithfully next morning? It would sometimes appear that every crank in England is busily engaged in airing his crazy views in its correspondence columns. It would sometimes appear that the three greatest highbrows in the country had laid their heads together to write the leading article. It would sometimes appear that conscientious objectors were really the only generous, manly and heroic people left in this mad world.

Let me tell you a true story of a man who for years has been, and still is, on the staff of *The Manchester Guardian*. I tell this strange story, partly because it *is* strange, and partly because it illustrates so finely the kind of reverence that so many citizens of Manchester have for the best paper in the world.

Some thirty years ago a male child was born to a worthy and not unprosperous man in Manchester. Now this man had one faith, one gospel, one ambition. His faith was of the Liberal persuasion. (Why, may I ask in passing, do people refer to Jews as men and women of the Jewish "persuasion"? Can a man, indeed, be persuaded to Jewry?) But to resume. His faith, as I said, was Liberal, his gospel *The Manchester Guardian*, his ambition to have some close connection with that paper. Being unfitted by the nature of his own talents to join the staff, he resolved that in the fullness of time that distinction should belong to his son. So he wrote to the editor, thus:

Sir,—I have the honour to inform you that last night my wife gave birth to a son. It is my ambition that, when his intellect is ripe and his powers mature, he shall be chosen by you as a member of your staff. His education, his whole upbringing, shall be directed to that end. I shall report to you his progress from time to time.

I have the honour to be, sir, your obedient servant,

—— —— ——.

I have not this letter before me; indeed, I have never seen it. But I am assured it was couched in those or similar terms.

Years passed. Harry—we will call him Harry—survived the perils of babyhood and was sent to a school for the sons of gentlemen, and the editor was duly apprised of the fact. Harry studied hard, for his ambition was even that of his father. Harry took scholarships, Harry had a private tutor, and, eventually, Harry went to the 'varsity. In the meantime, reports passed at regular intervals from Harry's father to the editor of *The Manchester Guardian*, who now, as nurses say, began to sit up and take notice. He desired to meet Harry. He did meet him. Harry took an honours degree, came back to Manchester, and was duly installed among the blessed, where he still is. Harry's dream, Harry's father's dream, is fulfilled. But are those reports, I wonder, still being written. As, for example:

Sir,—I have the honour to inform you that my son, Harold, contemplates marriage. It has always appeared to me that the married state is peculiarly useful in developing....

But not all the members of *The Manchester Guardian* staff are 'varsity men: for which, indeed, one may be thankful. The men of letters whom they admire most—Bernard Shaw, H. G. Wells, Joseph Conrad and Arnold Bennett—never even dimly espied the towers and spires of Oxford and Cambridge. But the paper has the manner of Oxford, though not Oxford's intellectual outlook.

For myself, I have never been on the staff of this paper, though I have written scores of articles for its commercial pages. Some of the most distinguished intellects in the country write for it regularly—Allan Monkhouse, whose play, *Mary Broome*, has not been and scarcely can be sufficiently praised; C. E. Montague, now in the Army; Professor C. H. Herford, whose scholarship is in excess of his human feeling; Samuel Langford, whom I have dealt with elsewhere in this book; J. E. Agate, whose fastidious style is a pure delight. Indeed, nearly every man who can write and who has something definitely new to say will find the columns of this paper open to him.

The drawback to social life in Manchester is that there is no central meeting-place where kindred spirits can foregather. It is true, there is the Arts Club, but when you have said the Arts Club is there, you have said all that it is necessary to say about the Arts Club. It is true, also, that if you stroll into the American bar of the Midland Hotel at almost any hour of the day, you are pretty sure to meet someone amusing; but you really can't make music, or rehearse plays, or play the fool (at least, not to any great extent) in an American bar. The consequence of this lack of a good democratic club is that all kinds of little coteries are formed, and it is about one of these little coteries that I wish to tell you.

Of course, Manchester is not London. You know that. In London, if you don't like one play, you can go to another. If the music that Sir Henry J. Wood gives you is not to your taste, you can go to hear Mr Landon Ronald, or (if truly desperate) join the Philharmonic Society. But in Manchester this is not so. You have either to like the music or do without it. Well, some years ago we didn't like it, and Jack Kahane, talking to me one day in a mood of disgust, casually remarked:

"I'm going to kick Richter out of Manchester. We've had enough of him."

With Kahane, to think is to act, and within a week he had formed the Manchester Musical Society and begun a Press campaign against the famous old conductor. This Society was Kahane's new toy, and he played with it to some purpose. We talked a great deal, gave innumerable concerts, hired lecturers, wrote articles, and held enormously thrilling committee meetings. Our programmes consisted almost exclusively of new and very "modern" music, just the kind of music that the guarantors of the Hallé Concerts Society detested. We were all for the new spirit in music, and some of us in our enthusiasm liked new music just because it *was* new. In three months Richter began to totter on his throne and, later on, he resigned his post, and now Sir Thomas Beecham most fitly reigns in his stead.

This little Society was extremely typical of Manchester. It was typical because it was enthusiastic, because every member of it worked hard for no monetary reward, and because it had a definite object in view and achieved that object. Above all, it was young; the spirit of it was young. I have never found in London a band of young men and women putting their noses to the grindstone for months on end with the sole object of achieving an artistic ideal. People in London exploit art, but they do not work at art for art's sake. Manchester is England's musical metropolis. Elgar said so ten years ago; Beecham echoed his words the other day. I claim for Manchester also that the level of culture is much higher than it is in London. In proportion to its size Manchester has during the last fifty years given to England more writers, musicians, politicians, actors, business men, reformers and social workers of distinction than any other city.... But all this, I think, is a little offensive— —

And yet how difficult it is for the stranger to understand Manchester!— and difficult in spite of the fact that Manchester loves being understood.

Mr J. Nicol Dunn, who, as editor of *The Morning Post* and, later, of *The Johannesburg Star*, did most brilliant work, utterly failed to understand Lancashire people when he came to edit *The Manchester Courier*. I think he regarded them as a peculiar race of savages. "A wealthy Lancashire manufacturer," he said to me once, "will ask you to dinner and will order a bumper of champagne. But if you ask him for a half-guinea subscription for a political society, he will give you a curt refusal. What is to be done with such folk?" Dunn thought us hard and unimaginative, incapable of seeing in what direction lay our best interests, and utterly childish in our notions of political economy.

"Cumberland," he said, unexpectedly, one evening, "is your father a Conservative?"

"He is," said I.

"What paper does he take?"

"*The Manchester Guardian.*"

"I *knew* he did! Of course he would take *The Manchester Guardian*! Good Lord! To what a strange set of people have I come!"

And he grunted and went on with his work.

My native town is young and strenuous and guileless. Its vanity is the vanity of the clever youngster who loves "showing off" in his exuberant way. So young and guileless is it that it is the easiest thing in the world to deceive it. How easy it is to deceive Manchester is illustrated by the case of Captain Schlagintweit, the German consul for some years in that city.

Schlagintweit was an enormous German whose mission in life it was to induce Manchester to believe that Germany was our bosom friend, that Germany's first thought was to help Great Britain, and that the two peoples were so closely akin in their spiritual aims that a quarrel between them, even a temporary misunderstanding, was utterly and for ever impossible. As I have said, he was enormous: a great man with a fair round belly: a man who talked a lot and ate a lot, and who, when he talked even with a solitary companion, spoke as though he were addressing a huge audience. He "bounded" beautifully and with so much aplomb and zest that it seemed right he should bound and do nothing else.

I met him everywhere—in the Press Club, at concerts, at the Schiller Anstalt, in restaurants; and nine times out of ten he was in the company either of a journalist, a member of the City Council, or a Member of Parliament. I never knew any man who worked so hard for his country as he did. He distilled sweet poison into our ears and we believed him every time.

I must confess I felt rather flattered by the way in which he constantly sought my company. I thought for a long time that he loved me for my own sweet sake, and it was not until the, for him, tragic *dénouement* came that I realised that it was because I was a journalist, and for that reason alone, he dined and wined me and talked discreetly of Germany's heartache for Great Britain. As I very rarely wrote on international politics, I do not think his evil counsel had any appreciable effect on my work, but it is impossible to imagine that his overflowing bonhomie, his cleverness, his subtle scheming did not greatly influence the thought of Manchester. He was made much of by more than one member of *The Manchester Guardian* staff.

His daughter came to sing at a concert I organised, and it was after this concert that he so overwhelmed me with flattery that I looked at him in amazement. I said to myself: "You are a humbug." But on looking at him again, I said: "No; you're not a humbug: you're a fool." A third scrutiny, however, left me in doubt, and I said: "I'm damned if I know what you are." Certainly I never suspected he was first cousin to a spy, that he was paid handsomely by his Government for his propaganda work in Manchester, and that he secretly despised and hated us.

Shortly after war broke out, many things were discovered about Schlagintweit that had hitherto been unknown, and he was led, handcuffed, to Knutsford gaol, but not before he had broken through the five-mile radius to which, as a German, he was confined, and not before he had motored through a far-off district where tens of thousands of our soldiers were encamped.

I do not believe London would have been deceived by him, and I am sure that Ecclefechan wouldn't. Yet Manchester was.

Manchester is young, ingenuous, trusting, guileless.

Have you ever noticed (but you must have done!) that the self-made man—and half the prosperous men in Manchester are self-made—will frequently part with a ten-pound note much more readily than he will with a few pence? The economical habits of his youth still cling to and dominate him, and he counts the halfpence and is careless of the pounds.

One Saturday night in the summer, I was taking a walk with a friend in the country ten or twelve miles from Manchester. Our talk was of County cricket, in which my companion—a most magnificent person, with ships sailing on half the oceans of the world—was greatly interested. For three days Lancashire had been playing Yorkshire a very close match, and we knew that by now the game would be over.

"We sha'n't know the result till we get *The Sunday Chronicle* to-morrow," said X. regretfully.

But, five minutes later, we met, most miraculously, a newsboy with a bundle of papers under his arm.

X. took a penny from his pocket, handed it to the boy, and received *The Evening News* in exchange.

"Very sorry, sir," said the boy, "but I've got no change. I've got no halfpennies."

X. turned to me.

"Oh, I've no change either," said I, amused.

With an exclamation of annoyance, X. handed the paper back to the boy and pocketed his penny.

After we had proceeded a few paces:

"Lancashire has won by two wickets," he said. "I saw it in the corner in the Stop Press news."

Now, X. had great riches.

An incredible story, isn't it? But it is true, and it gives you the self-made Manchester man—at least, one side of him—in a nutshell.

It used to be a great delight to me to see Dr J. Kendrick Pyne walking near the Cathedral or in Albert Square, for he used to suggest to me a bygone age and a remote place. His short, thick-set figure used to move with the utmost precision, unhurried, unperturbed. His plump, clean-shaven face, his well-shaped head, surmounted by a new silk hat of old-fashioned shape, his gold-rimmed spectacles with the peering eyes behind them, his inevitable umbrella, and his correct dress—all these conspired to make a figure of great dignity, a figure that always seemed to carry about with it the atmosphere of the Cathedral whose organ he played for so many smooth years. There hung about him the tradition of the famous Dr Wesley.

In character and disposition also he belonged to a different era. He never underestimated the importance of the position he held in the city as Cathedral organist, City organist, and Professor at the Manchester Royal College of Music, and wherever he went and in the execution of whatever work to which he set his mind, his word was law. A very fine type of Englishman. He would brook no interference from Bishop or Dean, and his combative, upright spirit fought unceasingly to uphold the dignity of his art.

His childlike vanity was most alluring, and I used to love him for it and respect him for the way he clung to his belief in himself.

One day he took me to the town hall to look once more at the wonderful series of frescoes that Ford Madox Brown painted in the great hall. When he came to the fresco picturing the Duke of Bridgewater at the ceremonial "opening" of the Bridgewater Canal, he pointed to the features of the Duke, and inquired:

"Whom do you think he resembles?"

There was just a note of anxiety in his voice as though he were afraid I should not be able to answer his question. For the life of me I could not think of anyone who resembled Madox Brown's Duke, and I stood silent. Pyne then turned his face full upon me, and again inquired, somewhat imperiously:

"Whom do you think he resembles?"

"Why," exclaimed I, guessing wildly, "it is a portrait of you!"

"Yes," said he, with naïve satisfaction, "it is. I sat to Madox Brown for the great Duke. The portrait is immortal."

But whether the portrait was immortal because Kendrick Pyne had sat for it, or Madox Brown had painted it, I did not gather.

On another occasion he again used the word "immortal," but this time it was in reference to one of his own works.

"You know," said he, apropos of something I have forgotten, "I should have made a name as a writer if I had gone in for literature, but I felt that music had stronger claims upon me. My organ-playing will not, so to speak, live, because the art of the executant necessarily dies with him. But my Mass in A flat is, in itself, enough to keep my name immortal."

There was such innocent satisfaction in his tone, such a bland look upon his face, that he seemed to me like a delicious grown-up child.

But have not all men of genius this superb confidence in themselves? I am convinced they have. Could they possibly "carry on" without it? But only a few men of genius have the courage, or the artlessness, to speak what is really in their hearts.

One of the "characters" of Manchester, a man who loves being a character, is Mr Charles Rowley, who for an unconscionable number of years has been doing splendid educational and recreative work in Ancoats, a congeries of slums, a district of appalling poverty. Here, in the Islington Hall, on most Sunday afternoons, one can hear first-rate chamber music and, as a rule, a lecture delivered by some local or London celebrity. I myself have heard Bernard Shaw and Hilaire Belloc lecture there and, after the lectures, I have gone to the clean little cottage where Mr Rowley occasionally entertains a few chosen friends to tea and talk.

I do not know if Mr Rowley is a Manchester man, but he is of a type that I have found only in that city. He is combative and energetic; he is a little red flame of enthusiasm. Though, no doubt, interested in and pleased with himself, he is equally interested in local public affairs and equally pleased with the people for whom he works. His broad and pungent humour is just the kind of humour the so-called lower classes understand, and his energy of mind and readiness of wit are remarkable. I have seen him on several occasions talking to—or, perhaps, talking *with* is what I really mean—a huge audience in order to keep them in good humour until the arrival of the lecturer of the afternoon. He bandies jokes with anybody who cares to shout to him, and he has the true democrat's gift—he never by a look, a word or a gesture implies that he is in any way superior to the meanest member of his audience. These rough people love him, admire him and laugh at him. And, of course, he is able to laugh at himself. Perhaps, all things considered, he is the most human man I have met, and I like to think that in him the spirit of Manchester is embodied. I do not mean you to infer that I think the spirit of Manchester is the finest spirit in the world, but I do believe that it is a spirit that might well be emulated by many other towns.

What is that spirit? Well, Manchester has a sincere and very proper respect for success, and particularly for success that has been won in the face of great difficulties. Manchester loves education and knowledge, not only because these things are useful in achieving success, but also for their own sake. Manchester is public-spirited, proud of its traditions, loyal to its principles. It is cultured—not in the super-refined, lily-fingered sense, but in the sense that it loves literature, music, art. It is enthusiastic about these things; it works hard to come by them and treasures them when they are obtained.

One could, of course, say many disagreeable and true things about Manchester, but as these have been said frequently by other people, I refrain from repeating what is already known.

CHAPTER XIV
CHELSEA AND AUGUSTUS JOHN

THERE is a prevalent opinion that Chelsea is the British counterpart of the Quartier Latin, but the resemblance each bears to the other is only superficial. The Quartier Latin and respectability are poles asunder; its population does not only never think of respectability, but it does not know what it is. Parisian Bohemians have no use for it. They do not condemn it, for it may suit others; for themselves, it is as useless as yesterday's dinner.

Chelsea is not in revolt against morals or anything else; for the most part, it is quiet, law-abiding and hard-working. Very little is demanded of new-comers; in order to obtain entrance to that magic land, you must be a "good fellow," you must have personality and a real love of the arts, and you must be a democrat through and through. One thing is never forgiven—a reference, however remote, to your own success. You may be as successful as you like without creating the slightest envy, but you must not thrust your success down other people's throats.

My own introduction to Chelsea was rather of a wholesale kind; indeed, it would be truer to say that Chelsea was introduced to me. One evening Ivan Heald and I finished a rather strenuous day's work at the same time. I had just finished my daily column of chat for *The Daily Citizen* when the telephone rang. "Is that you, Gerald? ... Yes, Ivan speaking.... Finished? ... Cheshire Cheese? Right-o! It's now thirteen minutes past seven; we'll meet at sixteen minutes past." So while he ran down Shoe Lane, I ran up Bouverie Street and we met at the door of that caravanserai where, sooner or later, one comes across all the bright spirits of Fleet Street and every American sightseer who sets his foot on our shores. We feasted and, replete, adjourned to the bar for gossip. But there was no one there to gossip with and, presently, Ivan said:

"Come to my flat and play Irish songs."

"But your piano's such a poor one. Much better come to my place and listen to Wagner."

So we jumped into a taxi and were soon racing through Sloane Square for Chelsea Bridge on the way to my flat in Prince of Wales's Road, opposite Battersea Park. At the Bridge Heald tapped the window, and, the taxi having stopped, he jumped out on to the pathway and promptly closed the door upon me inside.

"And now," said Ivan, "do you know what you are going to do?"

"Whatever you tell me, I suppose. What is it?"

"You're going home in this cab to prepare your wife for a lot of visitors. Tell her there will be ten or maybe twenty. We sha'n't want any food; we'll bring that with us. All we shall want is coffee. Ask her if she'll make gallons of coffee, Gerald. For the women, you know. There'll be whisky for us, won't there?" he added rather wistfully. "Now trot along. I sha'n't be a quarter of an hour behind you."

"But, Ivan——"

"But me not a single but," he said, grinning, and turned away.

Half-an-hour later a taxi-cab full of strangers carrying parcels arrived at my flat. Heald was not with them. In answer to their ring, my wife and I went to open the door to welcome them.

"Come right in," we said. And then they told us who they were and we told them who we were. A couple of minutes later another taxi full of strangers arrived. Still no Ivan Heald. It was now about ten o'clock, and during the following hour Chelsea people still kept arriving, some in cabs, some on foot. It appeared that Heald had routed up half the people he knew in Chelsea and told them that he had found someone "new," that we were just "it," and that the sooner we all got to know each other the better.

This "surprise party"—so dear to Americans—turned out a complete success, though half the people had to sit on the floor. Norman Morrow, away in a corner behind a pile of books, sang Irish songs, Herbert Hughes played the piano in his brilliant way, and Harry Low and Eddie Morrow, with two clever girl-models, acted plays that they invented on the spur of the moment. Heald came in late, armed with loaves, butter, cakes and fruit. Not until dawn (the month was June) did we separate. I was to meet these delightful people many, many times later, but so casual yet intimate was our relationship that I never heard—or, if I heard, I soon forgot—the surnames of a few of them. We called each other by our Christian names or by nicknames.

Perhaps of all the Chelsea people Augustus John is the most interesting. We became acquainted at the Six Bells, the famous King's Road hostelry, and he took me to his studio near at hand. It was a big barn-like place with a ridiculous little stove that burned fussily somewhere near the entrance and from which you never felt any heat unless, absent-mindedly, you sat on the stove itself. The studio was crowded with work of all kinds, the most conspicuous canvas being a huge crayon drawing of a group of gipsies. Augustus John planted me in a chair in front of this, seated himself on another chair and stared—not at the picture, but—at me! Now, I had been told that John does not suffer fools gladly, and I suspected from his inquisitorial glance that he was waiting to see if I was of the detested brood. Sooner or later I should have to speak, and I groped despairingly in my mind for something sensible yet not obvious to say about his bold, vivid and arresting picture. Through sheer apprehensiveness I found nothing, so, after gazing at the canvas for a few minutes, I rose and passed on to the next picture. John's large, luminous eyes followed me.

"You don't like it," he said, softly but decisively.

"Oh yes, I do," I answered, "or, rather—what I mean is that 'like' is not the right word. It attracts me and repels me at the same time. It makes me curious—curious about the gipsies themselves, but more curious still about the man who has drawn them. But you didn't make it for anyone to 'like,' did you?"

"No; I don't suppose I thought of anyone at all. There the thing is, to be taken or left, to be accepted by the onlooker or rejected."

"Quite. But to me it is not a passive kind of picture at all. It thrusts itself on to you very violently, I think, and it rather demands to be 'taken,' as you put it. It is not like your *Smiling Woman*, for instance, who mysteriously glides into one's mind, wheedling her way as she goes. Your gipsies assault the mind. Your picture is quite contemptuous of opinion."

He appeared to be satisfied, for he smiled; if I had proved myself a fool, it was clear I was not the kind of fool he detested.

We met often after that. I would see him two or three times a week in the Six Bells. He used to drink beer, and he would talk in his slow way, or listen to me, nodding occasionally and saying just a word now and again. But John is the least loquacious of men. His presence makes you feel comfortable, not only because his personality is tolerant and roomy, but because you know that if you are boring him he will not think twice about edging away to the billiard-room or telling you abruptly that he must be "off." Like so many very hard workers, he appears to be an accomplished loafer. I have never seen him at work; I don't know anybody who has. I have never heard anybody say: "John can't come to-night because he's busy." I expect that when the fever is on him, he keeps at his easel night and day.

But perhaps you are wondering what Augustus John looks like? Have you seen Epstein's bust of him? Wonderfully good, of course; extraordinarily good; but it is rather solemn—heavy, I mean. John is not ponderous, and he does not wear the air of a prophet, and I have never seen him look precisely like *that*. His hair is long.... Of course, most of you will feel disposed to sneer at that; so should I if it were anybody but John.... But he carries it off splendidly. You know, even Liszt (at all events in his photographs) looked frightfully conscious of his locks, but though John's hair makes him conspicuous, he does not appear conscious of his conspicuousness. He is tall, deliberate in his movements, deep-voiced, very self-contained. His shortish beard is red, and he has large eyes that, in some extraordinary way, seem separate from his face; I mean, they belie it. His features are so composed that one might think them expressionless; but his eyes are brooding and deep and quiet. He has not the noisy, fussy little eyes of the "trained observer," the man who notices everything and remembers nothing; he notices only what is essential to him, the things that are necessary for him to notice.... Of course, I haven't described him in the least; I might have known I could not when I began to try.... But it seems to me that the essential thing about Augustus John is the quiet, lazy exterior which, in some peculiar way, contrives to suggest hidden fires and volcanic energies. A Celt, of course, and the mystery of the Celt hangs about him.

I think John loves few things so much as simply sitting back in a chair and looking at people: ruminating upon them, as it were; chewing the cud of his thoughts. I remember his coming to my flat on one occasion at one o'clock in the morning when he knew there was a party there. His eyes were very bright and he came in rather eagerly, and rather eagerly also he sat and watched us, sipping cold coffee as he did so and occasionally raising his voice into a half-shout when something happened that amused him. But though he sat until nearly all our guests had departed, he scarcely spoke at all.

And yet another evening I remember very vividly, an evening at Herbert Hughes's studio where, by candle-light, we used to have music every Sunday evening and where, in the half darkness at the far end of that long room, one could, if one wished, just sit and look on and perhaps talk a little to one's neighbour. There John sat in the dark, like a Velasquez painting, his limbs thrown carelessly about, his head turned gently towards a sparkling Irish girl who seemed to be teasing him.

It is only now, when I have set myself to write about him, that I realise how little, after all, I know about Augustus John, though I have met him so often. He reveals himself most generously in his work, though even there he keeps back more than he discloses. But I think that even to his closest friends he reveals very little, and that perhaps is why so many legendary stories about him are afloat. He has the mystery of Leonardo. One feels that his personality hides a great and important secret, but one feels also that that secret will remain hidden for ever. Sombre he is, sombre yet vital, sombre and full of humour.

Allusion to the impression that Augustus John gives of habitually loafing reminds me that this characteristic is typical of Chelsea. They are the most casual people in the world, and it is their casualness that the worker-by-rote cannot understand. I know a score of studios where one could walk in at any time of the day and be welcomed or, if not welcomed, treated with most disarming frankness. If the owner of the studio were busy on some work that had to be finished, he would say: "There's a drink there on the table and a smoke. Do what you like but, for God's sake, don't talk!" Or: "Go round to the Bells, Old Thing. I like you very much and all that sort of nonsense, but even you can be a bit of a nuisance at ten in the morning. It's like drinking Benedictine before breakfast." But receptions such as this latter are very rare, and most artists—because they *are* artists, I suppose—are ready enough to throw down their work and play for half-an-hour.

I always think of Norman and Edwin Morrow as typical artists. Norman, who died almost in harness a short time ago, was absolutely disdainful of success, or perhaps it would be truer to say that he was disdainful of the means by which success is usually won. I imagine him looking upon certain successful men and their work and saying to himself: "Only the distinguished nowadays are unknown." But he would say this with his tongue in his cheek, laughing at himself, and knowing that the dictum is only half true. He liked admiration—what artist does not?—but people who liked things of his that he himself did not approve of made him "tired."

Of course, those people who worship success—or, at all events, admire it—are very difficult to bring to the belief that many artists are almost indifferent to it. "Artists may *pretend* to care nothing for success, especially those who have failed to achieve it," they say, "but surely it is a case of sour grapes?" No man except a fool, it is true, is wholly indifferent to money, but the type of artist of whom I am now writing is tremendously casual about it. If money comes his way, as it has in John's case, well and good; if not, it can very well be done without. The artist lives almost entirely for the moment, for the moment is the only thing of which he is certain. Yesterday has gone and has melted into yesterday's Seven Thousand Years; to-morrow is not yet here and may never arrive; therefore, *carpe diem*.

Norman Morrow had the kind of subtlety and refinement that one finds in the work of Henry James. I very rarely came away from his studio without feeling that I had given myself "away," that he had seen through all my insincerities, that he was aware of the precise motives of my acts even when I was not aware of them myself. But, being a swift analyst of his own emotions and a constant diver after the real motive in himself, he was tolerant of others and very slow to condemn.

It is incorrect to assume, as many people do, that there is in Chelsea anything of the atmosphere of Henri Murger's Bohemia. Nowadays, in London artistic and literary circles, only the idle and incompetent starve. Murger's young artists, moreover, are absurdly self-conscious and flabby and childish. Chelsea men and women are keen-witted, level-headed, and experienced people of the world.

All the faddists, of course, go to live at Letchworth, but there are in Chelsea a few groups of young "intellectuals" who are good enough to supply comic relief in the "between" days when one is bored. One Saturday evening, having been to the Chelsea Palace of Varieties and feeling restless and disinclined for bed, I remembered that I had a standing invitation to go to a certain studio where, I was told, I should be welcomed whenever I cared to go. I went and discovered a handful of young men sitting round the fire and directing the affairs of the Empire.

The little group of intellectuals (all from Cambridge—or was it Oxford?) hailed me and fell to talking about politics, socialism, Fabianism, Sidney Webbism, and so forth. All very bright and clever, and all very promising, but the wonderful conceit of it all! Some of them were men with brilliant university honours, but they had not even the wisdom, the sense of proportion, of children. They idolised Bernard Shaw and spoke of H. G. Wells in terms of contempt. They really thought that the destinies of our Empire were directed by the universities, and their priggish little minds were eager to "control" the poor, to direct their work, even to fix the size of their families....

I sat silent, wondering if these men represented the best—or even the average—that our universities produced in immediately pre-war days. I looked at their long, white fingers, their longish hair, their long noses, and I listened to their drawl which was not quite a drawl, and I thought that their conversation was, what Keats would have called it, "a little noiseless noise." They had brains, of course; they were smartish and "clever." But what are brains without experience and what is cleverness without judgment? These men, I felt, would never gain experience, for they saw in life only what they wished to see, denying the rest. Life to them was a vast disorder which Oxford and Cambridge, as represented by them, was about to put right. I imagine Mrs Sidney Webb and Mr Beatrice Webb (as *The New Age* once so happily called them) walking over from Grosvenor Road to Chelsea and smiling blandly, and with huge satisfaction, at their ridiculous disciples.

I have described these people because, though they do not represent Chelsea, they are to be met with there in considerable numbers. They have flats and studios full of knick-knacks, flats in which you will find art curtains, studios in which there is ascetic severity and where one has triscuits for breakfast.

CHAPTER XV
MISCELLANEOUS

I QUITE forget what particular concatenation of circumstances brought me into personal touch with Mr Arthur Henderson, M.P., but I rather think that when I waited for him at Waterloo Station I was acting the part of messenger-boy. Perhaps I delivered a letter or telegram to him, or I may have given him a verbal message. All I remember is, that something very important had happened, and it was necessary that Mr Arthur Henderson should be apprised of this happening at the earliest possible moment. So I volunteered to meet him at Waterloo.

We walked across the station together, and I was depressingly aware of a rather bulky form with a Manchester kind of face. He spoke heavily and uttered commonplaces that fell dead on his very lips. I could feel his self-importance radiating from him, and I gathered that I was supposed to be in the presence of a very exceptional person indeed. But I did not feel that he was exceptional. There has never been a moment since I reached manhood that I haven't known that my intellect is of finer texture than that of the five thousand who elbow each other on the Manchester Exchange, and it seemed to me that night at Waterloo Station that Mr Henderson would be very much at home on the Manchester Exchange. I recollect most vividly that he bored me very much and that, offering him some plausible excuse, I parted from him before we had crossed the river, and darted away to more congenial people.

A few weeks previous to this encounter I had heard Mr Henderson give an "address" in a Nonconformist chapel. An "address," I am given to understand, is a kind of homely sermon in which the speaker talks to his audience in a friendly and distinctly unbending manner. He seeks to improve them, to lead them to higher and better things: in a word, to make them more like himself.... I have not the faintest recollection of what drove me inside this Nonconformist chapel, but I cannot conceive I went there of my own free will. I suppose that someone paid me to go there. But my mind retains a very clear picture of a pulpit containing a man with a face so like other faces that, sometimes, when I examine it, it seems to belong to Mr Jackson of Messrs Jackson & Lemon, the famous auctioneers of Boodlestown, and at other times it is owned by Mr Brownjonesrobinson who, I need scarcely point out, is known everywhere.... Really, I have no intention of being violently rude. This question of faces is important. A face should express a soul. No great man whose portrait I have seen possessed a commonplace face.

The address was heavy, obvious and dull. I was taken back twenty years to my boyhood when stern parents compelled me to go to a Wesleyan chapel one hundred and three times a year (twice every Sunday and once on Christmas Day); on most of those hundred and three occasions I used to hear exhortations to be "good," not, so to speak, for the love of the thing, but because being "good" paid. Mr Arthur Henderson, Samuel Smiles *redivivus*, proved that it paid. He didn't say: "Look at me!" but, all the same, we did look at him. The spectacle to most of his congregation was, I suppose, encouraging; me, it didn't excite. I can well believe that, as I stepped out of the building, I said to myself: "No, Gerald. We will remain as we are. The penalties of virtue are much too heavy for us to pay."

One Saturday evening I journeyed to Liverpool with twenty or thirty other newspaper men to dine with Lord Derby. Pressmen are accustomed to this kind of entertainment from public men, and their host generally contrives to be exceptionally agreeable. It would be putting it very crudely to state that these dinners are intended as a bribe: let me therefore say that they serve the purpose of smoothing the way for the dissemination of some propaganda or other. To the best of my recollection, Lord Derby had no other purpose in view than the laudable and kindly intention of making the journalists of Manchester and Liverpool better acquainted with one another.

After dinner, various ladies and gentlemen from the neighbouring music halls provided us with an excellent entertainment, and I can now see Lord Derby smilingly and courteously receiving these artists and making them feel that they, like ourselves, were honoured guests, and not merely paid mimes. He seemed to me then, as he has always seemed to me, our dearly loved, bluff but unfailingly courteous national John Bull. He is, I think, the most British man with whom I have ever spoken—honest, brave, resourceful, self-sacrificing, fond of good company and good cheer, hail-fellow-well-met yet a trifle reserved and not a little cautious, blunt but considerate of others' feelings. Some of us collected signatures on the backs of our menus, but when Lord Derby had written his name on the top of mine I left it there alone, not caring to see other names mingling with his: perhaps feeling that no other name of those present was worthy to stand beneath his name.

He spoke to us, but his speech had nothing in it save welcome.

When I see, as I frequently do, the newspapers and reviews praising the works of Mrs Humphry Ward and describing her as the greatest of living British female writers, I rub my eyes in astonishment and wonder why Miss Elizabeth Robins is overlooked. Mrs Humphry Ward can, it is true, tell a story: she knows well much of the behind-the-scenes life of modern politics: moreover, she is a woman of the world with a highly cultivated mind and a varied experience of life. But if ever there was a woman without genius, without, indeed, the true literary gift, she is that woman. She cannot fire the imagination, quicken the pulse, or stir the heart. She plays with puppets and never reveals life. Miss Robins, on the contrary, strikes deep into life— cleaves it asunder, disrupts it, opens it out to our gaze. She has the gift of tragedy.... When I think concentratedly of Mrs Humphry Ward's books, I remember atmospheres, social environments, a few incidents, and I see dimly about half-a-dozen pictures. But when my mind dwells on *The Open Question* and *The Magnetic North*, I see and hear and touch live men and women.

I know nothing of Miss Elizabeth Robins' private affairs, but if my intuition guides me rightly, she has had a tragic life and her life is still and always will be tragic. Her temperament is not dissimilar to Charlotte Brontë's, that great little woman whose sense of the ridiculous was so great but whose power of expressing it was so small.

Miss Robins, as you all know, entered the ranks of the militant suffragettes, and it was at a meeting of the W.S.P.U. that I met her and heard her speak. In the real sense, she has no gift of speech. When she has to address an audience, she prepares her words beforehand, memorises them, and then delivers them with the lucidity, the passion and the eloquence of a great actress. I think I have heard all the best-known women speakers from Lady Henry Somerset up to Mrs Pankhurst, but though my admiration of Mrs Pankhurst's brave and proud gifts scarcely knows a limit, I consider that Miss Robins surpasses her in her power of sweeping an audience along with her and in her great gift of quickening the spirit and urging it upwards to the heights of an enthusiasm that does not quickly die....

Perhaps in reading this book you have not gathered the impression that I am afflicted by a devastating bashfulness that, always at the wrong moments, robs me of speech and makes me appear an imbecile. Nevertheless that affliction is mine. The more I like and reverence people, the more bereft of speech I become in their presence. It is so when I am with Orage, though we have been intimate enough for him to address me in letters as "My dear

Gerald"; it is so with Frank Harris (but perhaps you think I ought not to "reverence" him—yet his genius compels me to); and it is so with Ernest Newman and Granville Bantock. And when Miss Elizabeth Robins' hand met mine in a firm clasp and she spoke some words of greeting, I had not a word to say. Like an ashamed schoolboy, I walked, speechless and fuming, from the room and kicked myself in the passage outside.... I know this shyness has its origin in vanity, but then I *am* vain. But I am a fool to allow my vanity to gain the upper hand of my speech.

Frank Mullings!... Well, I have more than once said that singers bore me, but if a man is bored by Mullings, he is worse than a fool. One always has a special kind of affection for men whom one has known in obscurity and of whom one's prophecies of great things has come true. Mullings has, indeed, travelled far since those jolly days when we used to meet in Sydney Grew's little flat in Birmingham and make music with Grieg, Bantock and Wolf for company. A great "lad," as we say in Lancashire: a great fat boy without affectation, without jealousy, without even the pride that all great artists should possess: a generous, simple-hearted man who is capable of travelling a couple of hundred miles to sing, without fee, the songs of Bantock, just because he loved those songs and wanted others to love them.

He was always untidy, short-sighted, and either very depressed or very jolly. His moods were thorough, and they infected you. In Birmingham, in days when only a few, and those few powerless to help, were aware of his astonishing gifts, he was serene and happy. I remember him, Sydney Grew and myself sitting on the floor of Grew's very narrow drawing-room, our backs to the wall, and talking of our future. I was the oldest of the three, and for that reason spoke with simulated wisdom.

"Only one of us is marked down for real success, and you, Mullings, are the man," I said. "You have the successful temperament. Sydney here will do valuable work, but he hasn't the gifts that shine and blind. As for me, I shall make the most of my small but, I really think, engaging talent and swank about in a little circle of appreciators."

Mullings laughed.

"Do you really think I shall?" he asked. "Have another whisky, Cumberland, and go on talking; you give me confidence. And confidence is half the battle, isn't it?"

"So they say. But haven't you confidence already?"

"Well, it ebbs and it flows."

"Oh, *he's* all right," said Sydney Grew. "Don't worry about Mullings. But what do you mean when you say that I shall do valuable work?"

"You're an artist, and you've got personality and ideas. Haven't you often reproached me on the score that you meet me for an hour and, a month later, see all that you have told me in two or three articles that in the meantime I have written for the papers?"

"Well, you do pick my brains, Gerald. You know you do."

"Simply because they are worth picking. And if I didn't, they would be lost to the world. Why don't you yourself write? You must write more and talk less."

He took my advice, and began a career that promised much until the war interrupted it.

In the meantime, Mullings has "arrived" and I am longing to meet him again, for I know very well he will be still fat and jolly, that he will still allow me to play accompaniments for him on any old piano that is handy, and that we shall talk excitedly of Bantock and Julius Harrison, of the Manchester Musical Society and Phyllis Lett, of "Colonel" Anderton and Ernest Newman, and of everything and everybody that made those far-off days so full of interest and so sweet to remember.

Harold Bauer set out to conquer the world, and has done nothing more than arouse the interest of one or two countries. Yet he is a great pianist. But I am told that his personality stands between him and the real thing in the way of success. I have sat next to critics at his recitals who have squirmed in their stalls as he played.

"What is the matter?" I have asked.

"I don't quite know. But don't you feel it yourself?"

"Feel what?"

"Something. I don't quite know what. Something indefinable. His playing is too greasy. Did you ever hear Brahms played like that before?"

"No. I wish I had. I think his Brahms wonderfully fine."

Certainly, his temperament is not magnetic like the personality of Paderewski, of Kubelik, of Yvette Guilbert, and the public is a connoisseur of temperaments. I think I have elsewhere observed in this book that the public collects temperaments just as a few people collect china or autographs. Perhaps Bauer is not exotic or orchidaceous enough. He is too "straight," too downright.

"What are they like, these Manchester people?" Bauer asked me one afternoon before he was to play in England's musical metropolis.

"Well, they're 'difficult,' I think. They know something about music here. You are not in London now, you know. You have reached the centre of things."

"Seriously?"

"Quite. I mean it. These people really do know. You see, for the last fifty years they have had nothing but the best. They have a tradition and stick to it."

"The Clara Schumann tradition? Joachim and Brahms and Hallé and all that?"

"No, no! That is on its last legs, on its knees even. The tradition, I admit, is hard to define, but it's there all the same. If you get a couple of encores here, you may well consider that a success."

"Funny thing, the public," he muttered. "You never know where you have it. But, of course, there is no such entity as 'the public.' There are thousands of publics and they are all different."

Emil Sauer has a glittering style and had, fifteen years ago, a technique that no word but rapacious accurately describes. The piano recital he gave in Manchester nearly two decades ago was the first recital I ever attended, though I was a lad in my late teens; the occasion then seemed, and still seems, most romantic. It is true that, on the nursery piano at home, one of my elder brothers used to give recitals with me as sole auditor, and that I used to return the compliment the following evening, but though we took these affairs very seriously and even wrote lengthy criticisms of each other's playing, our performances were not of a high order. But one evening, defying parental authority and risking paternal anger, we slipped unseen from home and went to hear Sauer.

I think we must both have been much younger than our years—certainly we were much younger than the average educated boy of eighteen or nineteen to-day—and we were in a very high state of nervous excitement as we sat in the gallery of the Free Trade Hall waiting for the great man's appearance. His slim and, as it seemed at the time, spirit-like figure passed across the platform to the piano, and two hours of pure trance-like joy began for at least a couple of his listeners. My brother and I knew all there was to know about the great pianists of the past, and often we had tried to imagine what their playing was like; but neither he nor I had conceived that anything could be so gorgeous as what we now heard. For once, realisation was many more times finer than anticipation. Only one thing disturbed my complete happiness—and that was the notion that the pianist might possibly be disappointed with the amount of applause he was receiving, though, of a truth, he was receiving a great deal of applause. So I clapped my hands and stamped my feet as hard and as long as possible. The Appassionata Sonata almost frenzied me and a Liszt Rhapsody was like heady wine.

But all beautiful things come to a close, and towards ten o'clock my brother and I found ourselves on the wet pavement outside, feeling very exalted but at the same time uncertain whether we had done our utmost to make Sauer's welcome all that we thought it should have been.

"Let's wait for him outside the platform entrance and cheer him when he comes out," suggested my brother.

Very strange must that two-voiced cheer have sounded to Sauer as, in the dark side street, he stepped quickly into his cab, which began immediately to move away. As our voices died, he opened the window and leaned out, holding out to us his long-fingered hand. Running eagerly to him, we clasped his hand in turn and, amazed, listened to the few words of thanks he shouted to us.

For long after that, Sauer was one of our major gods, and we followed his triumphs both in England and on the Continent with the utmost interest and excitement. When we boasted to our friends that we had shaken hands with the great pianist, they evinced little interest in the matter. "Why, that's nothing!" exclaimed a Philistine; "last Saturday afternoon I touched the sleeve of Jim Valentine's coat!" Now, Jim Valentine was a great rugger player.

Perhaps the most exquisite and the most fragile thing in the world at present is the Chopin playing of Vladimir de Pachmann. For more than a quarter of a century writers have been attempting to reproduce his coloured music in coloured words: they have all failed. De Pachmann is an exotic, a hothouse plant. Not a hothouse plant among many other plants, but a plant living luxuriously and solitarily and with exaggerated self-consciousness in its own hothouse.

In thinking of him, one feels that he belongs to the very last minute of civilisation's progress. All the civilisations of the past have come and gone and returned; they have worked age-long with tireless industry; mankind has struggled upwards and rushed precipitately downwards through thousands of years; cities have been sacked and countries ravaged;

Babylon, Nineveh, Athens and Rome have bloomed flauntingly and wilted most tragically: and the most exquisite thing that has been produced by all this suffering, all this unimaginable labour, is the Chopin playing of de Pachmann. The world has toiled for thousands of years and has at last given us this thing more delicate than lace, more brittle than porcelain, more shining than gold....

There is the rather painful question of this pianist's eccentricities. One can discuss them publicly for de Pachmann himself continually thrusts them on the public. You know to what I refer: the running commentary of words, gestures, nods, smiles and leers which he almost invariably passes not only on the music he plays, but also on his manner of playing it. I refuse to believe that this most extraordinary behaviour is mere affectation: it seems to me a direct and irrepressible expression of the man's very soul. It is not ridiculous, because it is so serious and so natural. Nevertheless, it is entirely ineffective. It does not help in the least. Rather does it mar. To see the performer winking slyly at you when he has, as it were, "pulled off" a particularly delicate nuance does not give that nuance a more subtle flavour: it merely distracts the attention and sets one conjecturing what really *is* going on in the performer's mind. It has appeared to me that the pianist has been saying: "You noticed that, didn't you? Well, *you* couldn't do it if you spent a whole lifetime trying; yet how easily *I* achieved it!"

The large, smooth face, with its loose mouth and dizzied eyes, is the face of a magician out of a story book. It is not a real face. It has only one of the attributes of power—egotism. Egotism has furrowed every line on that countenance; it dilates the eyes. Egotism runs through the sensitive fingers. I have stood by his side and wilfully shut my ears on the music and fastened my eyes on his face; but I learned nothing. I do not know if his mind dwells aloof from all emotion, his intellect functioning automatically—as would seem to be the case; or if, experienced and cynical, he has the power of pouring the very essence of his spirit into sound, laughing at himself and us as he does so—but laughing more at us than at himself, for we are deceived whilst he is not.

It is strange that so exotic a personality should have a firm and unrelaxing hold on the public. He is not caviare to the general. Villiers de l'Isle Adam is worshipped by the few; Walter Pater cannot have more than a thousand sincere disciples, but de Pachmann is adored by millions. "Millions" is no exaggeration. People are taken out of themselves whilst he plays. You remember, don't you? the Paderewski craze in America fifteen years ago, when the platform was stormed and taken by assault night after night by society ladies. I witnessed pretty much the same kind of thing at a de Pachmann recital in a Lancashire town; but the latter pianist was stormed, not by society ladies, but by unemotional bank clerks, stockbrokers, merchants, working men and women. At the end of the concert, they flowed on to the platform in hundreds, and surrounded the pianist whilst he played encore after encore, smiling vacantly the while and enjoying himself immensely, pausing between each piece only to motion his ring of worshippers a little farther from the piano.

An enigmatic creature, this; a creature who will never give up his secret; perhaps, even, a creature who is not aware that he possesses a secret.

CHAPTER XVI
CATHEDRAL MUSICAL FESTIVALS

NO; I'm not going to be a chronicler in this chapter. It sounds a dull subject, I know, but many things happened in Gloucester, Hereford and Worcester in mellow September days that were vastly amusing and which were not reported in the papers, and it is about these I am going to tell you.

It used to be very charming to go to one of these cathedrals early each autumn, drink cider, listen to music six hours a day, walk by the river, have jolly "rags" in the hotel at night, and come home again at the end of a week or ten days. September is a tired month, I always think ... if not tired, a little languorous.... It has many days in which one wants to walk about just quietly, enjoying being alive. It would be wrong to fuss and work really hard. I suppose that in all those wonderful places in which I have spent so many happy weeks—Worcester, Lincoln, Gloucester, Hereford, Norwich—people ruminate and browse at all times. Certainly I have seen them browsing in herds in September days. I once watched the Bishop of Hereford browsing. He stood perfectly still and seemed to be contemplating and measuring and gently wondering about the growth of a healthy nasturtium.

Everybody used to migrate to these festivals. Well, not quite everybody ... but you know what I mean; just the very people you most awfully wanted to meet again and talk to and hear music with: people like Granville Bantock, Ernest Newman, Samuel Langford, John Coates, Dr McNaught, Frederic Austin, Herbert Hughes. London used to send thirty or forty critics, and the provinces about the same number. And from the surrounding towns would pour in county families, middle-class families anxious (poor deluded ones!) to keep abreast of the musical times (or do I mean *The Musical Times*?), maiden ladies still and for ever ecstatic over Mendelssohn's poor old *Elijah*, fierce choir-masters with ideas on choral singing, village organists who really believed that Dr Brewer was the Last Word, immaculate young men with æsthetic fever and a decided leaning towards Elgar's *The Dream of Gerontius* (always alluded to by them as *The Dream*), very "nee-ice" young ladies who when at home played the violin, and, last of all, deans (oh yes, lots of deans), minor canons, slim curates, parsons of all kinds, squires without money, squarsons.

It was hard for us musical critics to take these festivals quite as seriously as the festivals expected us to do, for it always seemed incredible to us that London or Birmingham or Glasgow should have the least desire to know how the choruses of Handel's *The Messiah* were sung in a little town like Gloucester. Moreover, many of us were amused at the tragic seriousness of these age-old festivals—festivals at which, as a rule, only two new works of any importance were produced and over which old oratorios—an impossible form of art—hung like a heavy cloud. So we used to amuse ourselves in our different ways, and the ringleaders in our occasional rags were generally Granville Bantock and Ernest Newman.

Almost every detail of one of these joyous occasions lingers in my memory. Dr McNaught, the doyen of us all, an experienced critic, a witty speaker, and a most profound musician, was the not unwilling victim. Bantock or, to give him his full title, Professor Granville Bantock, M.A., had brought from Birmingham two live eels in a tank. When he bought these sturdy creatures, he must have had in his mind some jollification or other, and when I met him in the streets of Hereford (I think it was Hereford) during the morning of the Festival's first day, he asked me what was the most amusing thing I could think of that could be done with two live eels.

"Eels!" exclaimed I, in amazement. "Do you mean to tell me that you really possess two live eels?"

"Yes, here in Hereford. One gets a little dull here after a couple of hours, and, after all, eels are very lively fry. They break the monotony of life." He paused a moment. "And," he added rather dreamily, "they swish their tails so busily. I suppose an eel's tail is the busiest thing in the world. Come and have a look; they're in my room at the hotel."

And there they were in a tank: dark objects in dark water, swirling about with enormous enthusiasm.

The day passed and no amusing idea occurred to me. Bantock conducted one of his works in the cathedral that evening—a very important and solemn occasion, and when we critics had left our "copy" at the post-office for telegraphic transmission to our respective newspapers, we foregathered in the hotel.

Now Dr McNaught had gone to spend the late hours with a friend and was not expected back till nearly midnight; it became obvious, therefore, both to Bantock and myself, that the eels must, in some way, be made to surprise him on his return. We placed the slimy creatures in a washhand basin in his bedroom, poured water upon them, and gazed down upon them with knitted brows.

"It is enough," said Bantock; "there is no need to think of anything else. Listen."

And, truly, there was a most stealthy and uncouth sort of noise. Eels may have soft skins, but their muscles are hard and, as they careered round the basin, one heard a continuous smooth sound as of people going about some nefarious business in the dark, and now and again, at unexpected moments, a loud thwack would be heard as one of the fish threw his tail upon the side of the basin.

Newman and Frederic Austin and one or two others collaborated in preparing our scheme. A female figure was made, carefully placed on the middle of Dr McNaught's pillow, and gently covered to the neck with the bedclothes.

These elaborate arrangements for Dr McNaught's entertainment were only just completed when the doctor himself returned. We waited in dark corners of the corridor for the result.

After an interval of a few minutes, a bell rang and a chambermaid appeared.

"There is some mistake, I think," said Dr McNaught genially. "Either this room is a bedroom, a larder, or an aquarium; it would be most good of you if you would decide as soon as possible which it really is."

The chambermaid entered the bedroom and we could just hear her quiet voice as, a moment later, she half whispered:

"But, sir, the room is already occupied. There is a lady in your bed."

Of course, the psychological moment had arrived, and we strolled casually into the bedroom to become witnesses of Dr McNaught's embarrassment. The jape was continued. McNaught was taken to the smoke-room, solemnly tried by judge and jury for having murdered a woman and concealed her body (it was at the time of the Crippen affair), and sentenced to death. Newman brought a hatchet from the cellar and, not long before dawn, the mock sentence was carried out with elaborate pantomime....

"Very childish—just like schoolboys!" I hear a reader (not you, of course) say, rather contemptuously. Yes, it was like schoolboys, and substitute "-like" for "-ish" in "childish" and I agree with you most heartily.

But not all our time was spent in this uproarious way. There were long hours of talk, great talk from Langford of *The Manchester Guardian*, a man of mature years whom to meet is a privilege and whom to know intimately is a blessing; witty, rather cruel, but vastly entertaining talk from Newman; pungent talk from Bantock; and general gossip from all kinds of people.

I do remember so regretfully—regretfully, because I do not think a like occasion can happen again—an afternoon that Langford and I spent sitting at a little rustic table under a just yellowing grove of poplars. Langford's mind is spacious, most richly stored. Nothing can happen that does not at once and without effort fit into his philosophy of life, and though his talk is profound it is so greatly human that, in listening to him, one feels completely at rest. He accepts everything.... I daresay you have noticed that many people have tried to describe the effect Walt Whitman's personality has had on them, and you will have observed how they have all failed. It is an impossible task.... And I feel that in writing about Langford it is impossible to convey to you what he stands for to his friends. I recollect Captain J. E. Agate once saying to me: "I never come away from speaking to Langford without feeling what an empty fool I am." Yes, that is true; yet, at the same time, you feel reconciled to your own empty folly; besides, you know well enough that if you were a fool Langford would not talk to you; he would just ask you to have a drink and then he would fumble clumsily in his waistcoat pocket to find you a cigarette.

Langford will never be "successful" in the worldly sense. Perhaps he looks with suspicion on success; certainly he has never attempted to achieve it. I imagine that his nature is very like that of Æ, and if what everyone says of Æ is true, one cannot conceive that anything finer could be said of anyone than that he resembles the great Irish poet.

It was these refreshing talks with various people that did something to mitigate the severity of the atmosphere of conventionality, of "respectability" in its worst sense, that made it rather difficult to breathe freely in these cathedral cities. Everyone wore new clothes; men perspired in kid gloves; girls carried prayer-books and copies of *Elijah*; deans were dapper; ostlers were clean and profoundly polite; and, wherever you went, you heard people saying that they had seen Lord Bertie and Lady Jane, and had you noticed that the dear Bishop had looked a little tired last evening? There was, too, about these festivals an air as of a society function. Music, an unwilling handmaid of charity, was "indulged" in. One did not have music every day, for that would have been frivolous; but one had it in great lumps every twelve months, and had it, not because one cannot live fully and vividly without art, but because it made a good excuse for a social "occasion." The music itself was excused—for in the minds of these people it required an excuse—by the fact that the entire festival was organised for charity, that vice which causes so many sins.

I myself came into rather violent conflict with the Norfolk and Norwich Musical Festival authorities on a question of artistic morality. Ten or eleven years ago they offered a prize of twenty-five guineas for a poem, and another prize of fifty guineas for the best musical setting of the poem. I entered the former competition and secured the prize. My "poem" was in blank verse and lyrics, its subject Cleopatra, and it contained the following passage:

Iris. And when with regal, arrogant step she passed

Across the portico, her white breasts gleamed;

Her neck seemed conscious of its loveliness;

Her lips, tired of tame kisses, parted with

The expectancy of proud assault; she was

As one who lives for a last carnival

Of love, in which she may be stabbed and torn

By large excess of passion.

*Charmion.*Oh! Our Queen

Has wine for blood; her tears are heavy drops

Of water stolen from some brackish sea

Or murderous waves; her heart now leaps with life

And now lies sleeping like a coilèd snake.

But in to-night's cold moon she burns and glows;

Her heart is housing many a mad desire,

And she is sick for Antony.

*Iris.*The day

Has gone, and soon they'll drink the heady wine

That sparkles in each other's eyes. Once more

Venus and Bacchus meet, and all the world

Stands still to watch the bliss of living gods.

There was a little more to the same effect, and when I wrote the stuff I thought it very fine and still think it rather pretty. But a section of the musical Press attacked it violently, and for a couple of months I was quite a notorious person. I gathered from the articles and letters that appeared that my dramatic poem was not likely to engender music that would carry on the tradition of Mendelssohn's *Elijah*. That had been my object in writing it. I was sick of that tradition. I wished to help to break it.

One day, while the little storm was still raging, I received a letter from Sir Henry J. Wood, who was to conduct the Festival at Norwich at which my work was to be given. (Mr Julius Harrison, who has since become prominent as one of Sir Thomas Beecham's assistant conductors, had gained the prize for the musical setting of my poem.) In his letter Sir Henry wrote: "Very much against my will, I am writing to ask you on behalf of the Committee of the Norfolk and Norwich Festival if it is possible for you to make any alternative version of the 'two objectionable lines' (I fail to find them myself) in your libretto, *Cleopatra*.... From my point of view, the whole thing is absurd and ridiculous."

I could not find the objectionable lines. I showed the poem to a most maiden aunt and watched her as she read it, hoping to tell by her sudden blush when her eyes had reached the evil place. She did not blush; she simply read the thing and said: "Oh, Gerald, how nice! I do think you have such pretty thoughts." So did I.

A few days later Mr Julius Harrison came to my aid. The committee, it appeared, objected to "her white breasts gleamed" and also to:

> Her lips, tired of tame kisses, parted with
>
> The expectancy of proud assault....

I changed those lines, and the work in due course was performed at Norwich, and in Queen's Hall, London. Later on, when my little poem was sung in Southport in its original form, with Mr Havergal Brian's music (for he also had honoured me), Mr Landon Ronald conducting, the members of the audience did not leave their seats when the "objectionable" lines occurred; rather did they seem to lean forward a little and listen more intently.

I have mentioned this incident, not because in itself it is important, but because it so beautifully illustrates the point of view of our Cathedral Festivals. Their "secular" concerts are echoes of the concerts given in the Cathedral. They hate (or else they are afraid of?) every emotion that is not a religious emotion. They think that God made our souls and the devil our bodies. They may be right; if they are, it is clear the devil is not lacking in consideration.

There is no doubt that our most ecstatic moments at the Cathedral Festivals were supplied by Wagner's *Parsifal*, which Mr J. F. Runciman, in his little book on this composer, describes as "this disastrous and evil opera." Only excerpts from it, of course, were given; all "objectionable lines" were cut out. If *Parsifal* is to be given on the platform at all—and, in view of the fact that we seldom have it on the stage, why not?—then it had better be given on a platform that has been erected in a spacious and beautiful cathedral. I remember those white voices floating down from a place out of sight near the roof, away above the clerestory. I always used to try to obtain a seat near some dimly stained window so that it might for me blot out the rather bewildered or consciously "rapt" faces of my fellow-creatures, for, in listening to noble music, I invariably feel much greater than, and curiously irritated by the presence of, other people.

And it used to be so fine to come forth from the Cathedral at noon, step into that mellow September English sunshine which I have not seen for nearly three years, and walk by the river ... walk perhaps a mile or so and come back to the hotel to eat cool meats and cool salads and drink cool wine. It was at these times I used to sigh and long for Bayreuth and wonder if I should ever see the grave of Wagner in the garden of Villa Wahnfried in that little Bavarian town.

It was at Gloucester, I think, that one year I was pursued by a certain hard-working, but not very talented, composer who, having gained a most extensive "popular" public for his work, was now anxious to win the suffrage of more cultivated people. Most unhappily for me, he took it into his head that my musical criticism had some influence in the north, and though he was quite wrong in this assumption, I was never able to convince him of his error. Wherever I went, lo! he was there with me. And always under his arm was a musical score, a score of his own composition. Something new, he assured me; something really quite modern. Would I look at it? I did. It was feeble, paltry and bombastic, but I did not like to tell him so. But when he pressed me for an opinion I said, what was near enough to the truth, that it was a great advance on his previous work. This seemed to please him, and he took to inviting me out to lunch. If ever I went into the hotel smoke-room for a quiet pipe, I would invariably notice a vague but self-important figure in the doorway, and presently would hear the unmistakable pop that a champagne bottle so deliciously makes when it is opened. A bubbling glass would be placed at my side.

"Now, Richard Strauss in his *Ein Heldenleben* ..." his voice would begin. And he would proceed to tell me all about *Ein Heldenleben* and its beauties. To bewilder him, I used to assert that *Carmen* seemed to me a much finer work than Strauss's *Elektra*, and, because he was very ignorant and because he had not the slightest appreciation of Strauss, he used to look at me rather pitifully, and would eventually confess that he too liked Bizet more than he liked Strauss and that, indeed, it appeared to him that Arthur Sullivan....

One day, when we were alone, he asked me if I would write a series of articles on his works. It was my turn to be bewildered.

"A series?" I asked, utterly stunned.

"Yes," answered he, "a series. First of all, there are my part-songs. Then there are my instrumental pieces. Last of all, my Cantatas." He pronounced cantatas with a capital C. "Just a short series: three articles in all."

I hesitated, but he looked at me most pleadingly. I tried a little sarcasm, but that made him more pertinacious than ever. So then I flatly refused, and kept on refusing, and did not stop refusing.

"Well, then," said he at length, "will you put in writing and sign what you said to me the other day about my new work? You will remember that you said it was the best thing I had ever done, that it was original, full of vigour, astonishingly fresh, subtle in harmony...."

"Oh, really," I protested, "did I say all that?"

"Yes, indeed, you did."

And then I became very, very rude indeed, and, after that, whenever we met, we used to bow to each other most politely and say never a word.

This kind of man, and there is quite a handful of them, haunts the more important Festivals, but it must be very rarely that one of them obtains what he desires.

Can you recall the most curious and most unlikely sight you have ever witnessed? Most of us, even in the course of a few years of a very ordinary existence, witness many strange things, but of all the strange things I have stumbled across nothing has been so wayward, so *outré*, so fundamentally silly, as the forty organists I saw sitting in one room at Worcester. One can imagine two, or even three, organists sitting talking together, but forty, and fifteen of the forty Cathedral organists, seems incredible.

Now, you have only to be fond of modern music to feel instinctively that a man who is an organist and nothing else is sitting on the wrong side of the fence. In ninety-nine cases out of a hundred he is helping to hold things back; he hates the rapid progress which music is making, and he has as much imagination as the *vox humana* stop.

Well, the forty organists were sitting and talking and smoking, and as I looked at them and at their mild, but worried, faces, it seemed to me and my companion that, in the interests of art, morality and ordinary decency, some protest should be made. And we decided that we were just the people to make it. We could have forgiven them if they had met together to discuss some professional question—*e.g.* how to get their salaries raised, how to get the better of their respective vicars, or how they could expand their minds so as to be able to appreciate Debussy or Ravel or even Max Reger. But they were gathered together merely because they liked it, just for the sake of enjoying each other's society. Monstrous absurdity! Could they not see how ridiculous they were? Forty organists in one room!—why, there ought not to be forty organists in the whole world.

Fortunately the room was on the ground floor and the hour late. My companion and I stepped outside the hotel, waited till the street was quiet, and then rapped a series of three tattoos upon the window-pane to secure silence within. We then sang in two parts, I in a high falsetto and my friend in a lugubrious bass, the "Baal" Chorus from *Elijah*. "Baal, we cry to thee! Baal, we cry to thee!"

We had not proceeded very far in this beautiful music—intended by the dear, delicious Mendelssohn for a shout of savagery, but really a quite charming cradle song—when a cry of delighted laughter came from the room, and two or three of the organists, hatless and earnest, rushed out into the street.

"Come inside!" they said; "come and join us. You belong to *us*!"

Too utterly flabbergasted at this invitation to make any reply, we turned and fled, rushed back to our hotel, and ordered whisky-and-sodas.

The great musician to whom we told the story next day said:

"Well, once more, you see, the biters were bit."

But my friend and I did not think so.

CHAPTER XVII
PEOPLE OF THE THEATRE

SIR HERBERT TREE never met a stranger without trying to impress him. He always succeeded. He would take the utmost pains about it: go to any lengths: use his last resource.... I am not now, of course, dealing with him as an actor. We all have our varying opinions of him as an actor. Some think he could; some think he couldn't.... But I am writing of him at the present moment as a man. A showman, if you like. As a man, as a man who "showed off" either as a wit, a mimic, a man of the world, a superman, or what not, he was supreme.

I met him in his private office at His Majesty's in the middle of the run of *Joseph and his Brethren*. He had invited me there in order to dictate an article to me, but, as he told me over the 'phone, he hadn't the remotest notion what the subject of the article was going to be. Could I help him with any ideas? His article was for a Labour paper. Did I know anything about Labour? If I didn't, did I know anybody who did?

In speaking to me over the 'phone, he appeared so anxious that I began to rack my brains for a subject. In the recesses of my meagre intellect I found the remnants of two or three subjects, and at nine o'clock that evening I presented myself at His Majesty's Theatre with them on the tip of my tongue.

His room was empty as I entered it. Opposite the door was a fireplace and above the fireplace a mirror; on the left of the door as you entered it was Sir Herbert's large desk. By the side of this, seated on a low chair, I waited. I had not to wait long, for presently I heard a soft, rather pulpy kind of sound coming down the passage and, a moment later, Sir Herbert entered, wearing a long white beard and the garments of a gentleman of the East. The play was still in the first act, and he had that minute come off the stage.

"Got a subject?" he asked, shaking hands. "So have I. The Influence of the Stage on the Masses! What do you think of it? Very trite, I know, but there are a few important things I want to say. Sit here, will you? Here you are—ink and paper."

And, sitting down, he began immediately to dictate the article. He got along swimmingly, and about a third of the article must have been down on paper when I heard a squeaky voice outside the door. It was the call-boy. Sir Herbert rose, stroked his beard, adjusted his gown, and walked outside; as he did these things he continued dictating, his voice stopping in the middle of a rather involved sentence when he was out in the passage.

After five or six minutes, I heard the same soft, pulpy sound approaching and, while yet outside the door, he began dictating at the precise point where he had left off, rounding off the sentence most beautifully. It was a remarkable feat of memory. After a very short period, we heard the high-pitched voice a second time, and once more he moved dreamily away, still dictating. Again he stopped, purposely as it seemed to me, in the middle of a sentence, and again, when he reappeared, he spoke the waiting word. Marvellous! He gave me a cautious, inquiring look, as if to discover if I had noticed his cleverness. I smiled back reassuringly. In a few minutes the article was finished.

"Do you like it?" he asked.

"Exactly the thing. *The Daily Citizen* readers will be delighted. But what an extraordinary memory you have!"

"Ah! You noticed that?" he said, seemingly well pleased.

He began to talk of *Joseph and his Brethren* and, in the middle of our conversation, Mr Temple Thurston, looking rather nervous, was shown in. I knew that, at that time, Thurston was writing for Tree a play on the subject of the Wandering Jew, and as I guessed they had business to transact, I withdrew as quickly as possible.

I saw Sir Herbert on another occasion, but whether it was soon before, or soon after, the incident I have just related I cannot recollect.

He was conducting a rehearsal on the stage of His Majesty's, and I stood in the wings, watching him. He had recently produced a play called, I think, *The Island*, by a Spanish or a Brazilian writer. It was a dead failure and was withdrawn after three or four nights. It was to talk of this play that I had come, and as he advanced to the wings I noticed that he looked rather worried.

"What *was* wrong with the play?" he asked. "All you critics have tried to tell me, but I'm blessed if I can understand what you are all talking about."

"To me the fault of the play was quite obvious. The author had got hold of a good idea and the drama had several fine situations; but, whereas the idea was poetical and mysterious and the situations tense and dramatic, the author or the translator had employed the most stilted kind of dialogue, and language as commonplace as that which I am now using. The play should have been translated or rewritten by a poet."

"Ah! It's very strange you should say that, for I myself had felt strongly disposed to ask John Masefield to prepare the thing for the stage. I wish I had done; but, of course, it's too late now. But a manager can never tell beforehand what play will be a success and what won't."

"Pardon me. That is often said, but I don't believe it's true. Some people really *do* know what the public wants. Arnold Bennett, for example, and Hall Caine, not to mention others. Do *they* ever make mistakes? Has Arnold Bennett ever been guilty of a failure?"

"No, perhaps not. But I can't engage Bennett as a reader. Even if he would consent to do the work, I should not be able to afford his fee."

"Yes, I know. But my contention is that there are people who can and do gauge to a nicety the taste of the public." And I mentioned the names of two critics who had, on many occasions, foretold most accurately the exact length of time new pieces would run.

Tree was called back to the rehearsal, and he glided away for a few moments, fluttering a handful of loose papers as he went. He soon returned, and this time he was cheerfulness itself.

"It's going very well," he said, referring to the rehearsal. "It's only a stop-gap, of course, but it'll make a little money. I must write to those critics you mentioned," he added musingly; "or perhaps it would be better if I seemed to run across them accidentally?"

But whether or not he did run across either of the critics accidentally, I do not know, for the war broke out soon after and disrupted everything.

It was when I was staying in Guilford Street, Bloomsbury, six or seven years ago, in a house opposite the Foundlings' Hospital, that, one morning, Gordon Craig came into the room. He was, I think, in search of Ernest Marriott, a most ingenious and original artist, who at that time and for long after was doing some sort of work for Craig. Marriott and I were staying at the same boarding-house.

When Craig's bulky form filled the doorway I recognised at once, from Marriott's description of him, who he was, and I introduced myself to him, telling him Marriott was out.

"Yes, I know he is," said Craig; "but I have often wanted to look at one of these fine old houses."

And he walked round and round the room, with his eyes on the cornice, telling me all sorts of things, which I have long forgotten, that I had never heard before. He seemed to have made a special study of English architecture of the early nineteenth century, and whilst he was in the house talked of nothing else, though I tried to lure him into gossip of the theatre.

He gave me the impression of a large, white man with hair which, if not entirely grey, was very fair. He had, I remember, hands much plumper than one would expect an artist to possess; his face also was rather plump. He seemed to fill the large room and radiate vitality. He left as suddenly and as inconsequently as he had come.

"How like he is to Miss Ellen Terry!" remarked my landlord, not knowing the identity of his visitor.

"Yes," said I, "now you mention it, I notice the extraordinary resemblance. But, after all, the resemblance is not so remarkable, for you see, he is her son."

On one occasion I was sent to interview Mr Henry Arthur Jones. Over the telephone I made an appointment with him for the morrow, and when I arrived at his house I found rather elaborate preparations had been made for the occasion. Mr H. A. Jones was standing in the middle of the drawing-room with outstretched hand, on a table near the open window (it was July, I think) was a tray with what one calls tea-things, a lady shorthand typist (specially engaged for the occasion) was waiting with notebook and pencil, and a maid was carrying into the room a teapot, and cress sandwiches.

The presence of the lady typist embarrassed me. She took down in shorthand my questions and Mr Jones' replies. Thinking it would be foolish to waste any time on preliminary politenesses, I plunged straight into the middle of my subject. The lady typist sipped her tea in the awkward little pauses that came from time to time. It was not an interview; it was a kind of official statement. It was like the proceedings at a police court. I felt I should be held responsible to a higher authority for every word I spoke.

However, at the end of an hour a good deal of excellent matter had been taken down, probably enough for a two-column article. But my news editor did not want a two-column article. He wanted a scrappy little paragraph or, at most, two scrappy little paragraphs. Now, in view of the fact that Mr Jones had gone to the trouble and expense of getting a shorthand typist specially from town, and, more particularly, in view of the fact that it was perfectly clear that he had not contemplated the possibility of an interview with him being used merely and solely for a snappy little paragraph, I felt it incumbent upon me to tell him just how matters stood. But how could I? Could you have told him? Well, I couldn't, though I tried and tried hard.

When the interview was over, he arranged that the shorthand typist should return to her office, type out her shorthand, and send the result to me in Fleet Street early that evening. In due course, ten foolscap sheets of valuable and most interesting matter came along, and I handed it in to the night-editor just as it stood.

Next morning, only two snippety paragraphs appeared in the paper, and I have often thought since that Mr H. A. Jones must have felt disgusted with the paper, a little more disgusted with himself, but most of all disgusted with me. After all, it was not entirely my fault, was it?... I mean, he should not have taken himself *quite* so importantly, should he?

I retain a very clear impression of his personality. He was short, rather dapper, and very deliberate. He always thought briefly before he answered a question, but when he did answer it he did so without hesitation, going straight into the middle of the matter. He struck me, as he sat on a rather low chair opposite the window, as essentially earnest, essentially honest-minded, essentially clear-headed. His manner was a little important. He may be said to have "pronounced" things rather than to have spoken them. He was formally courteous. I do not think one could justly say that he has the "artistic" temperament, and I imagine he possesses no particularly acute perception of beauty. There is no emotional enthusiasm about him; he has no unreliable "moods"; he does not think or feel one thing to-day and another to-morrow. By no means typically a man of this generation, and yet not a man who has outlived his own time. It appeared to me that he had little intuition; his very considerable knowledge of human nature is probably based on close observation and most careful deduction.

When we parted he gave me copies of two of his plays.

He was a man of considerable personal charm and no little intellectual weight: a man both kindly and stern: a man who could at all times be trusted to see the humour of things and who, on occasion, could be cruel to be kind.

Not so very long before the war, my journalistic duties took me to the first night of Mr Temple Thurston's *The Greatest Wish in the World,* a rather weak but quite innocuous play given by Mr Bourchier. If the play "succeeded," the audience assuredly didn't. When the curtain went down on the last act, there was a good deal of applause, chiefly from the gallery, and we who were seated in the stalls waited a moment to discover what the verdict of the house was going to be.

Now, every close observer of theatre audiences knows well enough that among the many different kinds of applause there is one kind that is very sinister: it is a kind difficult to describe, but unmistakable enough when heard: to the uninterested listener it sounds sincere and hearty, but if you listen carefully you will catch, beneath the heartiness, a derisive note—something viciously eager in the shouts, something malicious in the whistles. There was this sinister sound, a kind of ground-bass, in the applause that followed the last fall of the curtain at the first production of Mr Temple Thurston's play. The mimes had walked on and bowed their acknowledgments when, suddenly, there arose loud cries of "Author! Author!" Well did I know what those cries meant, and I told myself that the play had failed pitifully. I was edging my way out of the stalls when, to my amazement, I saw the curtain rise once more and disclose the nervous figure of Mr Temple Thurston. Instantly there went up from a section of the audience hisses and boos and cries of half-angry disappointment. Mr Thurston shrank and winced as though he had been struck in the face, and his exit was confused and awkward. It was as wanton an act of cruelty as I have ever witnessed: deliberate, heartless, stupid. This is not the place to discuss the propriety or otherwise of an audience insulting a writer who has failed to please it, but it is certain that in no other profession, in no other walk of life, do such savage traditions prevail as in the enticing and intoxicating world of the theatre.

Not long after this incident I was received by Mr Temple Thurston at his flat. I found him writing, and almost at once he began to talk most intimately about himself.

"Never again," said he, apropos of the episode I have just related, "shall I 'take a call.' I cannot even now think of those awful few moments on the stage without a shudder. It is distressing enough for an author to fail—distressing: not only because of his own disappointment, but chiefly because of the disappointment he brings to the actors who have done their best for his play—without having his failure hurled in his face, so to speak. But though I shall never again take a call, I shall continue writing plays. I have never yet written a really successful play, and no work of mine has had a longer run than sixty performances. I have had many chances, of course, but I shall have more."

He then told me of his early attempts to win fame. Like many other successful writers, he began in Fleet Street. The work there did not suit him, and he soon abandoned it. He married early, lived with his wife in a couple of rooms in Chancery Lane, and for a little time picked up a living as best he could. The story of his first wife's extraordinary success with *John Chilcote, M.P.*, is common knowledge. That success preceded his own by two or three years, but he had not long to wait before his own work found and pleased the public.

I saw Thurston on two or three other occasions, and found him a man avid of enjoyment, frank, a little bitter, combative, kindly, strong, sensitive, independent. He has a nature at once contradictory and baffling.

Twenty years must have passed since Miss Janet Achurch gave her astounding performance in Manchester of Cleopatra in Shakespeare's *Antony and Cleopatra*. It was a performance so remarkable, so electrifying, that the old Queen's Theatre in Quay Street became, for a time, the centre of theatrical interest for the whole of England. What London critic nowadays goes to Manchester, or anywhere else more than five miles from home, to witness a Shakespeare play? Yet they all went to see Miss Achurch. I remember a cheeky and brilliant article by Bernard Shaw in *The Saturday Review* on Miss Achurch, another by Clement Scott in *The Daily Telegraph*, a third by William Archer in (I think) *The World*.

For myself, I saw the play seventeen times, and though I have seen many other actresses interpret Cleopatra, I have not known one whose performance could rank with the gorgeous presentation by Miss Achurch.

All my visits to the Queen's were surreptitious, for I was brought up in a family that not only hated the theatre as an evil place but feared it also. Though I was but a boy I had a certain amount of freedom, for I was studying medicine at the Victoria University, and many afternoons that should have been spent in dissecting human feet and eyes were passed in the gallery of Flanagan's theatre.

I suppose I must have been in love with Miss Achurch, though the kind of feeling that a boy sometimes has for a great emotional actress is more akin to worship than love. I longed to approach my divinity, but feared to do so. I wrote about her in local papers, and I remember a curious weekly called *Northern Finance* which, for some dark reason or other, printed, among its news of stocks and shares, a crude, bubbling article of mine on Miss Achurch. I sent all my articles to her and, with the colossal impudence of youth, and driven by a schoolboy curiosity, asked for an interview.

She wrote to me. Reader, are you young enough to remember how you felt when you first saw Miss Ellen Terry? Can you recall your adoration, your devotion?... Those days of young worship, how fine they are! Novelists always laugh at calf love because they cannot write about it and make it as beautiful as it really is. Like many other things that are human, calf love is absurd and beautiful, noble and silly, profound and superficial. But, unlike so many things that are human, there is nothing about it that is mean and selfish, nothing that is not proud and good.

Yes, she wrote to me and invited me to visit her. She was kind and gracious.... Amused? Oh, I have no doubt she was amused, but she never betrayed it.

I used to hang about the stage door in the dark to watch her go into the theatre or come out of it. I scraped up an acquaintance with several members of the orchestra, for I thought I saw in them a kind of magic borrowed from her. Her hotel was a castle.

Those of my readers who never saw Miss Achurch in what theatrical writers call her "palmy" days can have only a very faint conception of her genius. She became ill: her beauty faded. Only rarely did one see her on the stage.

Years later I saw her in Ibsen's *Ghosts* and, again much later, in a small part in Masefield's adaptation of Wiers-Jennsen's *The Witch*. She was wonderful in both plays, but the grandeur had departed, the glory almost gone.

It is most sadly true that actors live only in their own generation. Janet Achurch ought to have lived for ever. She will not be forgotten while we who saw her live; but we cannot communicate to others the genius we witnessed and worshipped.

Miss Horniman is one of the many people I have never met. "Then why write about her?" you ask. I really don't know, except that I want to. She was (and, for all I know to the contrary, still is) something of a personality in Manchester, and she was so for a considerable period, she producing quite a few plays at the Gaiety Theatre that were well worth seeing.

But she was ridiculously overpraised. She was petted and spoiled by *The Manchester Guardian*, the Victoria University gave her an honorary Master of Art's degree, many literary and dramatic societies went down on their knees to her and implored her to come and speak to them, and she was regarded by the entire community as a woman of daring originality, great wisdom and vast experience. She could do nothing wrong. No play she produced, no matter how sour and Mancunian, was ever condemned by the local Press. Miss Horniman had given it, therefore it was "the right stuff." She knew about it all: *she knew*: she knew. Many Manchester dramatic critics were themselves writing plays, and Miss Horniman smiled upon them. She smiled upon Stanley Houghton, Harold Brighouse, Allan Monkhouse, all critics of *The Manchester Guardian*. She would have smiled upon the plays of J. E. Agate and C. E. Montague if they had written any. She was our benefactress, and we used to sit and watch her in her embroidered gown as she rather self-consciously queened it in a box at her own theatre.

Yet, after all, she had a rather depressing effect upon the city. She gave no new play that was perfectly beautiful. She appeared to detest romance and had little understanding of blank verse. Starting her public life as a patron of Bernard Shaw, she declined upon Shaw's fevered disciples. She spoke in public very frequently, and always said the same things. She had all the enthusiasm of a clever business woman. Wishing very much to make money (so she told us), she understood all the arts of self-advertisement. But, really, Manchester was not the place for her; it was sufficiently hard and provincial before she came— —

But perhaps I am allowing myself to run away with myself in writing down all these disagreeable things. Yet I believe them to be true, and they must stand. Her plays gave me several enjoyable evenings which, but for her, I should never have had, and I can never be too grateful to her for restoring to the Gaiety Theatre the drink licence that the Watch Committee had taken away some years before she came. That act, at all events, did in some degree help to make the Manchester plays a little less like Manchester plays.

CHAPTER XVIII
BERLIN AND SOME OF ITS PEOPLE

ONE winter, about ten years ago, I went to Berlin in the company of Mr Frederick Dawson, the famous English pianist, who had planned to give two recitals there. We stayed at the Fürstenhof, a luxurious and enervating hotel where we had a suite of rooms facing the front. In the large drawing-room that Karl Klindworth had engaged for Dawson was a good piano.

Now, music in Berlin is just a trade. Everyone plays or sings and everybody teaches somebody or other to play and sing. Unless you are an artist of colossal merit (and sometimes even if you are), you will find it practically impossible to persuade anybody to listen to you if you are not prepared to "square" the critics. In the season, twenty, thirty, forty concerts are given nightly, and by far the greater number of them are given to empty stalls. That does not matter: no artist of any European experience expects anything else. A musician does not go to Berlin to get money: he goes to get a reputation. Berlin's cachet is (or, most decidedly, I should say *was*) absolutely indispensable for any pianist, violinist or singer who wishes to make a permanent and wide reputation. Before the war, Mr Snooks could play as hard and as fiercely and as long in London as he liked, but unless he was known in Berlin, and unless it was known that he was known in Berlin, he was everywhere considered but as a second-rate kind of person, a mere talented outsider. So that it is quite within the facts to say that few artists have gone to sing or play in Berlin except for the purpose of obtaining Press notices, favourable Press notices, Press notices that glow with praise and reek of backstairs influence. An American, a French or a Danish artist will go to Berlin with a few years' savings, give a short series of recitals, cut his Press notices from the papers, go back to his native land, and then advertise freely—his advertisements, of course, consisting of judicious excerpts (not always very literally translated) from his Berlin notices. This visit to Berlin, with the hire of a concert hall, etc., may cost a couple of hundred pounds, but it is counted money well spent, well invested.

Frederick Dawson had already paid several visits to Berlin and Vienna, and was so well known in both cities that his appearance in either always attracted large and enthusiastic audiences; but, apart from Dawson himself, d'Albert and Lamond, no other British artist or semi-British artist had, I imagine, the power to do so.

I was introduced to many critics and many artists. The critic was almost invariably a Herr Doktor and the Herr Doktor was almost invariably a Herr Professor: they all had degrees and they all taught. They were overworked, "doing" five or six concerts a night and receiving very little pay. They would dash about from one concert hall to another in taxi-cabs, jot down a few notes, and look down their noses; when they wished to leave a particular hall, they would look round furtively, gather their coat-tails together, and sidle slimly or roll fatly to the door.

Some of these gentlemen, I heard, were very shady in their dealings with young and inexperienced artists. They plied a trade of gentle blackmail, kid-gloved blackmail, of course, but the kid gloves contained the claws of a hungry eagle. The following describes one of their pretty little customs.

Hearing of the arrival in Berlin of a singer or pianist whose agent had been advertising the fact that his client would shortly give a series of three recitals, the critic would call upon him, express interest in his work, and ask to have the pleasure of hearing the artist sing or play. The artist, flattered and already sure of one good "notice" at least, would immediately accede; having done his best or worst, something like the following conversation would take place:—

Critic. Quite good. But that A-minor study of Chopin's is, of course, rather hackneyed; you are not, I presume, including it in any of your programmes?

Artist (*rather taken aback*). I must confess I had intended doing so. But if you think....

Critic. I do. Most decidedly I do. There are in Berlin at least ten thousand people who play it; why should you be the ten thousand and first? Debussy, now. Why not Debussy? Or even Busoni. Busoni can write, you know.

Artist (*eagerly*). Yes, yes; I'm playing some Debussy: *Les Poissons d'Or* and *Clair de Lune*.

Critic. *Clair de Lune* is a little *vieux jeu*, don't you think? However, play it. Play it now, I mean.

The artist, half angry, but tremulously anxious to please, does as he is told.

Critic. Oh yes; you have talent. I think, yes, I rather think I shall be able to praise you in my paper. However, we shall see. But there is something, just a little of something, lacking in your style. Your rhythm is not sufficiently fluid. It should, if I may say so, *sway* more. And your use of *tempo rubato*.... Well, now, I could show you. You see, I have heard Debussy himself play that, and I know pre-cise-ly how it should go.

Artist (*absolutely staggered*). Oh ... er ... yes. Quite.

Critic (*having allowed time for his remarks to sink in*). Now what would you say if I were to suggest that I give you a few lessons—say a couple. I would charge you a guinea and a half each: lessons of half-an-hour, you know.

Artist (*looking wildly round*). If you were to suggest such a thing—of course, you haven't done so yet—but if you *were* to suggest it....

Critic (*with most un-German suavity*). Of course, when I said "lessons," I used entirely the wrong word. What I meant was hints and suggestions. Mere indications. A passing on of a tradition—passing it on, you understand, from Debussy to yourself. Not everyone, I need scarcely say, has heard Debussy play. If you were to play Debussy as I know he should be played, you would be one of the first to do so in Berlin, and I in my paper should record the fact.

Artist. I see. Yes, I do see. I think that perhaps you are right. You believe I could—I am rather at a loss for a word—you believe I could, shall we say "absorb," the tradition in a couple of lessons?

Critic. I don't see why you shouldn't, though, of course, I may decide—I mean, we may agree—that a third lesson is necessary. Shall we have our first lesson now?

Artist (*now quite at his ease, slyly*). Lesson? You mean my first "hint," "suggestion," "indication." Right-o.... Let's get along with it.

They are friends: they understand each other. Within twenty-four hours three guineas pass from the pocket of the artist to the pocket of the critic, and, in due time, half-a-dozen lines of praise, golden-guinea praise, appear in the critic's paper.

After all, how simple, how friendly, how altogether right and jovial!

You may think the artist a fool to pay so much for so little, but, really, you are quite wrong. It isn't "so little." It is a good deal. Those half-dozen lines, in the old pre-war days, would help to secure valuable engagements not only in New York, Boston, Philadelphia, Chicago, and the scores of large towns that lie in between, but also in London, Manchester, Bradford, Leeds; in Paris, Lyons, Rouen, Marseilles, Bordeaux, Brussels, Ghent, Antwerp. But not in Germany. Germany knows better. Not in Mannheim, Cologne,

Hanover, Dresden. The secrets of Berlin were known in all the cities and towns of Germany some years before the war, and the playful little habits of the critics of that most wonderful city were looked at askance ... were looked at askance ... were looked at askance *and imitated*. And the imitators had for their secret motto: *Honi soit.*

A beastly city was Berlin. And yet not all of Berlin was beastly. But the artistic, the musical, part of it was "low, very low," as Chawnley Montague said, on an historic occasion, of the slums of Sierra Leone.

But Karl Klindworth had nothing of beastliness in him. In writing about Klindworth I shall, I am convinced, feel rather old, and you, when reading about him, will, I greatly fear, also feel rather old. You see Klindworth belongs so awfully to the past. Yet he was a very great man in his day, and there must be still in London many people who knew him in those silly, savage days when stupid people (and they were brutally stupid) thought of Wagner what brutally stupid people think to-day of Richard Strauss.

Klindworth was not only a disciple of Wagner's but he was also one of Wagner's prophets: a forerunner. A great pianist, also: a great conductor: a great man. Frederick Dawson, one of the most generous-hearted of men, took me to Klindworth's, and said some jolly, flattering things about me to the great musician. Klindworth was very old, about eighty years, and, when he spoke, it was like listening to the voice of a man who had just got beyond the grave and was not unhappy there.

I egged him on to speak of Wagner.

"What can I say?" he mused. "Nothing. Wagner was from God."

His large eyes, two great ponds of colour in a face not white but stained with ivory, smouldered and suddenly burst into flame. His hands, always trembling a little, now shook rather violently. I could not help feeling, as I gazed upon this old man, that Wagner lived in him as strongly as he lives in the mighty scores of *Die Meistersinger* and *Tristan und Isolde*.

We sat silent. Frau Klindworth, an Englishwoman speaking English most charmingly with a foreign accent, folded her hands and gave a little sigh. Dawson shot me a significant look which meant: "Keep quiet; if you do, he will begin to talk."

And for a little while he did. Without a gesture, without a movement, Klindworth, looking with unfocussed eyes into space, began to talk. (He spoke in English, for he knew that I knew very little German.)

"No one," said he, "who was a gentleman, I mean no one who had ordinary feelings of chivalry, could meet Wagner without feeling that he was in the presence of one of the Kings of our world. Certain people, both in England and Germany, have written stupid things of him; they have pointed fingers at his faults, banged their fists upon his sins. I hate those people. Faults and sins? Who has not faults? Who has not committed sins? You English have a word 'uncanny.' Or is it you Scottish people? Wagner was uncanny. He dived into things. Yes, he dived. And every time he lost his body in the blue sea, he brought back a pearl. A pearl? No: pearls have no mystery. He brought back, each time, a hitherto undiscovered gem.... 'Gem'! What silly sounds you have in English.... Jem.... Djem!"

His old mind, outworn and very weary, appeared to cease its functioning. He sat with no sign of life in him. It was as though a clock had stopped, as though a light had gone out. And then, without any apparent cause, he came to life again.

"Let us go to the piano," he said, rising.

So we left the little room in which we were sitting and moved to the large music-room at the far end of which was a grand piano. Frau Klindworth, Dawson and I sat in the semi-darkness near the door; Klindworth's tall but rather shrunken figure moved down the room to the little light that hung above the keyboard. He played some almost unknown pieces of Liszt, interpreting them in a style at once noble and half-ruined. The excitement of playing seemed to increase rather than add strength to his physical weakness, and many wrong notes were struck.

It was very pathetic to see this old man trying to revive the fires within him, trying and failing; and I felt that if, by some miraculous effort, he had succeeded, if the ashes of long-spent fires had indeed broken into hot flame, his frail body would have been consumed.

He gave me his photograph and wrote on the back some message, and when I left him I thought I should never see him again. But, a few days later, I saw him in the front row of one of Frederick Dawson's recitals, and I occasionally heard from him a deep-noted "Bravo!" as Dawson electrified us with one of his stupendous performances.

Klindworth lingered on for some years later and, when I was in Macedonia last year, I saw in some newspaper a few lines recording his death. In the seventies he was a great figure in London, and Wagner-worshippers of those days worshipped Klindworth also, not only for his genius, but also for his loyalty, his noble-mindedness, his devotion to his art.

Out of curiosity on the last day of my stay in Berlin, I went to a famous concert agent's office, ostensibly to make some business inquiries, but, in reality, to have a look at the underworld of art; for the business side of all art has almost invariably an underworld of its own in which there is much irony and in which dwells a spirit of strangely sardonic humour.

The office was crowded with artists, most of them prosperous, all of them of recognised position. Though they were clients of the agent—that is to say, people able and eager to engage his services and pay handsomely for them—they were kept waiting an unconscionable time, as though they had come to beg favours. As, indeed, they had. For Herr Otto Zuggstein always made it perfectly clear by his manner that the favour was his to confer, the honour yours to accept. He had a hot, eager brain, cunning hands and hairy wrists.

And his work, his object in life? Well, he was the connecting-link between the artist and the public, just as a publisher is the connecting-link between authors and those who read. Otto Zuggstein "published" pianists, singers, violinists. He engaged concert halls for them, sold their tickets and collected the money, printed their programmes, distributed tickets to the Press, advertised their recitals, and so on. There are, of course, many such men, men engaged honourably in an honourable profession, in all the big cities of Europe; but Zuggstein was steeped in dishonour. It was freely said of him that he had all the powerful music critics of Berlin in the hollow of his hand. Instead of working for their respective editors they really worked for him. He could command a long and enthusiastic "notice" about almost any artist in almost any paper; he could also secure the publication of the most damning criticisms. If you were a really great artist desiring to "succeed" in Berlin and he, or his friends, considered it against his own and his friends' interest for you to succeed, he could and would prevent you doing so.

He occasionally emerged from the inner room in which he sat, moved among us for a minute or so, exchanging handshakes, smiles and other insincerities, and, singling out a man or a woman with special business claims upon him, returned with his companion to his private office. As he disappeared, some of those who waited smiled significantly at each other.

Zuggstein, as one used to write three or four years ago, "intrigued" me. He was such an efficient rogue: a rogue working, as it appeared, most openly, most flagrantly, but in reality working with an abundance of prepared camouflage.

I waited most patiently and, in the course of time, when he again issued from his private sanctum, he queried me with his right eyebrow, beckoned me almost imperceptibly with his left elbow and, preceding me, made a gangway to his room. I followed him with an air, recognising, as I did so, that I was in for a bit of an adventure, and resolved to lie like poor Beelzebub himself.

"Good-morning," said he in English when the door was closed upon us. "Will you take a chair and also a cigar?" Mysteriously, he produced a box from the region of his knees and looked hard at me. "And a whisky?" he added, with a smile. "I never drink myself," he apologised, "but you English!"

I accepted all three invitations.

"I have come," said I, when I had lit my cigar and savoured it, "I have come to see you about half-a-dozen recitals, piano recitals, that a Norwegian friend of mine wishes to give here in Berlin next January."

"To whom," asked he—and a little chill descended upon him as he asked the question—"to whom have I the honour of speaking?"

I smiled deprecatingly, and produced from my card-case a card bearing the name "Gerald Cumberland."

"I am staying at the Fürstenhof. Room 4001."

Disarmed, but still cautious, he wrote the number of my room on the pasteboard.

"I am, I think it is obvious, from England. This is my first visit to your great city. I am interested in art, in music." I used a careless, all-embracing gesture. "And my Norwegian friend, Mr Sigurd Falk, knowing that I was about to set out for Berlin, asked me to try to arrange certain matters with you. He got your name from a compatriot of his."

By this time he had poured out, and I had drunk most of, the whisky. A peculiar thing happened: whilst it was I who drank the whisky, it was he who became genial—more than genial: almost friendly.

"What," he inquired, "does your friend wish to do in Berlin?"

"Play the piano and make a little money."

He grunted sympathetically, if a man may ever be said to grunt sympathetically.

"Money is difficult to make in Berlin," he said, looking at me keenly, "but I will do my best for him. Six recitals, you say?"

"Six. And at this, our first interview, I wished to have just a rough estimate of what those six recitals are likely to cost."

"Why, it all depends.... Another whisky?... No?... It all depends. Depends on all kinds of things. What hall do you want? I ought, perhaps, to tell you, first of all, what hall you can *have*: you see, you come rather late, very late, in the day. It is now November, and your friend wishes to play in January. All the halls are usually booked months in advance."

We went into particulars of halls, dates, etc. And then he began to scribble figures on a sheet of paper.

"Press?" he queried.

"I *beg* your pardon?"

"You would, I mean your friend would, I imagine, like a favourable Press?"

"Why, yes."

"Audience?"

"Do you mean *any* kind of audience?"

"I am afraid they will be mostly women, though, of course, I can get you a certain number of male students. But the audience, I can promise you, will be well disposed. Three or four encores at least."

"Yes, then, both Press *and* audience."

He scribbled a little more.

"An inclusive estimate?" he asked.

"Please. You mean by inclusive...?"

"Everything," he said impressively; "the hall, the printing, the advertisements, a few invitations, the preliminary paragraphs, the audience, the critics' articles. And not only the critics' notices, but the presence of the critics themselves," he added.

He worked hard for five minutes, looked up data in books, and at length very gently pushed over to me, across the shining top of the table, a properly written out estimate for the recitals my imaginary friend intended to give. The total amount, as represented by English money, was £3.

"Thank you so much," said I; "I will call to see you to-morrow perhaps. But I must first of all get an estimate from Herr Dorn."

"Who is Herr Dorn?" he asked, in surprise.

I did not know: his name had slid into my mind that very moment, and I was not quite sure whether, in the whole world, there was such a name. Then, greatly daring, I greatly lied.

"He is a cousin of Sigurd Falk," said I.

As I left, he gave me another cigar, shook my hand most warmly, and looked me in the eyes very keenly.

Every night Dawson and I used to go either to the opera or to some concert, and, when the music was finished, which was generally very late, we would perhaps go to some supper-party or other.

I have a good appetite myself, but really some of the German ladies' gastronomic feats were superb. I remember myself one night sitting fascinated and awestruck as I saw a Wagner-heroine type of woman, full-breasted, high-browed and majestic, eat plateful after plateful of oysters, until I began to wonder how it was so many oysters came to be in Berlin at one and the same time.

Elena Gerhardt, in those days, was large, white and serene. She was a little bitter, perhaps, and certainly greatly disappointed. I met her in Manchester shortly after my return to England, and found her mind insipid, her soul tepid.

Egon Petri had phlegm almost British: a real slogger: most uninspired: the possessor of faultless technique: the possessor of a brain that retained everything but expounded nothing. He had business ability and pushed ahead all the time: pushed ahead all the time, but never arrived anywhere. Never will arrive anywhere in particular, except at his own well-cleaned doorstep, where the polished knocker will respond to his carefully gloved hand.

Richard Strauss I also met in Manchester at about the same time. I have always maintained that, in at least one case out of three, it is unwise to judge a man by his face.

But I must for a moment digress. This question of faces is most interesting. Every man, of course, makes his own face: even the most ugly of us will concede that much, for, if we are, and know we are, ugly, we always console ourselves with the thought: "Yes, but it is a special kind of ugliness. There is strength in my ugliness. There is character; there is soul. My ugliness is original. There is no ugliness *quite* like my ugliness." For, so long as we are different from other people, that is all that matters. Now, in making our faces—a process that is always continuous from the time we are born to the moment of death—some of us are full of anxiety to make, not a face, but a mask. Our faces do not express our souls: they hide them. The consequence of this is that you will sometimes, though not often, meet a man with a mean, insignificant face who is, in reality, the possessor of a first-rate brain. But it is difficult to repress some facial hint of intellect; try how one may, one can do little to modify the shape of one's brow or give the eye a sodden and unintelligent look.

Richard Strauss has disguised himself. At close quarters one sees at once that his head is both shapely and well poised: one notices the exceptionally high forehead, the firm rounded lips, the determined chin. "A financier," you say to yourself; "at all events, if not a financier, a man of affairs, a man accustomed to deal with and order facts. Certainly not a dreamer—not a poet or a musician or an artist of any kind."

He exhibits no emotion. Self-restrained, he speaks little but very much to the point. Even in moments of great success, he is reserved and businesslike. You can never take him unawares. He is guarded, on the alert, watchful. "All mind but no heart," you say; at least, you say that if you are a careless observer.

His tastes are of the simplest and though, for a composer, he has amassed a large amount of money, he is absurdly economical. He rather likes abuse, and when a critic makes a fool of himself he is inordinately amused. The spectacle of human vanity and human folly excites him. His handshake is firm, his regard direct.

His piano-playing is beautifully neat and polished, but he is not a virtuoso on the instrument.

CHAPTER XIX
SOME MUSICIANS

VERY many years have passed since, one cold winter's afternoon, I met Edvard Grieg on Adolph Brodsky's doorstep. A little figure buried, very deeply buried, in an overcoat at least six inches thick, came down the damp street, paused a minute at the gate, and then, rather hesitatingly, walked up the pathway. He saluted me as he reached the door and we waited together until my summons to those within was answered.

I found him very homely, completely without affectation, childlike, and a little melancholy. He was at that time in indifferent health, and it was at once made evident to me that both Grieg himself and those around him—especially Mrs Brodsky—were very anxious that he should be restored to complete fitness. He said nothing in the least degree noteworthy, but when he did speak he had such a gentle air, a manner so ingratiating and simple, that one found his conversation most unusually pleasant.

Ernest Newman once called Grieg "Griegkin," a most admirable name for this quite first-rate of third-rate composers. His music is diminutive. He could not think largely. He loved country dances, country scenes, the rhythm of homely life, the bounded horizon. Even so extended a work as his Pianoforte Concerto is a series of miniatures. And Grieg the man was precisely like Grieg the artist. He was Griegkin in his appearance, his manner, his way of speaking: a little man: a gracious little man. His attitude towards his host and hostess was that of an affectionate child. Such dear simplicity is, I think, in the artist found only among men of northern races.

Some years later, in an intimate little circle, I was to hear his widow sing and play many of her husband's songs. She was the feminine counterpart of himself—spirited, a little sad, simple yet wise, frank, and an artist through and through.

A great deal of comedy is lost to the world through lack of historians. It is almost impossible to conceive that Sir F. H. Cowen should ever have been in serious competition with Hans Richter: impossible to conceive that half the musical inhabitants of a large city should have been ranged fiercely on Sir Frederick's side, and the other half ranged on the side of Richter: impossible to conceive that both Cowen and Richter were candidates for the same post. Yet so it was.

Sir Charles Hallé, who had founded and conducted for about half-a-century the famous orchestral concerts in Manchester still known by his name, died and left no successor. Literally, there was no one to appoint in his place, no one quite good enough. Month after month went by, a good many distinguished and semi-distinguished musicians came to Manchester and conducted an odd concert or two, but it was very widely felt that no British musician would do. Sir Frederick Cowen, always an earnest and accomplished composer, came for a season or two and did some admirable work, but Cowen was not Hallé. Then the German element in Manchester discovered that Richter would come, if invited. The salary was large, the work not heavy, the climate awful, the people devoted, the position unusually powerful. All things considered, it was one of the few really good vacant musical posts in Europe.

All this is ancient history now, and I will record only briefly that ultimately Sir Frederick Cowen was, in effect, told (what, no doubt, he already knew) that Richter was the better man and that he (Cowen) must go. But before this decision was made a most severe fight was waged in the city. Cowen conducted, and thousands of partisans came and cheered him to the echo. Richter conducted, and thousands of partisans came and cheered him to the echo. People wrote to the newspapers. Leader writers solemnly summed up the situation from day to day. Protests were made, meetings were organised and held, votes of confidence were passed. London caught the infection, and passed its opinion, its opinions....

Sir F. H. Cowen (he was "Mr" then) received me in his rooms at the Manchester Grand Hotel. It was impossible not to like him, for, if he had no great positive qualities that seized upon you at once, he had a good many negative ones. He had no "side," no self-importance, no eccentricities. He had neither long hair nor a foreign accent. He did not use a cigarette-holder. He did not loll when he sat down, or posture when he stood up. And he had not just discovered a new composer of Dutch extraction.... These are small things, you say. But are they?...

I remember looking at him and wondering if he really *had* written *The Better Land*. It seemed so unlikely. Faultlessly dressed, immaculately groomed, how *could* he have written *The Better Land*—that luteous land that is so sloppy, so thickly covered with untidy debris?

He would not talk of the musical situation in Manchester, and I could see that he was very sensitive about his uncomfortable position.

"If I am wanted, I shall stay," was all he would give me.

"And are you going to write about me in the paper?" asked he, at the end of our interview; "how interesting that will be!" And he smiled with gentle satire.

"I shall make it as interesting as I can," I assured him, "but, you see, you have said so little."

"Does that matter?" he returned. "I have always heard that you gentlemen of the Press can at least—shall we say embroider?"

"But may I?" I asked.

"How can I prevent you? Do tell me how I can, and I will."

"Well, you can insist upon seeing the article before it appears in print."

"Oh, 'insist' is not a nice word, is it? But if you would be kind enough to send me the article before your Editor has it...."

Hans Richter was an autocrat, a tyrant. During the years he conducted in Manchester, he did much splendid work, but it may well be questioned if, on the whole, his influence was beneficial to Manchester citizens. He was so tremendously German! So tremendously German indeed, that he refused to recognise that there was any other than Teutonic music in the world. His intellect had stopped at Wagner. At middle age his mind had suddenly become set, and he looked with contempt at all Italian and French music, refusing also to see any merit in most of the very fine music that, during the last twenty years, has been written by British composers.

He irked the younger and more turbulent spirits in Manchester, and we were constantly attacking him in the Press. But with no effect. Richter was like that. He ignored attacks. He was arrogant and spoiled and bad-tempered.

"Why don't you occasionally give us some French music at your concerts?" he was asked.

"French music?" he roared; "there *is* no French music."

And, certainly, whenever he tried to play even Berlioz one could see that he did not regard his work as music. And he conducted Debussy, so to speak, with his fists. And as for Dukas...!

Young British musicians used to send him their compositions to read, but the parcels would come back, weeks later, unread and unopened. His mind never inquired. His intellect lay indolent and half-asleep on a bed of spiritual down. And the thousands of musical Germans in Manchester treated him so like a god that in course of time he came to believe he was a god. His manners were execrable. On one occasion, he bore down upon me in a corridor at the back of the platform in the Free Trade Hall. I stood on one side to allow him to pass, but Richter was very wide and the corridor very narrow. Breathing heavily, he kept his place in the middle of the passage.... I felt the impact of a mountain of fat and heard a snort as he brushed past me.

Everyone was afraid of him. Even famous musicians trembled in his presence. I remember dining with one of the most eminent of living pianists at a restaurant where, at a table close at hand, Richter also was dining. The previous evening Richter had conducted at a concert at which the pianist had played, and the great conductor had praised my friend in enthusiastic terms; moreover, they had met before on several occasions.

"I'll go and have a word with the Old Man, if you'll excuse me," said my friend.

I watched him go. Smiling a little, ingratiatingly, he bowed to Richter, and then bent slightly over the table at which the famous musician was dining alone. Richter took not the slightest notice. My friend, embarrassed, waited a minute or so, and I saw him speaking. But the diner continued dining. Again my friend spoke, and at length Richter looked up and barked three times. Hastily the pianist retreated, and when he had rejoined me I noticed that he was a little pale and breathless.

"The old pig!" he exclaimed.

"Why, what happened?"

"Didn't you see? First of all, he wouldn't take the slightest notice of me or even acknowledge my existence. I spoke to him in English three times before he would answer, and then, like the mannerless brute he is, he replied in German."

"What did he say?"

"How do I know? I don't speak his rotten language. But it sounded like: 'Zuzu westeben hab! Zuzu westeben hab! Zuzu westeben hab!' I only know that he was very angry. He was eating slabs of liver sausage. And he spoke right down in his chest."

He was, indeed, unapproachable.

Of course, he was a marvellous conductor, a conductor of genius; but long before he left Manchester his powers had begun to fail.

For two or three years I made a practice of attending his rehearsals. Nothing will persuade me that in the whole world there is a more depressing spot than the Manchester Free Trade Hall on a winter's morning. I used to sit shivering with my overcoat collar buttoned up. Richter always wore a round black-silk cap, which made him look like a Greek priest. He would walk ponderously to the conductor's desk, seize his baton, rattle it against the desk, and begin without a moment's loss of time. Perhaps it was an innocent work like Weber's *Der Freischütz* Overture. This would proceed swimmingly enough for a minute or so, when suddenly one would hear a bark and the music would stop. One could not say that Richter spoke or shouted: he merely made a disagreeable noise. Then, in English most broken, in English utterly smashed, he would correct the mistake that had been made, and recommence conducting without loss of a second.

He had no "secret." Great conductors never do have "secrets." Only charlatans "mesmerise" their orchestras. Simply, he knew his job, he was a great economiser of time, and he was a stern disciplinarian.

He could lose his temper easily. He hated those of us who were privileged to attend his rehearsals. He declared, quite unwarrantably, that we talked and disturbed him. But he never appeared to be in the least disturbed by the handful of weary women who, with long brushes, swept the seats and the floor of the hall, raising whirlpools of dust fantastically here and there, and banging doors in beautiful disregard of the Venusberg music and in protest against the exquisite Allegretto from the Seventh Symphony.

Sir Thomas Beecham (he was then plain "Mr") brought a tin of tobacco to the restaurant, placed it on the table, and proceeded to fill his pipe. He was not communicative. He simply sat back in his chair, smoking quietly, and behaving precisely as though he were alone, though, as a matter of fact, there were four or five people in his company. He was not shy: he was simply indifferent to us. If you spoke to him, he merely said "no" or "yes" and looked bored. He *was* bored.

And so he sat for ten minutes; then, with a little sigh, he rose and departed from among us, without a word, without a look. He just melted away and never returned.

I rather dreaded meeting Sir Charles Santley, and when I rang at his door-bell, I remember devoutly wishing that in a moment I should hear that he was out, or that he had changed his mind and no longer desired to see me. I dreaded meeting him because I realised that, temperamentally, we were opposed. I had read his reminiscences and disliked him intensely for the things he had said of Rossetti. Instinctively, I drew away from his robust, tough-fibred mind.

But he was in, and in half-a-minute I was talking to an old, but still vigorous, gentleman whose one desire appeared to be to put me at my ease. I do not think I ever met a man so honest, so blunt. I felt that his mind was direct and his judgment decisive, but I found him lacking in subtlety, unable to respond to the mystical in art, and wholly deficient in true imaginative qualities. He was Victorian.

Now, I don't suppose any of us who are living to-day (and when I say "living" I mean anyone whose mind is still developing—most people, say, under the age of forty-five) will be able to understand the point of view of the Victorian musician. It appears to me monstrous that anyone should still love Mendelssohn and hate Wagner, that anyone should sing J. L. Hatton in preference to Hugo Wolf, that anyone should still delight in Donizetti and Bellini. Those Victorian days were days when the singer wished that his own notions of the limitations of the human voice should control the free development of music. They loved *bel canto* and nothing else; they averred, indeed, that there was nothing else to love. They were admirable musicians from the technical point of view, and they had honest hearts and by no means feeble intellects. But they could never be brought to believe that music was a reflection of life, that there were in the human heart a thousand shades of feeling that not even Handel had expressed, that sound is capable of a million subtleties, that the ear of man is an organ that is, so to speak, only in its infancy.

It was a little pathetic, I thought, when speaking to Santley, that this very great singer had been living for at least thirty years entirely untouched by many of the finest compositions that had been written in that period.

And he declared, quite frankly, that "modern" music had no interest for him. When I mentioned Richard Strauss, he smiled. At the name of Debussy, he looked bewildered, and about Max Reger, Scriabin, Granville Bantock, Sibelius and Delius, he had not a word to say.

But soon we got on to his own subject—singing—and here again we were at cross-purposes. Singers who to me seem supreme artists he had either not heard of or had not heard.

"There is only one British singer to-day who carries on the old tradition," said he; "I mean Madame Kirkby Lunn. She has technique, style, personality. The others, compared with her, are nowhere."

Some general talk followed, and I soon discovered, beyond the possibility of doubt, that, like all great Victorians who have had their day, he was living in the past—in that particular past whose artistic spirit is embodied in the Albert Memorial, in the musical criticism of J. W. Davidson, in the pianoforte playing of Arabella Godard, in the poetry of Lord Tennyson, in the pictures of Lord Leighton, in the prose of Ruskin.

What had Santley to say to me, or I to him? Nothing, and less than nothing. We were from different worlds, different planets, for half-a-century divided us. In years, he was nearer to the Elizabethan age than I ... and yet how much farther away was he?

Perhaps Mr Landon Ronald will not be angry with me if I call him the most accomplished of British musicians. He would have every right to be angry if I said he was accomplished and nothing else.... How far back that word "accomplished" takes us, doesn't it? Twenty years, at least. For aught I know to the contrary, it may still be employed in Putney. I observe that Chambers defines "accomplishment" as an "ornamental acquirement," and, in my boyhood, that was precisely what it meant. Young ladies "acquired" the art of playing the piano, the art of painting, the art of recitation. Their skill in any art was not the result of developing a talent that was already there, but it was the result of a pertinacity that should have been spent on other things. But one no longer uses "accomplished" in that precise sense.

Landon Ronald has more than a streak of genius in his nature, and his cleverness is so abnormal as to be almost absurd. His genius and his cleverness are evident even in a few minutes' conversation. He radiates cleverness, and he is so splendidly alive that as soon as he enters a room you feel that something quick and electric has been added to your environment.

When I first met him—ten years ago, was it?—his one ambition was to be recognised throughout Europe as a great conductor. He was acknowledged as such in England, of course, and a visit to Rome had fired both the Italian public and critics with enthusiasm. But London and Rome are not Europe, whilst in those days Berlin most distinctly was. He was most charmingly frank about himself, full of enthusiasm for himself, full of delight in all life's adventures.

"Of course, I know my songs aren't *real* songs," he said. "I can write tunes and I'm a musician, and I'm just clever enough to be cleverer than most people at that sort of work. But you must not imagine I take my compositions seriously. I think they're rather nice—'nice' *is* the word, isn't it?—and I enjoy inventing them—and 'inventing' is also the word, don't you think? Besides, they make money; they help to boil the pot for me while I go on with my more serious work—that is to say, conducting."

Havergal Brian was in the room—we were in that fulsome and blowzy town, Blackpool—and he remarked, as so many extraordinarily able composers have from time to time remarked, that he found it impossible to write music that the public really liked.

"Nearly all my stuff," said he, "is on a big scale for the orchestra. I am always trying to do something new—something out of the common rut."

"Ah, but then," exclaimed Ronald, quite sincerely, "you are a composer, and I am not."

Brian was appeased, and I looked at Ronald with admiration for his tact. But he went even a little farther.

"I sometimes feel rather a pig," he continued, "making money by my trifles when so many men with much greater gifts can only rarely get their work performed and still more rarely get it published. You told us just now," said he, turning to Brian, "that you would like to make money by your compositions. Who wouldn't? Well, it would be foolish of me to advise you to try to write more simply, with less originality, and on a smaller scale. It would be foolish, because you simply couldn't do it. No; you must work out your own salvation: it is only a matter of waiting: success will come."

A month or two later, we met at Southport, I in the meantime having written an article on Ronald for a musical magazine. With this article he professed himself charmed. He was as jolly about it as a schoolboy, and expressed surprise that I could honestly say such nice things about him.

"It *is* good to be praised," said he, laughing; "I could live on praise for ever." And then, lighting a cigarette, he added: "Perhaps the reason why I like it so much is that I feel I really deserve it."

It was my turn to laugh.

"But I do feel that!" he protested; "if I didn't, I should hate you or anyone else to say such frightfully kind things about me and my work."

A month or two later he wrote me a long letter full of enthusiasm for some work of mine he had seen somewhere, and when I saw him the following week in London I protested against his undiluted praise.

"I believe you think I am a bit of a humbug," said he.

"I'm afraid I do," I replied. (For, really, I think almost all subtle and clever artists are bits of humbugs.)

"Very good, then!" exclaimed he, ridiculously hurt.

"What I mean is, that if you like anyone, your judgment is immediately prejudiced in their favour."

"So you think I like you?"

"I am sure of it."

"Well, you're quite right. But, really and truly, you mustn't call me, or even think me, the slightest bit of a humbug. You can call me impulsive, superficial, or anything horrid of that kind ... but insincere! Why, sincerity is the only real virtue I've got."

And I believe he believed himself. But who is sincere?—at least, who is sincere except at the moment? Are not all of us who are artists swayed hither and thither, from hour to hour, by the emotion of the moment? Do we not say one thing now, and an hour later mean exactly the opposite? Are we not driven by our enthusiasms to false positions, and do not glib, untrue words spring to our lips because the moment's mood forces them there?

I have not met Landon Ronald for four years, but the other day I heard him conduct, and I recognised in his interpretations the supreme qualities I have so often observed before. He himself is like his work—polished, highly strung, emotional, fluid, intense. His mind works with lightning-like quickness; he knows what you are going to say just a second before you have said it. And over his personality hangs the glamour that we call genius.

Many well-known singers have I met, but very few of them inspire me to burst into song. They are a dull, vain crew. Among the few most notable exceptions is Frederic Austin, a man with a temperament so refined, with a nature so retiring, that it is a constant source of wonder to me that he should be where he now is—in the front rank of vocalists.

Years ago Ernest Newman said to me:

"Frederic Austin has become a fine singer through sheer brain-work. He always had temperament, but his voice was never in the least remarkable until by ingenious training, by constant thought, and by the most arduous labour he developed it until it became an organ of sufficient strength and richness to enable him to interpret anything that appeals to him."

He is, I think, the only eminent singer in this country who is a distinguished composer. But perhaps the most remarkable thing about him is that you might very easily pass days in his company without guessing that he is a famous singer, for his personality suggests qualities that famous singers seldom possess. He is *distingué*, austere, and devoted to his art.

CHAPTER XX
TWO CHELSEA "RAGS," 1914 AND 1918

1914

IT used to begin as a rumour, a faint stirring and excitement in King's Road, Chelsea. The artist on the top floor of Joubert Studios—an artist who had a private income and a gently nursed hypochondria—received a parcel from home: a couple of cooked chickens, perhaps, a tongue, cakes, crystallised fruits, three bottles of wine and so on. The lady who occupied the studio below, and the musical critic who lived in the third studio from the top, were duly apprised of the fact, and Norman and Eddie Morrow were called in from near by for a consultation.

"Clearly," the lady remarked, "a rag is indicated. A rag must always have a beginning, and this undoubtedly is a most excellent beginning. Ring up Susie, somebody, and fetch Hearn over and Ivan and let the Cumberlands know; and, oh! Hughes, dear little Herbert, lend me your pots and pans and things. And, Warlow, just run round everywhere and tell all the people you meet. Don't forget John, and I think that Deane would like that girl with fuzzy hair. We'll begin at seven. No, we won't: we'll begin now."

And Warlow, nursing his hypochondria and being very biddable, sighed and moved away, saying beseechingly as he went:

"You *will* leave me a wing, won't you? I've had no breakfast yet."

But neither had the rest, and by the time Warlow, suffering in a resigned and patient kind of way from paleness and breathlessness, returned, one of the chickens had vanished, and the long table with its litter of paper, cardboard, pencils and paint, was now littered also with plates and knives and forks and breadcrumbs. The rag had begun.

The month was May, a true May with a warm wind, a warmer sun, and fluttering green leaves. The little party—the nucleus of the much larger party that was to meet there in the evening—drifted downstairs to Hughes's studio where there was a grand piano and a portable harmonium which appeared to belong to no one in particular. Hughes, looking a little ruefully at the MS. upon which he was engaged, put it away on a shelf, opened his wide windows and began to play. Harry Lowe, with his magnificent but untrained voice, appeared dramatically in the doorway and sang:

Largo grandioso	For he's a Scotsman, a bonny Scotsman, His feyther and his mither, His sister and his brither—
(Forte)	They are *all* Scotch, from the land of Roderick Dhu;
(Vivace)	And the whitewash brush in the middle of his kilt
(Piano)	Is all Sco-otch too.

This went to a great tune devised, invented, composed and arranged by Hughes and Lowe. The great air, heard with its cunning chatter of an accompaniment from the piano, put everyone in the right mood, and Norman Morrow, whose head was always full of ideas, began to prepare "stunts" for the evening, whilst Warlow, having nothing better to do, attired himself as an Italian Count, sat at the open window, and smiled sadly at all the girls whose attention he could attract in the street below.

Norman's idea was a revue—a revue of Any Old Thing: Mona Lisa, the sale of beautiful slaves, the Salome Dance by six-foot-two Harry Lowe, the Innocent Wench who took the Wrong Turning, etc., etc. He wanted to prepare the groundwork for the evening's performance; the details could be filled in on the spur of the moment. But, in the afternoon rehearsal, several scenes, exciting the actors, were studied carefully to the most minute particular. Kitty, in the meantime, was upstairs preparing food, her dainty hands fluttering over salads and sandwiches. At six, jolly, lovable little Susie rushed from her work, revitalised everybody, and sang in her funny little voice, holding a cigarette in one hand and a saucepan in the other.

But before the Rag Proper began, many charming idiocies were enacted. Warlow and Eddie Morrow walked to Sloane Square (it is conceivable that they called at the Six Bells on the way) for the sole purpose of riding back again in a taxi-cab, Warlow in a great Russian overcoat smothered in fur, Eddie a little unkempt and looking as though he had just stepped out of one of J. M. Synge's plays. Harry Lowe telephoned a number of telegrams to a far-off post office where it was supposed there was a lady who owned his heart and sold postage stamps. Norman Morrow sat in a corner daubing pieces of brown paper with yellow paint and chuckling inconsequently to himself. All three studios, one above the other, appeared to be in glorious disorder, but, as a matter of fact, nearly every brain was busy with preparations, and by seven o'clock everything was ready for the great rag....

I cannot re-create the scene for you. I do not know quite how it is, but the gaiety, the light-heartedness of that most jolly evening ooze from my heart as I write. I am not sufficient of an artist to sweep from my heart all the sad, irrecoverable things that my heart remembers. Especially, I cannot forget Ivan Heald, who now lies dead. (A year later he was to say to me, in that same studio: "This is a real good-bye, Gerald. It is not possible that both of us will survive this.".... And, of course, it is he who has gone. One feels mean in surviving, in enjoying the savour of life, when one's best friends have departed.) ...

The artistic Irishman is a perfect actor, an inimitable mimic, and the two Morrows surpassed everyone. If ever you have seen Eddie Morrow, it will appear to you inconceivable that he could ever make a good Mona Lisa. Yet his Mona Lisa was perfect. He smiled so mysteriously, so faintly, so imaginatively, that Walter Pater, had he seen him, would have rewritten that swooning chapter which contains so much of art's opiate.... I remember Edith Heald who, unexpectedly to me, revealed consummate art as a nigger-boy, her eyes rolling in rapt wonderment. I remember Hearn's eyeglasses, and the smiling eyes behind them, and the little scurry of words that occasionally came from his lips when something magical touched his spirit. And I can hear Herbert Hughes' contented voice saying: "Well, this is rather splendid, don't you know."

Hughes was awfully good to me on these occasions, for he would allow me to improvise the music for the dumb charades, though as an extempore player—and, indeed, as a player of any kind—he is worlds above me. And I used to love to invent Eastern Dances à la Bantock to fit the gyrations of Harry Lowe, or Debussy chords for anything shadowy and sentimental, or chromatic melodies—prolonged and melting things in the "O Star of Eve" manner—for luscious love scenes, or fat, bulgy discords when some real tomfoolery was afoot.

You must imagine everybody gay and, occasionally, just a little riotous; in remembrance, it seems to me very beautiful because so happy and childlike. And you must imagine everybody very friendly, even to complete strangers. There was a carnival atmosphere. Clever people were there with their brains burning bright. There were wit, music, wine, pretty women, courtesy, infinite good-will.

Perhaps, towards midnight, we would seek change in quietness, and, lying on rugs spread on the waxed floor, would listen to Norman singing, unaccompanied, an Irish Rebel song, and something a little hard would come into Irish Susie's eyes for a moment or two, and I remember with regret how, some months after war had broken out, I said after Norman had been singing that it was no longer pleasant to me to hear Rebel songs. Regret? Yes; for when I said that I was a prig and was imagining myself as something of a soldier-hero. If only Norman were alive now to sing whatsoever songs he liked!

Well, the evening lapsed into night and the night into morn, and again we became boisterous and new ideas were put into shape and little tragedies were given in the burlesque manner. The resourcefulness of the mimes! The devilishly clever satire! The good spirits that never failed!...

It is no use. I cannot describe for you one of those great nights, for the mood will not come. And one of the reasons why I cannot recapture the spirit of a Chelsea Rag as it was in the old days, is because whilst I am writing I have in my mind a picture of a very different kind.

1918

Early in 1918 I was in London for a brief period after an absence from England of more than two years spent in France, Egypt, Greece and Serbia. My health was broken, my spirits were low. The Chelsea people were dispersed; only Hearn, with his lame foot, was left of the men, but several of the women were to be found. Herbert Hughes, by some miracle, was on leave, and he turned up unexpectedly one night at my flat. We talked quietly, laughed a little, had some music, and fell into silence.

"Those great days!" said I, apropos of nothing.

"Yes. Nothing like them will come again. But all of us who remain alive and are still in England must meet. What about next Sunday? We'll meet at Madame's."

And so it was arranged. Next Sunday there were seven of us to make merry, whereas in former days there were forty or fifty. But we seven were together once more: we who, as it were, had been saved — saved perhaps only temporarily.

It is a long studio in which we sit, but screens enclose a piano, the fireplace, a few rugs and chairs, and a table. Madame is tall and quiet and distinguished; her light soprano voice conveys an impression of wistfulness, and her personality, full of charm and a sadness that does not conceal her courage, diffuses itself throughout the room. We have met together for a rag, but no one evinces the least desire to indulge in any violent jollity.

Hughes goes to the piano, for a piano always draws him as a magnet draws steel, and sometimes, half-consciously, he feels the pull of one before he has seen it. He goes to the piano and, perking his nose at an angle of about forty degrees with the horizontal, plays French songs very quietly, whilst we sit gazing into the heart of the fire, each with his own thoughts, and probably each with the same thoughts—thoughts of Harry Lowe in Greece, of Gordon Warlow in Mesopotamia, of those who lie dead, though but two years before they were more alive than we ourselves, of those who have gone to France and never returned....

And Madame, moving with our thoughts, gently rises and joins Hughes and begins, her hands clasped on her breast, to sing with most alluring grace things by Hahn, Debussy and Duparc. The music lulls us into a very luxury of sadness, into a mood in which grief loses its edge and sorrow its poignancy. To me, who have heard no music for two years, her singing is mercilessly beautiful, so beautiful, indeed, that my breathing becomes uneven and my eyes wet. And once again I feel that spinal shiver which, as a little boy, I used to experience when I heard an anthem by Gounod or just caught the sound of a military band as it marched down another road.... I never used to run from the house to see the band, for even in those early days I had an intuitive knowledge that beauty is mystery, and that to probe mysteries is to mar, if not altogether to kill, beauty.... And to-night, when Madame comes to the end of each song, I do not speak, I scarcely breathe, so fearful am I that the spell may be broken. But something of the spell lasts even when she ceases singing altogether and, looking at my wife, I know that she feels it too—that, indeed, all in our little company are more quietly happy, more reconciled to all the brutality and ugliness over the sea, than we have been for a long age.

We talk in quiet tones about the past, the present and the future, each contributing something to the common stock of conversation. Madame brings us tea and cakes, and we listen to the dim rumour of traffic in King's Road. And then, not very late, moved by a common impulse, we rise to leave, and talking softly as we go, make our way outside where, as we did in that spot three years ago, we say farewell, wondering as we do so what Fate has in store for each of us and whether for one or more of us this is the end of our life in Chelsea—a life in which we have worked hard and played hard, enjoying both work and play, and in which we have been carelessly unmindful of the danger lying in wait for our country.

CHAPTER XXI
SOME MORE MUSICIANS

AT the present moment there are only two names that are of vital importance in British creative music—Sir Edward Elgar and Granville Bantock. No two men could be in more violent contrast: Elgar, conservative, soured with the aristocratic point of view, super-refined, deeply religious; Bantock, democratic, Rabelaisian, free-thinking, gorgeously human.

Of the two, Bantock is the more original, the deeper thinker, the more broadly sympathetic.

It must be about ten years ago that, staying a week-end with Ernest Newman, I was taken by my host one evening to Bantock's house in Moseley. I remember Bantock's bulky form rising from the table at which he was scoring the first part of his setting of *Omar Khayyám*, and I recollect that, as soon as we had shaken hands, he took from his pocket an enormous cigar-case of many compartments that shut in upon themselves concertina-fashion. From another pocket he produced a huge match-box containing matches almost as large as the chips of wood commonly used for lighting fires. Having carefully selected a cigar for me, he struck a match that, spluttering like a firework, calmed down into a huge blaze. He gazed upon me very solemnly and rather critically all the time I was lighting up, but his face relaxed into a smile when, having plunged my cigar into the middle of the flame, I left it there for many seconds and did not withdraw it until the cigar itself had momentarily flamed and until it glowed like a miniature furnace.

I was destined to smoke very many of Bantock's cigars, and I hope that when the war is over I shall smoke many more; but I never lit a cigar he handed me without noticing that he invariably observed me very closely and a trifle anxiously, as though afraid I should fail in some detail of the holy rite. I do not think I ever did fail, for he never met me without offering me a cheroot, which he certainly would never have done if I had omitted any necessary observance of the lighting ceremonial.

That first evening we talked a good deal—at least, Newman and a few other friends did; but Bantock, never a very loquacious man, committed himself to nothing save a few generalities. By no means a cautious man in his mode of life, he is nevertheless cautious in his choice of friends, and no man can freeze more quickly than he when uncongenial company is thrust upon him. There were several strangers in our little circle, and Bantock was content for the most part to sit back in his easy-chair and listen.

The following night we met again at the Midland Institute, Birmingham, where Ernest Newman was giving one of his witty and brilliant lectures. Bantock insisted upon my sitting on the platform, though for what reason I do not know, unless it was to satisfy his impish instinct for putting shy and self-conscious people into prominent positions. At that time he and Newman were the closest of friends, and as Newman and I were on very friendly terms, Bantock was disposed to regard me very favourably; at all events, before we parted that evening, he showed me clearly enough that he did not actually dislike me, for he invited me to visit him for a week-end whenever I saw my way clear to do so. From that time onward I met him frequently in his own house, in Manchester, London, Wrexham, Gloucester, Liverpool, Birmingham and elsewhere.

Soon it became a regular practice of mine to run over from Manchester to Liverpool every alternate Saturday to attend the afternoon rehearsal and the evening concert of the Philharmonic Society, the orchestra of which Bantock conducted. These were very pleasant meetings, for a party of us used to stay at the London and North Western Hotel and we would sit until the small hours of Sunday morning talking music, returning to our respective homes on Sunday afternoon. At these times Bantock was at his best, and Bantock's best makes the finest company in the world. In his presence one always feels warm and deeply comfortable, and yet very much alive; he made a glow; he reconciled one to oneself. I would not call him a brilliant, or even a good, talker, but I can with truth call him a very wise one; and in argument he is unassailable.

Though I used frequently to go to Liverpool to hear Bantock conduct, I did not do so because I regarded him as a great artist with the baton. Of his ability in this direction, there is no doubt; but that he is an interpretative genius no qualified critic would assert. No: it was the personality of the man himself, and the new, modern works he used to include in his programmes that drew me to Liverpool. Bantock, at that period, was almost passionately modern. I remember with amusement how pettish he used sometimes to pretend to be when, perhaps in deference to public opinion (but perhaps he was overruled by a Committee?), he felt compelled to include a Beethoven symphony in one of his concerts.

On one occasion I met him at Lime Street Station, Liverpool, when he emerged from the train carrying a bundle of loose scores under his arm.

"Let me carry your books for you," said I.

He selected the least bulky and lightest of the scores he was carrying, and handed it to me.

"You are always a good chap, Cumberland," he remarked. "Do take this; it's the heaviest of the lot: Beethoven's Fifth Symphony. So very heavy." He sighed. "And so dry that merely to carry it makes me thirsty. How many times have you heard it?"

But he was poking a cigar into my mouth, and I could not answer until it was well alight.

"At least fifty or sixty. Oh, more than that! Eight times, say, every year for the last fifteen years—one hundred and twenty."

"Yes, always a good chap, and so very patient," he murmured to himself. "Do you know, Cumberland, I had to work—yes, to *work*—at that Symphony in the train. And I define work as doing something that gives you no pleasure. Talking about work, I must post these before I forget."

He took from his pocket a number of post cards all addressed to Ernest Newman. These post cards appeared to amuse him immensely, and he handed them to me with a smile. There were about a dozen of them, and each bore an anagram of the word "work"—KROW, WROK, ROWK, RWKO, etc.

"He'll receive these by the first post in the morning," Bantock explained, "and if they don't succeed in making him jump out of bed and finish his analysis of my *Omar Khayyám* for Breitkopf and Härtel, nothing will."

Point was added to the jest by the fact that Newman has always been a particularly hard, and generally very heavily pressed worker.

In his early manhood Bantock travelled a good deal in the East, not so much by choice, but because circumstances drove him thither. Yet I often feel that the East is his natural home. Whether or not he has any close acquaintance with Eastern languages, I do not know, but he certainly likes his friends to think he has, and many of the letters he has sent me contain quotations and odd words written in what I take to be Persian and Chinese characters. I should not, however, be in the least surprised to learn that these are "faked," for Bantock loves nothing so much as gently pulling the legs of his friends.

He has not, however, the foresight of Eastern people. His enthusiasms drive him into extremes and into monetary extravagances. When he lived at Broadmeadow, with its extensive wooded grounds, outside Birmingham, he had a mania for bulbs, and I remember his showing me a stable the floor of which was covered with crocus, daffodil, jonquil and narcissus bulbs.

"But," protested I, "these ought to have been planted months ago."

"I know, I know," he said sadly. "But the gardener is so busy. Still, there they are."

His philosophic outlook has been largely directed by Eastern philosophy. He admires cunning and takes a beautiful and childlike delight in believing that he possesses that quality in abundance. But in reality, he cannot deceive. Even his card tricks are amateurish, and his chess-playing is only just good.

Apropos of his chess-playing, I remember that some years ago a chess enthusiast—a bore of the vilest description—used to visit him regularly and stay to a very late hour for the purpose of playing a game. These visits soon became intolerable, and, one evening, as Bantock, irritated and petulant, sat opposite his opponent, he resolved to put an end to the nuisance.

"Excuse me a moment," said he; "I have left my cigar-box upstairs, and I really can't do without a smoke."

He left the room, and went straight to bed and to sleep. Next time he met his visitor, they merely bowed.

Bantock used to relate this story with the greatest glee, and in the course of time the yarn grew to colossal dimensions. It became epical. One was told how his visitor was heard calling: "Bantock! Bantock! I've taken your Queen," how strange noises proceeded from dark rooms, and how, next morning, his visitor, having sat up all night, was found wide awake trying the effect of certain combinations of moves on the board. When a thing is said three times, it is, of course, true, but Bantock never told exactly the same story three times. He believes, I think, that consistency is the refuge and the consolation of the dull-witted.

Frederick Delius, a Yorkshireman, has chosen to live most of his artistic life abroad, and for this reason is not familiarly known to his countrymen, though he is a great personage in European music. A pale man, ascetic, monkish; a man with a waspish wit; a man who allows his wit to run away with him so far that he is tempted to express opinions he does not really hold.

I met him for a short hour in Liverpool, where, over food and drink snatched between a rehearsal and a concert, he showed a keen intellect and a fine strain of malice. Like most men of genius, he is curiously self-centred, and I gathered from his remarks that he is not particularly interested in any music except his own. He is (or was) greatly esteemed in Germany, and if in his own country he has not a large following, he alone is to blame.

He is a man who pursues a path of his own, indifferent to criticism, and perhaps indifferent to indifference. Decidedly a man of most distinguished intellect and a quick, eager but not responsive personality, but not a musician who marks an epoch as does Richard Strauss, and not a man who has formed a school, as Debussy has done.

Joseph Holbrooke, for sheer cleverness, for capacity for hard work, and for intellectual energy, has no equal among our composers. It was Newman who first spoke to me about him, and it was Newman who made me curious to meet this extraordinary genius.

Holbrooke's weakness—but I do not consider it a weakness—is his pugnacity. He has fought the critics times without number and, in many cases, with excellent results for British music, though Holbrooke must know much better than I do that in fighting for his colleagues he has incidentally injured himself. A chastised critic is the last person in the world likely to write a fair and unbiassed article on a new work produced by the hand that chastised him. But not only the critics have felt the lash of Holbrooke's scorn: conductors, musical institutions, some very prosperous so-called composers, committees, publishers and, indeed, almost every kind of man who has power in the musical world, have felt his sting.

But if he is clever and witty in his writing, he is much cleverer and wittier in his talk. I do not suppose I shall ever forget one Sunday I spent with him, for by midday he had reduced my mind to chaos and my body to limpness by his consuming energy. When he was not playing, he was talking, and he did both as though the day were the last he was going to spend on earth, so eager and convulsive was his speech, so vehement his playing.

Perhaps his most remarkable quality is his power of concentration. I remember his telling me that when he was yachting with Lord Howard de Walden in the Mediterranean, he was engaged on the composition of *Dylan*, an opera containing some of the most gorgeous and weirdly uncanny music that has been written in our generation. At this opera he worked, not in hours of inspiration (for, like Arnold Bennett, he does not believe in inspiration), but when he had nothing more exciting or more necessary to do. For example, he would begin work in the morning, cheerfully and without regret lay down his pen at lunch-time, return to his music immediately lunch was finished, and unhesitatingly recommence writing at the point at which he had left off. Interruptions that arouse the anger of the ordinary creative artist do not disturb him in the least. He can work just as composedly and as fluently when a heated argument is being conducted in the room as he can in a room that is absolutely quiet. Music, indeed, flows from him, and if moods come to him which render his brain numb and his soul barren, I doubt if they last more than a day or two.

Of the truly vast quantity of music he has written, I, to my regret, know only a portion, and that belongs chiefly to his very early period, when he was under the influence of Edgar Allan Poe. Poe is his spiritual affinity, and Holbrooke's setting of *Annabel Lee*—a work which I can play backwards from memory—is more beautiful and haunting than the beautiful and haunting poem itself.

I have called Holbrooke pugnacious and, some years ago, much to his amusement and, I think, gratification, I called him the stormy petrel of music. But what makes him stormy? What are the defects in our musical life that he so persistently attacks? First of all, he hates incompetence, especially official incompetence, and the incompetence that makes vast sums of money. He hates commercialism in art, and by that phrase I mean the various enterprises that exploit art for the sole purpose of making money. He hates publishers who issue trash; he hates critics who write rubbish. He hates the obscurity in which so many of his gifted colleagues live, and he hates the love of the British public for foreign music inferior to that which is being written at home. And I believe he hates the system that presents editors of newspapers with free concert tickets for the use of their critics.

But, in dwelling at such length on Holbrooke's combativeness, I feel I am giving a rather one-sided view of his true character. For he is not all hate. Indeed, it is true to state that no composer has written more in appreciation of men who may be considered his rivals. He is anxious and quick to study the work of men of the younger generation, and whenever any of that work appeals to him he either performs it in public or writes to the papers about it.

I have heard him called perverse, unreliable, injudicious, and many other disagreeable things. He may be. But Holbrooke is not an angel. He is simply a composer of genius working under conditions that tend to thwart and paralyse genius.

Dr Walford Davies!... Well, what can I say about Dr Walford Davies except that he represents all the things in which I have no deep faith?— asceticism, fine-fingeredism, religiosity, "mutual improvement," narrowness of intellect, physical coldness. I love some of his songs—simple things of exquisite tenderness, but it would be futile to regard him as anything more than a cultured gentleman with considerable musical gifts.

On two or three occasions I have been thrown into his company, but I have never been able to decide whether he is ignorant of my existence or whether he dislikes me so intensely that he cannot bring himself to recognise my existence.

He is terribly in earnest—in earnest about Brahms and perhaps about Frau Schumann also. He wrinkles his forehead about Brahms and poises a white hand in the air.... Please do not imagine that I do not love Brahms: I adore him. But Brahms was not God. He was not even a god. Whereas Wagner.... It was in 1911, I think, that I heard Dr Walford Davies preaching about Brahms. Now, if you preach about Brahms, you are eternally lost, for you exclude both Wagner and Hugo Wolf.

How exasperating it must be to possess a temperament that can accept only part of what is admirable! It seems to me that Walford Davies distrusts his intellect: in estimating the worth of music, he seems to say, intellectual standards, artistic standards, are of no value. To him the only sure test is temperamental affinity. And he wishes all temperaments to conform to his own limitations.

I have seen Dr Davies near Temple Gardens with choir-boys hanging on his arm, with choir-boys prancing before him and following faithfully behind him. A shepherd with his sheep! I am sure he exerts upon them what is known as a "good influence." But in matters of art how bad that good influence may be! Did ever a worshipper of Wagner walk the rooms of the Y.M.C.A.?

I have a very bad memory for the names of public-houses and hotels (though I love these places dearly), and I regret that I am unable to recall the name of that very attractive hotel in Birmingham where, early one evening, Dr Vaughan Williams, travel-stained and brown with the sun, walked into the lounge and began a conversation with me. He had walked an incredible distance, and though, physically, he was very tired, his mind was most alert, and we fell to talking about music. He told me that he had studied with Ravel, and when he told me this I reviewed in my mind in rapid succession all Vaughan Williams' compositions I could remember, trying to detect in any of them traces of Ravel's influence. But I was unsuccessful. To me he, with his essential British downrightness, his love of space, his freedom from all mannerisms and tricks of style, seemed Ravel's very antithesis.

Like myself, he had come to Birmingham to listen to music, and the following evening, after we had heard a long choral work of Bantock's, we had what might have developed into a very hot argument. With him was Dr Cyril Rootham, a very charming and cultivated musician, and both these composers were amazed and amused when, having asked my opinion of Bantock's work, I became dithyrambic in its praise.

"But I thought you were modern?" asked Williams.

"I am anything you please," said I; "when I hear Richard Strauss I am modern, and when I listen to Bach I am prehistoric. But why do you ask?"

"Moody and Sankey," murmured Rootham.

Williams laughed.

"Good! damned good!" he exclaimed, turning to his companion. "You've got it. Hasn't he, Cumberland?"

"Got what?"

"It. Him. Bantock, I mean. Now, don't you think—concede us this one little point—don't you think that this thirty-two-part choral work of Bantock's is just Moody and Sankey over again? Glorified, of course: gilt-edged, tooled, diamond-studded, bound in lizard-skin, if you like: but still Moody and still Sankey."

I clutched the sleeve of a passing waiter and ordered a double whisky.

"One can only drink," said I. "And when people disagree so fundamentally as we do, whisky is the only tipple that makes one forget."

But, either late that night or late the following night, we found music in which we could both take keen pleasure. Herbert Hughes played us some of his songs, and I remember Samuel Langford, breathing rather heavily behind me, becoming more and more enthusiastic as the night wore on. Williams, to whom also the songs were new, took a vivid interest in them.

"I like your Herbert Hughes," said Langford.

"*My* Herbert Hughes?"

"Well, you do rather monopolise him. And I don't wonder. He's what one calls the ... the ..."

"The goods?"

Langford laughed in his beard and his eyes disappeared.

The last glimpse I had of Vaughan Williams was two or three years later, outside Hughes' studio in Chelsea. We stood for a minute in the darkened street.

"Going to see Hughes?" I asked.

But he was busy with preparations for enlisting, and a few weeks later he, Hughes and myself and nearly all our Chelsea circle were swept into the army.

In June or July, 1917, I missed Vaughan Williams at Summerhill, near Salonica, by a day. But perhaps when the war is finished...?

Dr W. G. McNaught, though a musician of the older school, is one of the youngest, most up-to-date and most powerful of our musical scholars. By one means or another, the influence of his personality is felt in every town and village in the British Isles. He is the editor of the best of our musical papers, a faultless and ubiquitous adjudicator at our great musical festivals, a witty and most reliable writer, a profound scholar, and a man of such natural geniality and spontaneity that he is liked by everyone. As a rule, I detest men who are liked on all hands, but I could never detest Dr McNaught even if he were to detest me and tell me so.

I do not remember when I first met him, and I do not think I have any special anecdotes to relate about him. But, in thinking of him now, and reviewing our friendly acquaintanceship of eight or ten years, I recall that I have never been able to persuade him to take me seriously. He has printed all the articles I have sent him, but he has always laughed indulgently at both them and me. I cannot help wondering why. Perhaps his exasperatingly clever son has betrayed the secrets I have entrusted to him: the facts that my piano-playing is amateurish, my scholarship nil, and my ear fatally defective. And I think I once showed McNaught, jun., some of my compositions. One should never show (but of course I mean "show off") one's compositions when one cannot compose.

Unless you are something of a musician yourself, you will probably never have heard the name of Julius Harrison, for though he has fame of a kind, and of the best kind, he is scarcely known to the man in the street. Just as Rossetti is primarily a poet for poets, so is Julius Harrison a musician for musicians. Only one word describes him: distinguished. Very distinguished he is, with the refinement and sensitiveness of a poet, the intuition of a novelist, and the waywardness of all men who allow themselves to be governed by impulse.

When I first met him he was little more than a brilliant boy full of rich promise. He lived at Stourport, where I used to go occasionally and pass a few days with him on the river. I knew of nothing against him save that he was an organist, and I feared that he might be tempted to remain an organist and build up a teaching "practice," just as a doctor builds up a practice. But I was mistaken. He ventured on London, suffered obscurity for a year or two, worked like a fiery little devil, and at length threw up the hack-work that kept him alive. Then he emerged, very engaging and very likeable, into the real musical world of London. Sir Thomas Beecham gave him *Tristan und Isolde* and other operas to conduct, the London Philharmonic Society invited him to interpret to it one of his own works, and concerts devoted entirely to his compositions were given in several provincial towns. In five years he will be recognised as the greatest conductor England has yet given us; in ten years he will have a European reputation as a composer.

What is he like? He is mercurial, passionate, loyal, snobbish, charming, outspoken, very open to his friends.

"I *am* snobbish, Gerald; we have agreed about that, so you won't quarrel with me, will you?" he has asked several times.

"Apropos?" I have answered.

"Well, I really can't stick your pal, So-and-so. An out-and-out bounder."

"Yes, Julius. But he bounds so beautifully. Besides, he has real talent."

"But you'll never ask me to meet him, will you?"

"When I'm rich, Julius, I shall have two flats—one where you and your friends can come, and another where my bounderish friends may foregather. But I'm afraid I shall be oftener at the flat you visit than at the other. You *are* a beast—what makes you so snobbish? And why do you continue to like me, who am not 'quite' a gentleman in your eyes?"

"Oh, but you are, Gerald. Well, perhaps you're not. Only in your case it doesn't seem to matter. You are so full of affectations—jolly little affectations, I admit, but still...."

I don't think anything will break our friendship, for Julius is good and generous enough to allow me to say the rudest things in the world to him. He only laughs. For my part, I can forgive him anything, for he admires my poems. And I suppose he will always forgive me much for I admire without stint his genius as a conductor and his genius as a composer. I think that at heart he will always remain a boy, a boy full of passionate dignity, of untarnished ideals, of frequent impulses.

Of all unhappy artists the most unhappy are those who are impelled by temperament to mingle social propaganda with their artistic work. Rutland Boughton has the soul of the artist-preacher. He has persuaded me to many things: he almost persuaded me to "try" vegetarianism, and I remember one morning very well when, sitting on the end of my bed, he pointed a finger at me and enumerated all the evils that infallibly follow on the immoderate drinking of whisky.

I regret this tendency in him: it does not strengthen his art, and it exhausts a good deal of his energy and time. A practical mystic, a man of intense and sometimes difficult moods, a man so honest himself that he is incapable of suspecting dishonesty in others, a man who is always poor, for he loves his art better than riches: he is all these things. Now, a man who endures poverty as cheerfully as he may, who is continually bashing his head against the brick-wall indifference of others, and who at the same time is extraordinarily sensitive, may seek happiness, but, if he does, it will always elude him. Boughton, of course, would deny this. I can hear him saying: "But of course I'm happy!" At times, Rutland, you are happy. You are happy when you are immersed in a new composition, when you are playing Beethoven (do you remember that evening when, on a poorish piano, you played so bravely a couple of sonatas for Edward Carpenter and me?), when you are lecturing, when you have made a convert. But when you believe, as you do, that the world is awry, has always been awry, and shows every sign of continuing indefinitely to be awry, how can you, with your ardour for rightness, for justice, for goodness, be happy?

For years Boughton has done very special Festival work at Glastonbury where, when the war has spent itself, I hope to go for a week's music, for at Glastonbury strange things are being done—things that are destined, perhaps, to divert in some measure the stream of our native music.

In the early days of August, 1914, Boughton burst into my flat. I was still in civilian clothes and was reading Ernest Dowson to discover how he stood the war atmosphere: I thought he stood it very well.

"What, Gerald!" Boughton exclaimed; "not enlisted yet?"

"My *dear* chap," I protested, "I am old and married and have a family. Besides, I don't like killing people: I've tried it. And I strongly object to being killed."

"Oh, you can help without killing people. There's the A.S.C., for example."

"A.S.C.? What's that?"

"I'm going to enlist as a cook. Come along with me."

But I told him that I was reading Dowson, that I was presently going to read a volume of Æ, and after that I had the fullest intention of strangling Debussy on the piano.

So he went away to enlist as a cook. I heard, however, that when he was told that, in addition to his duties as an army cook, he might be called upon to slaughter animals, he came away sad and dejected, and, I think, turned his mind to other things.

Where he is now, I do not know. The war has blotted most of us out, and few men know whether their best friends are at the other end of the world or fighting in the trenches in the very next sector on their right or left.

I have said somewhere that singers do not interest me. Nor do they. But John Coates is something more than a singer—superb artist, generous friend, unflagging enthusiast, maker of reputations. He is at once a grown-up boy full of high spirits and a profound mystic. There are many men who have seen him on the stage in some light opera who have never guessed that his buoyant spirits are the outcome of a soul that is content with its own destiny. To me, his interpretation of Elgar's *Gerontius* is one of the great things of modern times—as great as Ackté's *Salome*, as great as Kreisler's violin-playing, as wonderful as the genius of Augustus John. "Honest John Coates!" is his title: I have heard him so described many times in London and the provinces. A man you can trust with anything: a very fine and noble gentleman, humble yet proud.

His reverence for Elgar is extraordinary. I have been told that, on one occasion, after being in the company of the distinguished composer for an hour or so, he joined a few friends who were sitting in another room.

"I have just been talking to the greatest man living," said he, with deep impressiveness and in the manner of one who has been in the presence of someone holy.

I love such hero-worship. The man who can feel as Coates does about Elgar is himself noble and not far removed from greatness.

Cyril Scott possesses a mind of such exquisite refinement that it can react only to the most delicate of appeals. He is perhaps a little exotic, like his swaying and deliciously scented *Lotus Flower*. Many years ago I was introduced to his music, and in pre-war days I very rarely let a week go by without playing something of his. On only one occasion was I thrown into his company, and even then I was not aware of the identity of the somewhat excited and, to me, extraordinarily interesting man who sat restlessly in his chair and spoke a little vehemently. He struck me as a man easily carried away by his ideals, carried away into a world where logic is useless and facts are worse than dust.

CHAPTER XXII
PEOPLE I WOULD LIKE TO MEET

I SUPPOSE that even the most outrageously sincere of men are to some extent *poseurs*, if not to themselves, then to other people. The artistic temperament must either attitudinise or die. Posturing is the most delicate, the most dangerous, of all the arts. To pose before others is risky, but to pose before oneself is most hazardous, for no one in the world is so easy to deceive, and so ready to be deceived, as oneself, and to be deluded by a fancy picture that one has drawn and painted in hectic moments is to appear to the world as a fantastic clown.

Deluded thus, it appears to me, is W. B. Yeats. He is, of course, a fine though not a great poet: no reasonable man can question that. And there are lines and verses of his that have become woven into the very texture of my mind. Moreover, I recognise that it is futile to quarrel with a man because he is not other than he is. Yet I do quarrel with him. I remember a photograph of Yeats, a photograph I have not seen for ten or twelve years, wherein he appears conscious of nothing in the world but himself, conscious of nothing but his hair, his eyes, his hands—especially his hands. His fingers are so long that one is surprised that, his palm resting on his knee, they do not reach to the floor. It is, I concede, a human weakness for a man whom Nature has gifted (or do I mean cursed?) with the appearance of a poet, to play up to Nature and help her by delicate titivations. But to do this successfully, one must have an overwhelming personality—a personality like that of Shelley, of Byron, of Swinburne. It is a simple matter to look like a poet, but to impose that look on mankind is given to few. It is not given to W. B. Yeats.

How is it, I wonder, that one rather admires Æ for believing in the objective existence of strange gods and spirits, and yet despises Yeats for sharing this belief? It is, I think, because one feels that Æ has a solid, even massive, intellect controlling his fantasy, whereas Yeats' intellect is not distinguished either by subtlety or massiveness. Yeats believes what he wishes to believe; Æ believes only what he must. Yeats has an incurable aching for the picturesque, and whilst he believes that he is "helped" by the supernatural, I think that this help is derived from his own imaginings, if indeed the question of "help" comes in at all.

Why, then, should I wish to meet this man whom, it is clear, I regard as self-deluded and for whom my respect is mingled with a feeling that is not very far removed from dislike? Really, I do not know. His attitude of mind is not uncommon, and I have met many men and women his equal in intellectual force. I think that perhaps I wish to study at first hand a mind that is so exquisite in its refinement, so sensitive in its moods, so invariably right in its choice of words. From all the tens of thousands of words that exist, how difficult it is to select the one word that is inevitable! And how slender and fragile a man's work becomes when his mind must perforce invariably pounce upon the one only word! The great writers were not so fastidious. Scott, Byron, Shelley, Keats, Balzac and a hundred others: take, if you wish, any half-dozen words from almost any page of their writings and substitute six others, and what will be lost thereby? Scott and Byron and Balzac, and even Shelley and Keats, have, I think, not more than a hundred or so pages that could not with safety be tampered with in this manner.

There is something lily-fingered and, to me, something disagreeable and effeminate in a writer who, at all times and seasons, searches and burrows for the *mot juste*. I am curious about such writers, curious though I know instinctively that they love letters more than they love life. To me such men are incomprehensible, and in them, somewhere, something is wrong. Men who do not feel lust for life have thin necks, or shallow pates, or neurasthenia.... Perhaps, after all, I am something of a student of nerve trouble, and wish to meet Yeats in order to satisfy myself what precisely is lacking in him.

It is a popular fallacy that versatility is invariably accompanied by shallowness, whereas, of course, almost all men of great genius have been peculiarly and even marvellously versatile. For me, versatility has most powerful attraction. The man with only one talent is as uninteresting as the man with no talent at all. Perhaps Hilaire Belloc has retained his hold on me because he is continually surprising me. He has done so many different and opposed things so admirably, that it seems impossible he should strike out in yet another line; but I know very well that before twelve months have gone he will have turned his amazing powers in still another direction, and will accomplish his task better than any other living man can do it.

Nearly twenty years have gone since early one spring I walked alone across Devon from Ilfracombe to Exeter and from Exeter to Land's End. Now, I went alone simply because Belloc had walked alone across much of France and Italy, and the spirit of imitation was then, as it is now, very strong within me. I had just read his glorious *Path to Rome*, and I carried a copy of the first edition in my haversack, reading it by the wayside and forgetting my loneliness (for I was many times pathetically lonely) in Belloc's most excellent company. I pondered over the nature of this man for many hours, envying him, and thinking that a man with such great and diverse gifts must be reckoned among the happiest people alive. I remember that during the weeks I walked in Devon and Cornwall I copied him as far as I could in the most minute particular, and at Clovelly, one golden evening as I stood talking with some tall, Spanish-looking fishermen, I suddenly made up my mind that I would write to him. I do not know what I wrote, but a couple of days later a reply came from him telling me that my letter had given him more pleasure than any of the enthusiastic reviews in the papers. This letter I pasted in my copy of *The Path to Rome*, and in 1915 a friend begged me to allow him to take it with him to France. He had a copy of his own, but he wished to take mine. That friend (our worship of Belloc was one of the many things we had in common) now lies dead, and I like to think that his comrades buried my precious book with him.

My imitation of, and devotion to, Belloc led me into several amusing scrapes, and I recollect arriving ruefully at Helston one wet afternoon and seeking shelter at an inn called, I think, The Angel. Having arranged to proceed to Penzance by train early in the evening, I went to bed whilst they dried my clothes. Whilst in bed, I recalled that Belloc had often praised Beaune and that I had never tasted it. So I ordered a bottle, drank it at about 4 p.m.—and promptly went to sleep for twelve hours!

Even now, on the borderland of middle age, I cannot pick up a new book of Belloc's without a little thrill: he is so clean, so bravely prejudiced, so courageous. He is a lover of wine and beer, of literature, of the Sussex downs, of the great small things of life: a mystic, a man of affairs, a poet. What, indeed, is he not that is fine and noble and free?

In the musical world one is accustomed to infant prodigies; very rarely do they develop their powers. But in the literary world infant prodigies are rare, and at the moment I can recall among writers of the past the boy Chatterton and that not quite so remarkable but, nevertheless, very distinguished youth, Oliver Madox Brown. In our own days we have had two or three men of letters whose first work, written in their late teens or early twenties, promised more, I think, than their later books have fulfilled. I am thinking more particularly of Edwin Pugh and William Romaine Paterson, the latter of whom usually writes under the pseudonym of "Benjamin Swift."

Many of us must remember Benjamin Swift's *Nancy Noon*, a strange novel that jerked the literary world into excitement two decades ago. The writer of it was but a boy, and though a few critics declared that he "derived" from Meredith, it was almost universally acknowledged that, for sheer originality both in style and in its general outlook upon the world, the novel was head and shoulders above any contemporary literature. So we all kept a close watch upon Benjamin Swift, reading each fresh work (and there were many fresh works, for the new-comer was very productive) with an eager anticipation which, alas! was foiled again and again. I remember six or eight of his books, each lit with genius, but all a little crude and violent and not one of them indicating that the writer's mind was becoming more mature. It was a vigorous, eruptive mind with which one was in contact, but it was also a mind in such incessant turmoil that one searched in vain in each of its products for that "point of rest" which Coventry Patmore maintains is a *sine qua non* of all fine works of art.

In some way that I forget Benjamin Swift and I got into correspondence, and I still possess a bundle of his letters, mostly about his work. I remember that in one of my letters I ventured to indicate what I thought were some of his faults: I called in question his knowledge of music, I expressed disapproval of his violence, and I told him I feared that he was in danger of settling down to being a mere "eccentric" writer. My letter, as might have been expected, produced no effect, and though I have not read his latest works (in dug-outs and trenches one reads everything that comes to hand, but Benjamin Swift has to be sought), I am given to understand that they are in many ways like his first efforts—*outré*, violent, eruptive, yet distinguished and glowing here and there with a genius that is always hectic.

Years ago, Swift invited me to call on him whenever I should happen to be in town, and though I should very much like to meet him, I have never accepted his invitation. One is like that. One shrinks from satisfying one's curiosity. I picture Benjamin Swift as bearing a resemblance to Strindberg, but in my mind's eye his lips are thinner and straighter than Strindberg's, and his eyes are more vehement.

What is it, I wonder, that prevents this writer from ranking among the great? His intellect is wide and deep enough, his literary talent is very considerable, and his experience of life has been exceptionally varied. There is a twist in his genius, a maggot in his brain. He sees life grotesquely; some of the people he creates are like the men and women one meets in nightmares.

Sometimes I amuse myself by inventing conversations between people opposed in temperament—*e.g.* Sir Owen Seaman and Mr Hall Caine, Mr John Galsworthy and "Marmaduke," Little Tich and Lord Morley, and I often wish a brain much brighter than my own (Mr Max Beerbohm's, for example) would occupy its idle hours in writing a book of such conversations.

I commend the idea to Mr E. V. Lucas, also, and to Messrs A. A. Milne and Bernard Shaw (only Shaw's fun is apt to be so distressingly emphatic and double-fisted).

Among the dead, I make Sir Richard Burton meet and talk with Herbert Spencer, and I always call this conversation *The Man and the Mummy*. It is strange, but we have not, so far as I am aware, any record of Burton's rich and provocative conversation, though I have been assured by men who knew him well that his talk was the best they had heard. Sir Richard Burton is one of the men whom I most wish to meet, and perhaps when my happy sojourn on this planet comes to a close, I shall be allowed to serve him in some humble capacity. To me he has always seemed to belong to Elizabethan times, and I think that he must often have cursed at Fate for placing him in the middle of a century that could not fully understand or appreciate him.

In our own days we have many young men of a spirit akin to that of Burton, though not one of them may possess a tithe of his genius or of his colossal intellect. I refer, of course, to our numerous soldier-poets—gallant young men of thought and action, of quick and generous sympathy, of noble aspiration. Most of you who read what I am now writing must know at least one man belonging to this type, for there are hundreds, perhaps thousands, of them—men who, but for the war, would probably never have written a line of poetry, but whose souls have been stirred and whose hearts have been fired by the grandest emotion that can urge mankind to self-sacrifice: I mean the never-dying emotion of patriotism—that emotion at which the sexless sneer, which the "cosmopolitan" regards with amusement, and for which men of imagination and grit gladly die.

One soldier of this type I knew intimately, and I would gladly know many of those others who have thrilled us with their poems. Let me describe my friend to you. He is no longer young: his precise age is thirty-five: but he was among those who, early in August, 1914, after first putting his small affairs in order, enlisted in Lord Kitchener's Army. He made no fuss about it, and told none but his most intimate friends what he had done. I met him a few months after he had joined up; he was then a Corporal, and seemed to me the happiest man I had met for many a day. He told me that he had begun to write "seriously," for hitherto his scribbling had been of a cursory and trivial nature. But he showed me none of his work, and it was not until he had been in France some little time that his verses began to appear in one or two reviews. Having been granted a commission, he quickly rose to the rank of Captain. He was mentioned in dispatches twice and, having led a particularly successful bombing raid on the enemy's trenches, was awarded the Military Cross.

There is, I know, nothing very unusual in this bare record as I have set it down; the unusual, indeed extraordinary, nature of this case is that before the war my friend had been a reserved, unadventurous but very capable bank clerk, quite undistinguished and apparently without ambition. But hidden fires must from his youth have been smouldering in his heart, and it required the war's disturbance and excitement to blow these ashes into flame, and the war's opportunity was needed to disclose of what fine material he was made. I flatter myself that I had always known his nature was fine and distinguished, for though he was a bank clerk one would never have guessed it from his conversation and demeanour. I also know that, generations ago, his forbears played a by-no-means ignoble part in our country's history, and for that reason alone I felt that, though concealed, there were imagination and aspiration abiding in his soul.

One of my friends, Anna Wickham, knows D. H. Lawrence very well, and one day I asked her if she would arrange for me to meet him at her house. But she brushed aside the suggestion with the few words that she was not particularly interested in Lawrence and that my time might be wasted if spent with him. Such a suggestion amazed, and still amazes me, and I cannot but think that Anna Wickham had never troubled to read any of D. H. Lawrence's writings, for it often happens among literary people that close friends do not look at each other's work.

To me D. H. Lawrence is perhaps the most peculiarly original English writer living. In his poems he is so egoistic as almost to seem like an egomaniac, and in two or three of his novels he is obsessed and overwhelmed by the passion of sex. Yet in *Sons and Lovers*, and in that wonderful first book of his called, I think, *The Red Peacock*, he gets clean away from himself, and is as objective as all great creative artists are and should be. Every writer must, of course, portray life in terms of himself, but only small men continually thrust themselves and themselves only on to an embarrassed public. But Lawrence has an insatiable curiosity about himself, and it seems at times as though he is not anxious to discover or uncover life, but to penetrate to the deeps of his own nature and shout out at the top of his voice what he has found there. In such egoism, there is, of course, strength as well as weakness, and the very fault, so grave and so calamitous, that bars him from achieving great work is, nevertheless, an attraction to those who are much intrigued by psychology.

There are, are there not? two kinds of imaginative literature: the kind we read without more than a passing thought for the man or woman who has written it; and the kind we read primarily because we are enormously interested in the personality and temperament of the man or woman from whom that literature comes. In removing himself to Italy instead of throwing himself heart and soul into the ugly but extraordinary life that these years are giving us, D. H. Lawrence is, I believe, evading his destiny and is thereby weakening the gifts and tampering with the intellect of a man whose name should stand near the head of all contemporary writers.

If Mr Lawrence should by chance read these pages, he will acquit me of impertinence if he remembers that he has taken the public into his confidence, and that he must expect the public to make some comment upon what he, uninvited, has told us.

CHAPTER XXIII
NIGHT CLUBS

AFTER what I have written you may find it difficult, if not altogether impossible, to regard me as a guileless youth. Yet I ask you so to regard me. For, if I be not guileless, how can one explain the whole-hearted enjoyment I used to derive from my occasional visits to the Crab Tree Club in Soho, and the Cabaret Club in Heddon Street during the twelve months before the war?

I had been a considerable time in London before it occurred to me that there was any other way of spending the night except in bed. Evenings, of course, were spent either at home, the theatre, the Café Royal, a concert hall, a music hall, or at friends' flats and studios, and though it is true that sometimes friends induced you to stay, or you induced friends to stay, until dawn, yet these long hours were never deliberately planned beforehand.

But I had the Café Royal habit, and the Café Royal, in a sort of way, used to be an ante-chamber to various night clubs. At midnight, or shortly after, when I left the Café with my friends, I used to find that, instead of proceeding to their respective homes, they went to one place or another where you made revelry and talked nonsense and, perchance, drank what proved at eight o'clock next morning to have been a little more than was good for you.

"Come with us to the Crab Tree," said two or three friends on one of these occasions.

And go I did. It was my very first visit to a night club, and I expected to find I know not what scenes of dissipation and naughtiness. I imagined that I should meet women even more strange than some of the strange women of the Café Royal, that I should behold dresses so daring that they could no longer be called dresses at all, that the music would be ravishing, the conversation sparkling, the men distinguished, the food delicate beyond words, the wine of a perfect bouquet. Instead, after walking up a flight of stairs, I found a large bare room with five men in it, one of them being the bar-tender who, behind rows of bottles of whisky and stout, was polishing glasses. Of the other men, three were members who had just arrived, and the fourth was the pianist who, later on, was to play rag-time for the dancers.

I stood for a moment on the threshold of this empty room, feeling rather exasperated that I had come hither.

"It's all right," said one of my friends, a little pugnacious Scotsman with a nose and chin like Wagner's; "wait a bit. Things will soon brighten up."

So we stepped to the bar and engaged the pianist in conversation. He was something of a scholar and had made a study of rag-time from the historical point of view. He played me two or three examples of rag-time which he declared occurred in Bach, and I accepted his word, though I looked at him incredulously.

The note of that night was youth. There was no hectic excitement, no Bacchic frenzy: everybody was jolly glad to be alive. Somebody has defined happiness as conscious pleasure. If that definition holds good, then I was happy that night, for I remember saying to myself: "I am coming here again." I loved the feeling of life the place gave me; the exhilaration of it seemed to pierce into my marrow. I did not want to talk to anybody. I merely wanted to sit back and watch everything: the furtive smiles of half-shy women who, happy in the arms of those they loved, were afraid to reveal too much of their happiness; the most delicate ankles of a slim girl I knew, but whose name (was it Kitty or Mimi?) I only half remembered; the kaleidoscope of colour on the platform where the dancers were. The women were like flowers—orchids suddenly endowed with movement.... I compared the scene with the spectacle afforded me by Murray's Club a few nights previously, when Ivan Heald and I were taken there for an hour or two. Some ladies at Murray's had had green hair, but only a poet like Baudelaire can wear green hair with success. But at Murray's the people were all old. Young girls of twenty were old. Everybody was old except the aged, and they pranced and frisked to prove their unconquerable youth.... But at this jolly Crab Tree youth was in the air, in the music, in the laughter.

And, feeling a little intoxicated with happiness, I allowed a gentle melancholy to steal over me, as one sometimes does in certain moods. I thought of Paris, for this scene reminded me of Paris: I was full of longing for Paris, and I remembered how in the spring of 1912 I used to sit in an attic in the Quartier Latin wondering and wondering. By that curious power that the mind, when a little excited, seems to possess—I mean the power of transferring one from a scene where one is happy to a scene where one would be still happier—I saw myself aimlessly strolling beneath the plane-trees on the banks of the Seine. I took out a pencil and wrote:

PARIS DAYS

These days, the bright days and white days,
These nights of blue between the days,
These streets a-glimmer in the haze:
These are for you, but you come not these ways:
Paris is empty in the light days.

These songs, the glad songs and sad songs,
This amber wine between the songs,
This scented laughter from dim throngs:
These are for you, Paris to you belongs:
Paris is mournful with her mad songs.

These breezes, the high breezes and dry breezes,
These stillnesses between the breezes,
These purple clouds the sunset seizes:
These are for you, but underneath the trees is
Paris a-sighing with her shy breezes.

These days, these breezes and these nights,
These streets, this wine, these songs, these sighs;
Paris with all her myriad lights,
Paris so careless yet so wise:
All in the black sea would I spew
If I could win an hour of you.

These verses (though you would hardly think so) cost me infinite trouble, and when I had finished them I looked up from my scrawl and saw that the room was half-empty.

"Is it so late then?" I asked a man sitting next to me. I saw it was Aleister Crowley, and he looked at me rather balefully.

"No: so early. Six o'clock, to be precise."

And he turned his back on me and gazed at a wall on which no pictures hung.

So I picked up my straw hat and tried to find my Scots friend. He was sitting behind the piano, talking very earnestly to a man I did not know.

"Oh, Nicol Bain," said I, "I *am* so hungry."

The streets were strewn with sunshine, and Bain took off his hat and looked long and long at the blue sky.

"How damned fine to be alive!" he exclaimed.

"How long have you been alive?" I asked.

"Only since I came to London."

"I was alive for three years in Manchester, but during all those years I sat at a desk pretending to be a clerk, I was dead, quite dead. So, you see, we really *are* young. You are about five, and I am nearly seven."

He steered me into a restaurant which appeared to cater specially for night-birds, and Bain ate bacon and eggs, whilst I feasted on a dish of strawberries, brown bread and coffee.

"I would," said I, "much prefer to have bacon and eggs, but strawberries seem to be more in the picture, don't you think? I am sure I am behaving very nobly to fit into the picture at the expense of my yearning inside.... And now, where can we get a bath?"

After that first visit I went frequently to the Crab Tree Club. There I met many poets and journalists and artists, and there, one night, a poet—a great strapping fellow, all bone and sinew and muscle—loudly challenged me to fight him. He is a man of some genius, well known both here and in America. The exact cause of his quarrel with me I have forgotten, but it appeared that, unwittingly, I had done him some real injury—or he thought I had. He spoke heatedly to me and I replied still more heatedly. Suddenly, he rose, faced me menacingly, and shouted:

"All right, then. Come and fight it out. Come and fight it out downstairs."

He looked at me with loathing.

I must have paled, I think, for I know that his terrific anger was like an onslaught. But I realised that I must accept his challenge. I hated the thought of what was before me, and hoped it would soon be over.

"Very good. We'll go downstairs."

I felt a hand tighten approvingly on my arm and, looking round, saw Ivan Heald. He came with me.

"Slog him, Gerald," he said earnestly.

But I felt most unheroic, and I know that as I made my way to the door I was trembling a little.

The whole room was interested now, and I realised that we were going to have spectators. And then the unexpected happened. The Club Secretary and a few committee men rushed between us, dragging my sudden enemy away. I was glad to be separated, for I was afraid of him.... Is it possible that he was afraid of me?

Augustus John used to come sometimes, and I remember chatting with P. G. Konody about Byzantine architecture, about which I think I know something. But one did not go to the Crab Tree for serious conversation. It was the diversion of excitement we all sought....

I think that for some weeks in the spring of 1914 I felt like a character in a rather second-rate novel. Literally, I was intoxicated with life. And so full of vitality did I feel that I scarcely found time for sleep. I remember walking with my wife from Soho to Battersea Park in the early hours of a June or July morning after being up all night. Several friends accompanied us, and though we ought to have felt extremely jaded, we were as fresh as paint at our seven o'clock breakfast of cherries and coffee and honey. I tried to feel like George Meredith as I ate, for I had read somewhere that he frequently breakfasted on honey and coffee and fruit.... The imitative instincts that we little artists have! How strange it is! We can never be ourselves for long. We are always imagining ourselves to be someone else more distinguished, or more interesting. We are always insatiably curious about the feelings and thoughts of others. Pale imitators we are. And when we snatch at our personalities, how feeble they seem ... how feeble they are.

One frightfully busy week an invitation came to us from Madame Strindberg to sup with her at the Sign of the Golden Calf, popularly known as The Cabaret. We did not particularly want to go, but I had been deeply interested in August Strindberg ever since I had read Max Nordau's *Degeneration* (that, I think, is not the title, but you know the book I mean) and I had wished to learn more about this strange vitriolic personality, and since Strindberg himself was dead, Madame Strindberg seemed to be the best person to whom to go for information.

The Cabaret was in a large cellar at the end of Heddon Street, and the narrow way was blocked up with taxis as our own cab sped round the corner from Regent Street. The place was nearly full, and a Frenchman with a little waxed moustache was singing *Two Eyes of Grey*, with his eyes glued to the ceiling in a stupidly sentimental manner, and I recollect that our first impulse was to turn and flee. One hears such songs, I am told, in Bolton and Oldham, and, I dare say, in the London suburbs, but that Madame Strindberg should come all the way from Sweden and bring a man all the way from France to sing the latest inanity was incredible. But my eye caught some fantastically carved figures that leered and leaned from the great, thick posts supporting the roof. These painted creatures were attractive and promising and futuristic, and:

"At all events, we'll drink a bottle of champagne before we go," said I, as a waiter drew us to a table and announced that supper was about to be served. "For champagne always helps," I added.

And, really, for an hour or two I required a little artificial stimulus in order to survive the dullness of the musical programme.

"Whoever the people are who run this place," I said to a pale, elderly man who sat opposite to me, "they are extraordinarily stupid. They get Frank Harris to lecture one evening and give us inane music the next. One doesn't come to a night club to be flapdoodled."

"Flap— —?" he queried.

"Flapdoodled. Yes. I mean these people who sing and recite like a Penny Reading. They do these things in Higher Wycombe and Bluzzerby-on-Stream. They should not be done here."

The pale man did not understand. He coughed behind a very white hand and delicately selected a nut.

And then Madame Strindberg approached our table. She had been pointed out to me half-an-hour previously and I had noted a pale little woman who appeared to examine her guests rather nervously. She looked cold and careworn. She was very silent, and her black clothing and white face struck a sombre note in all the moving light and colour of the large, warm room.

She came to the table and introduced herself to us, sitting down and placing a nervous little hand in mine. I soon discovered she had no conversation, for, try how she might, she could not say anything that mattered in the least. She chattered a little, made a few exclamations, and then sat silent. To me she seemed full of negations, denials. Personality she had, I daresay, but it did not arouse my interest in the least, and after I had paid her a few insincere compliments concerning the Club, I also sat silent. After a while, she was taken away to another table by some friends.

On subsequent occasions I saw her, but I do not remember that I had further communication with her except when I was made an honorary member of the Club, when I wrote to her a short note of thanks. She was no key to Strindberg: at all events, no key I could use.

Later on that night, the room roused itself from its semi-lethargy, and golden confetti and balls of coloured paper were thrown about by ladies and gentlemen who, not knowing each other, desired an acquaintanceship. The balls of paper unrolled themselves into long ribbons which, catching on to projections from the supporting pillars, hung in long loops and festoons which, thickening, soon began to resemble a gigantic spider's web. Silly musical toys were given us, and men and women—but especially women— made silly noises on them and giggled, or else shrieked uproariously.... Except for the supper, which was excellent, the evening was not a success, and I do not suppose I should have gone there again if I had not been in search of Frank Harris, or if Jack Kahane had not insisted upon my accompanying him.

I made a fairly extensive examination of London night clubs during the ensuing few months. One, near Blackfriars, admitted me to full membership on the payment of the sum of one shilling, and I used to go there—why, I know not—and throw darts at a board and drink beer. If I did not throw darts, I found I was deemed eccentric. So I threw darts.

Murray's was beyond my means, and I found the people there untalented and plethoric. They ate too much. And another club devoted to "the" profession was full of trifling women and jaunty men. Actresses are dear children, but at night they become tiresome. And actors always want me to praise them. They always pretended to be quite familiar with my name, and invariably invited me to "have one." Quite nice people, though, I assure you.

A night club is never for the old. Grey-haired people should always be at home after midnight. And there should be no card-playing. Dancing one would have of course, and music of the finest. And wine, and many pretty women, and a certain quietness, and invisible waiters, and a perfume of roses.... As I write, I ask myself: "Why should I not establish a night-club different from all the others?" It would be so easy to be different; it would be so difficult for me not to be different.... One wants space, of course: I hate being crushed against very full-bosomed ladies.... Oh, and above all, I would have a big room set apart for the hour that comes after dawn. Empty bottles, spilt wine, stale tobacco-smoke, cigarette ends, all kinds of untidiness: how horrible these are in the sun of a May or June morning! Yes, we would all go at dawn into another room, a room coloured green, with narcissi, and jonquils and hyacinths on the tables: a room with open windows: a room with fruit spread invitingly: a room where one could still be gay and in which one need not feel sordid and spiritually jaded and spiritually unclean.... If you have the right mental outlook, you will never feel spiritually unclean after a night of riot, but all our London night clubs in pre-war days seemed to conspire together to make enjoyment unhealthy, gaiety a matter for after-regret, and exaltation a little disgraceful.... If someone will lend me a lot of money (or give it me—why shouldn't he?) I will found a night club that will knock all the others into a cocked hat....

INDEX

Behn, Aphra,

Behrens, Gustave,

Bellini,

Belloc, Hilaire,

Bennett, Arnold,

Bennett, Joseph,

Berlioz, H.,

Besant, Annie,

Binyon, L.,

Bishop, Stanley,

Bizet,

Bjornson, B.,

Blackmore, R. D.,

Blavatsky, Madame,

Boughton, Rutland,

Bourchier, Arthur,

Bradlaugh, Charles,

Brahms, J.,

Brewer, Herbert,

Brian, Havergal,

Brieux, E.,

Brighouse, Harold,

Brodsky, A.,

Brontë, Charlotte,

Brown, F. Madox,

Brown, Oliver Madox,

Brown, T. E.,

Browning, Robert,

Burton, Richard,

Busoni, F.,

Butt, Clara,

Byron, H. J.,

Byron, Lord,

C

D

Hahn, Reynaldo,
Hallé, Charles,
Handel, G. F.,
Hardy, T.,
Harris, Frank,
Harrison, Austin,
Harrison, Julius,
Hauptmann,
Hatton, J. L.,
Heald, Edith,
Heald, Ivan,
Hemans, F.,
Henderson, Arthur,
Henley, W. E.,
Herford, C. H.,
Hobbes, John Oliver,
Holbrooke, J.,
Horniman, A.,
Horsley, Victor,
Houghton, Stanley,
Housman, Laurence,
Hueffer, F. M.,
Hughes, Herbert,

I

Ibsen, H.,
Irving, H. B.,

J

James, Henry,
Jerome, J. K.,
Joachim,
John, Augustus,
Jones, Henry Arthur,
Joubert,

Paterson, W. R.,

Patmore, Coventry,

Patti, Adelina,

Petri, Egon,

Plato,

Poe, E. A.,

Pond, Major,

Price-Heywood, W. P.,

Pugh, Edwin,

Punch,

Pyne, Kendrick,

R

Ravel,

Reger, Max,

Richardson, Frank,

Richter, Hans,

Robins, Elizabeth,

Ronald, Landon,

Rootham, Cyril,

Ross, Adrian,

Rossetti, D. G.,

Rowley, Charles,

Runciman, J. F.,

Ruskin, John,

S

Santley, Charles,

Sauer, Emil,

Schlagintweit, Capt.,

Schumann, Clara,

Scott, Clement,

Scott, Cyril,

Scott, Dixon,

Scott, Walter,